T Minus 36
Chain of Deceit, Book 3

By

D.A. McIntosh

ISBN -13   978-0-9856276-1-4

Table of Contents

Characters (In alphabetical order)..5
Preface...7
Prelude, South Caribbean Sea...9
Chapter 1 Sunrise over the Bahamas 25
Chapter 2 Anne Bonny's Gold...37
Chapter 3 Old Friends...45
Chapter 4 Life and Death on a Soviet Nuclear Submarine.........53
Chapter 5 Surprises 59
Chapter 6 Family Tree 65
Chapter 7 Who Let the Cat Out of the Bag? 71
Chapter 8 Decisions of Another Color......................................75
Chapter 9 In Search of Pirate Plunder (ISOPP) 81
Chapter 10 What Else Is Missing?...85
Chapter 11 Departure..87
Chapter 12 More Secrets...91
Chapter 13 Executive Privileges 95
Chapter 14 Pirates Code..101
Chapter 15 Capital Exposure 105
Chapter 16 Changing Faces 109
Chapter 17 You Did What?..115
Chapter 18 Discovery 123
Chapter 19 Chekov's Quest 133
Chapter 20 Who Are the Bad Guys?.......................................139
Chapter 21 Shots Fired..145
Chapter 22 Getting Involved..151
Chapter 23 Deadly Nights..157
Chapter 24 Complications of the Worst Kind...........................161
Chapter 25 I.S.O.P.P. 173
Chapter 26 White House Blues...177
Chapter 27 Call to Action 185
Chapter 27 Call to Action 185
Chapter 28 Don't Touch the Blue Wire...................................189
Chapter 29 Sorry Mr. President 197
Chapter 30 Cruising on the High Seas 201

Chapter 31 I.S.O.P.P. in the Bahamas 207
Chapter 32 Running Deep.. 211
Chapter 33 Norfolk Naval Yard.. 219
Chapter 34 Soviet Nuclear Boat "The Terminator"...................... 225
Chapter 35 Norfolk Naval Yard.. 233
Chapter 36 Nine Hundred Miles from Norfolk and 700 Feet Deep 241
Chapter 37 Nine Hours and 48 Minutes 245
Chapter 38 Treasure Hunters – Bimini Bahamas 253
Chapter 39 Which Way Did They Go?... 263
Chapter 40 FBI Headquarters Los Angeles 267
Chapter 41 The Terminator.. 273
Chapter 42 Eight Miles from 29 Palms Marine Base 277
Chapter 43 The Terminator Missile Room 281
Chapter 44 Norfolk Naval Yard.. 289
Chapter 45 Dallas, Texas 295
Chapter 46 Coast Guard Cutter Intrepid, Bahamas 297
Chapter 47 Twenty-nine Palms Marine Base 301
Chapter 48 The Terminator Launch Ready 305
Chapter 49 Washington DC 317
Chapter 50 Prepare to Surface Again... 319
Chapter 51 Aircraft Carrier Group, USS George H. W. Bush........ 329
Chapter 52 Final Warning.. 331
Chapter 53 Coming Home 339
Chapter 54 Dallas International Airport, Air Force One 343
Chapter 55 Norfolk Naval Yard Airport.. 347
Chapter 56 Epilog - Let's Get Wet 355

Characters (In alphabetical order)

Admiral Compton, Commander of Norfolk Naval Yard and head of Security
Admiral Ivanovich Rostov – Head of Soviet Submarine Fleet
Admiral Scott Hamner – Commander of the Atlantic Fleet
Admiral Sergio Kuznetsov – Commander of Soviet Naval Intelligence
Agent Frank Robertson – FBI agent in Los Angeles
Agent Janet Day – FBI agent in Washington Office
Agent Smith – FBI agent in Washington Office
Agents Douglas – FBI agent in Washington Office
Agents Lamplighter – FBI agent in Washington Office
Anne Bonny – Female pirate
Boris – Soviet Missile Sub, crewmember
Captain Adam T. Duncan – Pirate captain, aka "Greybeard", Harry Duncan's older brother, Captain of the ship Cortez, aka Captain Smith
Captain Harry Duncan – Captain of the pirate ship *Bonecrusher*
Captain Jack Rackham, aka "Calico Jack" – Pirate Captain
Captain Mike Morrow – Commander Norfolk Naval Yard Special Projects
Captain Mikhail Petrovich Viktorov – Captain of Soviet Nuclear Submarine
Captain Todd Henderson aka "Bear", US Nuclear Submarine captain, waiting for his new boat to be finished at Navy Yard, known as Bear because of his size, six foot five inches and two hundred thirty-five pounds, solid muscle
Chidley Bayard – Anne Bonny's second husband
Chief Brewster – Virginia Highway Patrol Commander
Chief Sharp – Chief of the Boat
Commander Anthony Basil – Diving Officer
Commander Chekov – Female Soviet Intelligence officer with Naval Intelligence working for the new FSB (old KGB), spy
Commander Harriet Lanstrom – Nuclear Specialist
Commander Tom Sanchez – Weapons Officer
Connie Pierce – Wife of Davin, FBI agent
Crocket, Sims, Fletcher, Dominic, Hightower, Ring, Wagner - *Terminator* US Crew
Daniel Drakes - Senior Service agent in Washington DC
Darrel Mitchell – President of the United States
Davin Pierce – Treasure hunter, ex-CIA, ex-US Army First Sergeant
Dennis Quaid – Captain of the *Undersea Adventurer*; manager of the Pirate museum
Director Carson – FBI Washington Office
Director Harrison – Director of FBI in Los Angeles
Director Donald Wilson – FBI Director – Washington DC
Director Doug Williams – Director U.S. Secret Service
Ensign Cheryl Kent – Liaison officer at Norfolk Naval Yard
Eric – Food service officer from the Soviet Missile Boat – *Terminator*
Fernando Lucanciano – Passenger on the ship *Cortez*, aka Anne Bonny
Gerardo Sanchez – passenger on the pirate ship *Bonecrusher*

Characters (continued)

Henry – FBI Agent in Los Angeles
Henry Wilson – NSA Intelligence Operative, Communications Intelligence Collection specialist
Hosteller – crewmember on *Bonecrusher*
Jackson – crewmember on *Undersea Adventurer*
James Bonny – Anne Bonny's first husband
Janco – Steward on Gulfstream 749
Janie Kelsey – Secret Service agent, girl friend of Henry Wilson of the NSA
Jerry Hancock – U.S. Secret Service Agent, special assignment to the President
Josh Randal – CIA agent
Lord Edward Fenwick - aka Lord Ripon owner of Fenwick Castle
LT Commander Anne Rackham, Special Intelligence Operations Executive Officer
LT Jerry Blair – *Terminator* inspector, Naval Intelligence
Manny – Museum security guard
Mary Brennen – mother of Anne Bonny
Mickel – Soviet Missile Sub, crewmember
Mike Olson – Maryland Highway Patrol Office, assigned to Jerry Hancock
Morton – crewmember on *Bonecrusher*
Natasha Haynes – curator for the Pirate museum
Officer Henry Banister – Virginia Highway Patrol
Officer Jacob Hawks – Virginia Highway Patrol
Officer Linda Blazer – Virginia Highway Patrol
Rick – works for Quaid, crewmember on *Undersea Adventure*
Robert Gants – FBI agent in South Carolina
Seaman Centrino - *Terminator* US Crew
Seaman Glascock - *Terminator* US Crew
Seaman Sandia – *Terminator* US Crew
Senior Agent Doug Williams – FBI Washington Office
Special Agent Donald O'Neil – FBI Washington Office
Stephanie Randal – Davin Pierce's ex-secretary, Josh Randal's wife
TK-17 Soviet Typhoon Class Nuclear Submarine – aka *Terminator*
Tony Sands – undercover FBI Agent out of Miami
Vice Captain Viktor Mikhailovich – Executive officer of Soviet Nuclear Submarine
William Cormac – father of Anne Bonny

Preface

Early Tuesday morning off the coast of a small uninhabited island in the southern Caribbean, Captain Mikhail Petrovich Viktorov sat quietly in his stateroom, sipping vodka. His boat sat at idle in a shallow cove with his crew working hard just outside his door. He was waiting for his crew to finish preparation of the TK-17, a Soviet Typhoon Class Nuclear Submarine, lovingly known to the crew and most of the world as *"Terminator"*. The island that was two hundred yards off the bow had a few palm trees, a couple of small hills and not much else; at least that's how it looked to the average boater anyway. While several of the crew were moving supplies to a small cave they had located, they discovered the bones of a dozen humans and a small stash of gold, several cutlasses and what appeared to be a the burial site of more than twenty-five lost souls. The crosses were crude and very old, no markings and no clues as to who they were or how they died.

Two days after dropping anchor, they were finished hiding items from the boat. They also left four life rafts with outboard motors, fuel and rations. The plan was to return later and retrieve them.

Captain Viktorov gave the order to head out to sea and start the next phase of the plan, ah yes, the plan; they had the gold paid to them for firing a missile at London; they also had a lot of nuclear warheads to use in the execution of holding the United States of America hostage. In the next few days, they would be leaving this boat adrift off the coast of Florida and head on shore in the remaining life boats. Most of the crew had been dropped off in a secluded cove on the north shore of Abaco, leaving only the most senior members of the crew to run the boat to the final departure point and head to a beach north of Fort Pierce, where they had arranged for several other members of the crew to meet them with several vans and three large sedans. Six crewmembers had been dropped off early the week before to secure vehicles and accommodations for the twenty remaining members left to bring the boat to its final resting place, about five hundred yards off the coast of Florida.

Unknown to the Captain, some of the remaining members had other plans and they were about to execute their own bit of terror on the United States. And if the Captain did not agree with it then he would have to be eliminated.

After loading the vehicles, they started north up A1A, crossed the bridge and then continued north on I-95. Their first overnight stop was Jacksonville. They had a plan that would make them richer than Bill Gates.

Prelude, South Caribbean Sea
Sept 25, 1714

The storm was raging, and getting stronger by the minute. Captain Harry Duncan of the pirate ship *Bonecrusher* was beginning to get worried. He had never seen a storm of this intensity and only hoped he and his crew of misfits would survive to deposit their latest booty on the island just over the horizon. The storm had already taken three of his crew, the top half of his main mast, and half of their sails. To say he was worried would be an understatement. As he turned his ship into the wind once again, he prayed to make it through this. Pray. This was something he had never done before. Duncan felt an odd sensation when he started to pray and he was not sure who to pray to, but pray is what he did.

Two hours later the storm broke and he looked around to see what was left of his ship and crew. Eighteen men were missing as well as all of his main mast and much of the forward mast. The *Bonecrusher* was dead in the water. She was listing badly to port and taking on water. His beloved ship was sinking.

"Run up all the sail we have left." he yelled to his remaining crew. "There is an island dead ahead; let's get there before we go under."

Two hours later, the *Bonecrusher* was scraping the bottom a hundred yards from shore. "Salvage what you can and abandon ship." he ordered while watching the long boats being lowered into the water. "We can come back and retrieve supplies once we get established on shore." he commented to his passenger, Geraldo Sanchez.

Over the next three days, the remainder of the crew salvaged the treasure and supplies from the doomed ship; the waves were beating her to pieces. They located a small cave several hundred yards inland and placed the treasure, water, food and other supplies there for protection from the weather and potential pirates. There was no way of knowing how long they would be stuck on this island. It did not take long to explore the island since it was only about eight miles long at its max and no more than a half mile wide at its widest. They started to build small huts and a fortified camp in the cove near the wreck of the *Bonecrusher*.

Eighteen survivors from a crew of thirty-six along with Captain Duncan did what they could to survive. They fished daily, planted crops using the seeds they had on board, and built a cistern to catch fresh water. Even though they did what they could to survive, the elements were not good to them. After two months, only five of the crew, one passenger and Duncan were still alive. Most died from illnesses they had when they were stranded here.

"Boson, bring me a mug of rum." Captain Duncan yelled across the sandy beach.

Boson Gibbons ran over to where his captain was resting under a tall palm tree, and explained in a rather meek voice "Captain, I am sorry to say we are out of rum. The last mug you had was all there was."

"Out of rum! Now I know we are doomed. How is the food and water holding out?" Captain Duncan yelled at his crewman. He then smiled and laughed.

"Since more of the crew died last night, we have plenty of food and water for several months. There are plenty of fish in the waters around here and that fresh water spring we located over the hill seems to be endless. If only we could just find a way to get rid of these biting bugs, life would be easier, sir."

The food and water were not a problem; the mosquitoes were a major problem, and the lack of rum caused minor problems.

"Have them buried with the rest of the crew."

"It's already done, sir. We are down to six plus you, sir. Not enough to man a boat, but the ones left seem to be in good spirit and their health is holding."

Three months later

The night was extremely dark. It was raining and extremely windy. The tiny ship *Cortez* was being tossed about like cork on a rocky sea. The sea was indeed rough and visibility was near zero. Captain Smith of the frigate *Cortez* was worried; he had never seen a storm as bad as this one. He feared his tiny ship would not stay together and he was probably correct. His main mast was already broken and dragging over the port side. He was taking in water faster than they could pump it out. Two crewmen had been washed overboard and there was no way to recover them; they were lost at sea. There was only one other thing that could happen to make things worse, but right now he could not think of what that would be. The best he could do was hang on and attempt to keep the ship on a course that would not put them on the rocks of some uncharted island.

Why had he let that Spanish idiot dictate this course? He knew that this was going to be a nightmare, but he really had expected to die at the hand of the pirates that sailed these waters, not this damn storm. Little did he know that the man who had convinced him to take this trip was in fact a deadly pirate in disguise! The promise of gold and silver had been tempting carrots for this poor ship captain. He was two days from the island that was not on any chart that he had, but which that Spanish idiot had insisted he knew where it was and promised they would get there and back without running into any pirates. However, there had been no talk of a storm like this one. They had been tossed around for three days and the ship was coming apart.

Suddenly the seas calmed and the sky cleared. Looking around, the captain could see the storm all around his tiny ship and wondered what kind of storm would do that. He had been sailing for twenty years and had never encountered this kind of storm. "Fernando" the captain yelled down the hatch for the Spaniard to come up. "Get your lazy ass up here; you have to see this and tell me which way we need to go." Then he turned to his crew and yelled, "We don't have much time, clear the deck, batten down the loose gear and clear that broken mast off the deck."

His crew jumped into action, clearing the broken mast and securing the deck as best as they could.

"What do you want, Captain?" Fernando Lucanciano asked as he stepped up on deck, "Are we out of the storm? Seems to be." he said asking and answering his own question. As he looked around, his jaw dropped as he gazed in amazement at the perfectly circular storm ring around the ship. Fernando was a small man with boyish features and slight of build. He wore his hair long and always dressed in a white shirt, buttoned up to the neck, a dark heavy wool coat, high boots, a cutlass strapped to his waist, pistol in his belt and a curved knife. If this had been the 21st century, he looked as if he might have just stepped off the stage of a Broadway theatrical production of the <u>Pirates of the Caribbean</u>.

The storm seemed to be about twenty miles across with movement in a circular motion, and moving toward them at a speed faster than their tiny ship could sail. They had never seen a hurricane of this size or intensity. In fact, they had never seen or heard of a hurricane and were lucky to be alive at all.

"I wanted you to see this." the captain replied as he waved his hand across the horizon. "What do you make of this? Have you ever seen anything like it?"

"No, Captain, never, and I do not believe I want to see it again. Do you know where we are?" he said, lying because just three months earlier he had been not far from here and had seen the same thing.

"I will in a couple of minutes. We are taking some sightings, but with the daylight and no stars it is difficult."

"Captain," the navigator said as he approached. "I have a fix". He stopped, spread out a map of the south Atlantic, and while pointing to a spot on the map where he had placed a small "x" stated "We are right about here".

"Fernando, where is the island? That pirate bitch Anne Bonny was supposed to have hidden it on that island, so where is it?"

"If your man is correct on his location, we need to go to this spot here." Fernando said, pointing to a spot that, if calculations were correct, would put the island just over the horizon in the band of storm directly ahead of them.

"I wish you had not said that. I don't think this ship can take anymore beating. We may not make your island. I don't believe we can turn back, and I know we can't go ahead. So we have no choice, do we, Fernando?"

"What are we going to do, Captain?"

"Sail straight ahead into that storm and die within sight of Anne Bonny's gold. Well, we may never see it, but we will be close, very close. Our bones will wash up on shore along with the remains of this ship."

Eight hours later, the small ship entered the storm again. It was tossed like a cork on a rough sea. The sea was extremely rough, even rougher than it had been earlier on this cruise.

Four hours later, the second mast snapped and fell overboard taking what little sail they had left with it. This left the ship without sails to move. The steering links had also broken causing the rudder to flop back and forth. The ship became a cork. Without a way to control her speed or direction, she was doomed to ride the waves and bounce around uncontrollably.

The captain looked at his crew and shook his head. They were not going to make it to the island alive. Twenty minutes later, the ship slid up the side of a wave, crested the top, dove into the next wave, and broke into thousands of pieces. They were two hundred yards from the island and never saw it.

The rain pounded the sea, winds grew, and the waves crashed down on the beaches of the four islands just within sight of the ship. Unfortunately, no one was able to see the islands. The survivors could only see the rain pounding the surf about them ferociously. Seven of them had survived the destruction of the ship and now hung on for dear life. They rode the waves on bits and pieces of the ship for even their long boat had been destroyed.

As the unseen sun slowly set in the west, several of the crew washed up on the shore of the largest of the four islands. Three were dead when they finally landed; the Captain, two crew members and Fernando were among the living, but just. The storm still raged on. Dragging themselves up the beach to a small area of rocks and fallen trees, they took shelter. What there was at least kept the rain off their heads, but the ground was wet and the wind blew at a speed they had never encountered before. It took all their strength to keep from being blown back into the sea.

For three days, they stayed under this small cover. Finally the rain slacked and the winds slowly died down to a light breeze. The captain crawled out from under the cover and looked up at the sky to see blue between the clouds and the sun shining. Morning had arrived and so did a calming of the weather.

"Captain, is it safe to come out?" Morton, one of the surviving crewmen asked in a very weak voice.

"Yes, son, come out. We need to find food and water." Captain Smith commented as he looked around the island. It was small, and seemed to be uninhabited. At least it seemed to be that way from where he stood. There was not much to be seen. He crawled up the small hill behind the shelter where they had taken cover. From the top of the hill, he saw what he expected to see. There were several palm trees, a few small hills and valleys, and lots of ocean all around. The island was long and he estimated about five miles long and maybe a half mile wide. Not much to look at and not much cover from the storm they had just lived through.

"Where are we, captain?" Fernando asked, acting weak and rejected, crawling out to the sunshine. He then realized where they were. He had been here three months ago; the bodies of the crew of the *Bonecrusher* were buried just over the hill.

"I do believe we are on Anne Bonny's little treasure island, but I cannot be sure without being able to see the stars and the other islands, if they still exist." Captain Smith replied and slowly stood and looked around. "Morton, when you can move, go to the top of that hill and see if you can locate some clean drinking water and food. When, what's his name wakes up, have him help you collect anything to put water in. I really do not think you will find much in the way of food, unless some of the stores from the ship washed up with us. Get going."

"Captain, if this is Bonny's island, we will need to locate the entrance to the cave. It is all there, all her gold and much more. She brought me here once, many years ago and showed me the cave. I think I can find it again but with all the destruction, it may be difficult. As soon as I am able to walk, I will take you to the cave." Fernando stated as he ran his hand through damp tangled hair while making sure his shirt was buttoned. He looked around for his jacket which he hoped had washed up on shore when they did. His jacket did not make the trip, but he still had his pistol, knife and cutlass; this alone made him smile.

"Fernando, get your skinny ass up and let's go. We have not eaten or drunk in three days. Morton, stand by on my last request. And wake up what's his name."

Minutes later the four of them were staggering over the hill and into a small partially flooded valley.

"Captain, you have to see this, there are bodies everywhere." yelled Morton. "No. not bodies, bones, human bones, must be a dozen or more."

'Yes, the storm must have uncovered my brother's crew,' Captain Smith thought to himself. "It must be the remains from a ship that landed here a while back." he stated to his men.

There were no high mountains. There were only a few hills with what was a small forest of trees. Most of them were palm trees, but there were a few other types, such as kapok. Unfortunately, most of the trees had been knocked down by the hurricane making the island look more like a war zone than a tropical island. Somewhere on this island, and this was the right island, was a stash of gold, silver and jewelry that could support a mid-sized country for years.

"Just over this hill to the next and behind those trees; oh, well, where those trees are supposed to be standing, we will have to move a couple of large rocks." Fernando stated before he slipped and slid down the side of the hill. Coming to a stop at the bottom of the hill, he rolled over and stood. "Ahh, it should be over here;" he said as he pointed to the large rocks on the other side of the valley about one hundred yards away.

"How do you know where the cave is Fernando?" Captain Smith asked looking at his Spanish passenger with a questionable eye. "All of a sudden you seem very knowledgeable about our location. How is that?"

Fernando ignored the questions and started to walk toward the cave entrance. Captain Smith with the remainder of his crew followed closely behind. He started to worry about his Spanish passenger that now suddenly knew more than he had let on from the beginning of this trip. They walked across the valley, avoiding the many human remains. They saw several rusted cutlasses, knives, and pistols dropped there by their previous owners, now long dead.

"You expect us to move those?" Morton asked as they approached the other side of the valley and looked at the large rocks that were covering the entrance to the cave.

"Yes I do, and quickly." Captain Smith stated; "Now you two get on the other side and Fernando and I will push from here. On the count of three, we push. Fernando, is this the only way in?"

"It is the only way I know. Bonny did not talk about or show me any other way Captain, and I hope the cave is not flooded."

After several failed attempts to move the rocks, they stopped and sat down to contemplate their next move. "Captain, why don't we try to slide a limb or something at the top and use leverage to move this thing? But I feel that with our reduced strength, we may never be able to move these rocks."

"Giving up so soon? I thought you Spaniards were tough." Captain Smith stated as he looked around his surroundings. "Not much to use to move these rocks. But anyway," he started to say, but abruptly stopped as he looked closely at Fernando. "Fernando, your shirt is open, and I see something that a young man should not have."

Looking down, Fernando saw that his shirt was open almost to the waist exposing a left breast to the captain and his crew.

"Ok, I guess you have a few questions." Fernando commented while slowly pulling a cutlass from her belt. "Well, first, my dear Captain, I am not really a man or a Spaniard looking for gold. You may find this hard to believe, because of my appearance and soiled clothing but as you can truly see, I am a woman. And I am not just any woman. I am really Anne Bonny; and yes, I am the bitch Pirate and I will kill you if you don't move that rock now. Yes, pirate! Now, my good captain, let's get this rock moved," she said pointing her cutlass at the rock and then at him. "And you blaming me for this is not wise, Captain Smith. I know who you are, Greybeard, and I have been tracking you ever since your brother seized my ship. I had heard that several of his crew were rescued from an island near here but did not know which one until now. I thought I had killed all of them, guess I missed a couple. Now I wish to thank you for bringing me here to retrieve my belongings. You have been very helpful. And had you known my loot was here, you probably would have killed me, taken it and we would not be here now."

"Miss Bonny, it was a pleasure to finally meet you and I am saddened to believe that my brother was so close to finding your treasure and died within feet of it. Had I know you had stashed it on the same island as where he and his crew died, I would have taken it with me when we rescued them. But first, you need to get behind this boulder to retrieve it; and second, you are just as stranded on this piece of rock as we are. How do you propose to get away with our treasure?" Captain Greybeard asked, bowing to the famous lady pirate. "I guess we all have our little secrets, don't we?"

"Guess so Captain. That is the easy part; I have had a ship following us since we left Port Royal. Now get the rock moved and let's get a look at my belongings."

"Why didn't you tell me this before? Why the deception? I have been a pirate in these waters for the past twenty years and have heard the tales about you. You are supposed to be dead. So why aren't you dead?" Looking down at the pointy end of her cutlass he said, "I heard you died in the governor's jail."

"The stories of my death are greatly overstated. Mary, my best friend did not survive giving birth; her son is safe. The governor took pity on my state of pregnancy and gave Mary's son to me and sent me down the road, so to speak. Not exactly how it happened, but that is all I will say for now. And why, you ask? Think about it my good captain; would you have risked your ship and crew to bring me here knowing I was a very nasty pirate, Anne Bonny, that, as the story goes, will kill just for the fun of it?" pausing to catch her breath she then continued.

"Yes, you did enough damage to the *Grimreaper* that she barely made it to port. She is now sitting on the bottom just off the coast of Port Royal. I salvaged what I could and got another ship, a forty gun slope that is fast and can withstand a tough beating, courtesy of the British Royal Navy. They will miss her soon. She will be here in a day or so to pick us up."

"I see; now that you have your belongings back, what are you going to do with us?" Greybeard asked.

"No magic, my good captain." Anne Bonny stated, "I will get off this island when the time is right, and well, you can join me or stay here and die, like your brother. But right now we need to get these rocks moved. Morton, get the strongest limbs you can break off from those trees and bring them over here."

"Miss Bonny, I don't want to die and I know my two able body seamen here are not ready to meet Davy Jones either, so we will pledge to you and join your crew."

"Wise choice Captain, or should I call you my first mate? After we leave this rock, I may tell you the entire story of my escape from the hangman's rope."

"I can live with First Mate. Now, let's move this rock. Hearing your story would be my pleasure. Maybe you could write it down to let the world know that you are not a nasty pirate, but a true servant of her crew."

"Don't get too far out of line; I have killed and will again. But for now, I need a trusting crew and our ship will be here soon. Let's get that rock moved."

Two hours later the first of the rocks had been moved and Bonny was sliding down behind it with Morton following behind. Once behind the rock and with the Captain and the kid using the sticks, they started to move the next and final rock.

Within a half hour, this rock was away from the cave entrance and all were standing looking into the dark abyss.

"Aye, Ms. Bonny, what now?" Captain Duncan asked as he looked down behind the rocks.

"Follow me, gentlemen." Bonny said and turned and started down the cave entrance. Minutes later she stopped, sat down on a small wooden crate, leaned over and picked up a candle and a fire starter, lit the candle, and with it, lit several torches located on the walls around the cavern. "Gentlemen, there is water in the bottles over there, food in the crates around me here. Do not open the boxes against the back wall; you will die a horrible death if you do."

After eating and filling up on water and rum, the men had lain down and slept. The storm which had almost killed them had calmed and left them alone; the sun was shining and a light breeze was blowing. Anne did not sleep, and she was the only one to leave the island alive. Dead men tell no tales or for that matter they don't say much at all.

Chapter 1 Sunrise over the Bahamas

April 1, Present Day

The day had started with a light breeze and no clouds could be seen anywhere; the sea was calm and clear. The fifty foot cigarette boat sat anchored about a mile off the largest island of the chain of islands known as the Abacos. Some people would not even call these small sand bars islands, but they were big enough to attract many people looking for seclusion and beautiful sandy beaches without the hot dog vendors, drug pushers and prostitutes. There were cities on the main islands and many tourists visited to enjoy those tranquil islands. But the cities were miles away from the cigarette boat, allowing this small group of friends to enjoy the sun, beautiful blue water and privacy without worry. It was completely private and secluded here. There was not a ship, another boat or rowboat nearby. It was a nearly perfect get away. There were no phones, no television, no radio or no bothersome vendors. This area was very remote, the use of cell phones had no signals, and only satellite phones had any use at all.

It was quiet here; a person could get used to the serenity and seclusion. Davin Pierce, Josh Randal, Connie and Stephanie had arrived only yesterday and had enjoyed total seclusion except for a couple of dolphins and a small whale. They had been doing some diving, sunning and a lot of consumption of adult beverages, aka beer, tequila and rum.

Connie and Stephanie had been working on their tans, while Davin and Josh attempted a little fishing with little success, but they did not care. Tomorrow they planned on doing a bit more diving and this spot was as good as any around these islands. The water's depth ranged from sixty to one hundred feet. The depth finder showed a possible reef with great relief. There were a lot of old wrecks to explore and new things to see down below. The only thing missing was a larger supply of adult beverages, but the boat could only hold a limited quantity, about six days worth at their present rate of consumption.

"Josh, there is an old story about a cache of gold and silver located on one of these islands around here, but no one has ever located it. The story is that a ship with Captain Adam T. Duncan, a pirate, killer, rapist and all around bad guy of the 18th century, had set sail with a hold full of treasure and was never seen or heard from again. The story goes, he had killed all of his crew and disguised himself as a Spanish merchant known as Fernando Lucanciano; the real Fernando was also dead. As Fernando, he conned a ship's captain into taking him to the island where the gold and silver was hidden. There is no proof they made it to the island and picked up the gold and silver, and there is no proof that they didn't. But wouldn't it be cool to find out what really happened to old Grey Beard?" Davin Pierce said as he sipped a cold beer on the stern of his fifty foot cigarette boat, the *Gold Digger*. He had purchased this boat new after he, Josh, Connie and Stephanie helped bring up the treasure and contraband from the freighter *MaryJane* last year. The money they made from that discovery had made the four of them extremely rich and now they lived the life of the rich and famous, well, just rich. The famous part was something they did not want,

but they were written up in several newspapers and magazines about the discovery and

subsequent recovery.

"Davin, I heard it differently. This Captain Duncan plundered many ships

and was sailing back to Port Royal when he ran into a storm. He lost his ship and most

of the crew during that storm; but not before stashing his loot. The story, I heard was

that he got another ship and crew, picked up a passenger named Fernando and headed

back to get his loot. But they never made it back. What happened next is still out for

speculation. Nobody knows for sure what happened. They might have been lost at sea,

attacked by other pirates, meaner ones, or run into a hurricane. As I said, nobody

knows for sure what happened."

"Well, both stories sound good. Either one may leave the loot out here

somewhere. It's probably deep in the ocean;" Davin commented as he picked up his

beer.

"Yeah, but that was about three hundred years ago and there were no records

kept, and even if there were, where would we start to look?" After stopping to take a

sip of beer and looking at the horizon and the small chain of islands that were about a

mile away from them to the south, Josh continued. "You know about these rumors and

pirate stories, they get told and retold so many times that no one really knows the real

story and besides, if they disappeared and were never seen or heard from again, where

did the stories come from? Damn beautiful day, isn't it?"

"Sure is my friend, sure is." Davin said as he set his empty beer can down on the deck. "Stephanie, are you down in the galley or still on the bow?"

"I am heading for the galley, Davin. Do you need anything?" she replied as she stepped up behind the guys.

"Yea, if you are going down below would you toss up a couple beers?" Davin asked and turned to face her, but was looking directly at her exposed chest. He then smiled and glanced up to her smiling face.

Moments later, after she had gone done below, she yelled up to Davin; "Catch!", and two cans of cold beer flew up from the galley.

Davin caught the first one, but missed the second as it bounced on the deck and started to roll toward the side. Josh reached out and while almost falling out of his chair, grabbed it just in time.

"Hey, you know that is considered beer abuse and is punishable by, well I am not sure what the punishment is, but it is severe." Josh yelled up to the bow; "Hey, Connie baby, do you two want to go diving in the morning?"

"Sure, honey, but not too early," Connie yelled back up from the bow as Stephanie came up and headed for the bow to join her with two beers for themselves.

Several hours passed and after a dinner of fresh caught grouper in a sweet lemon sauce followed by frozen margaritas and a little bit of star gazing, Stephanie looked over at Connie and asked, "Did you hear these two talking about pirate gold on one of these islands? Stories about pirates are a dime a dozen out here in the islands." She shook her head in disagreement.

"Yes, it is a bit wild, but fascinating. I always dreamed of sailing the seas as a pirate. Kind of romantic, don't you think?" Connie sat there daydreaming and looking at the stars, "Would have been nice to be out on the high seas, eating stale food, drinking hot rum, being worried every day if someone with a bigger boat and more crew would come over and kill you and take your boat. But there is the fact that a woman on a boat back then could make a lot of money selling her body. Being the only women on board could have been fun and profitable; if they allowed that on board. Yeah, a female pirate, there were some, right?"

"Come on ladies, a female pirate, no way. There were superstitions about women on ships as being bad luck and they would not allow it." Josh commented sipping his drink and leaning back to look up at the stars. "And you are right about the bad food, cramped shipping arrangements, scurvy, and well you would have a lot of rum; that would be good. It's your favorite drink and don't forget the only women were on shore."

"No, no, you don't understand, there were female pirates. Two famous ones sailed around these waters disguised as men, fighting, killing, and stealing with the best of the men. Let me think, ah, one, if I recall her name was Anne something. Ah, I can't remember her last name but she ran with a guy that called himself Jack, Cal or something like that." Connie commented and sipped her margarita.

"Interesting, but let's not speculate, the facts are there were supposed to have been female pirates that raped, plundered and stole all over the Caribbean. Well, maybe not raped, but then again, maybe." Davin added then reached over to retrieve his cold beer before it got hot.

"I'm tired, think I will go down to bed, you coming honey?" Stephanie said as she stood and stretched. "It's late and you want to dive in the morning, remember, not too early, it has been a long day."

"Right behind you babe," Davin said smiling, as he started to head below behind Stephanie.

"No you don't Hotshot. I meant my baby, Josh over there." Stephanie stated, smiling at Davin and grabbed Josh's hand, pulling him through the hatch. "

"Guess it is bedtime; see you two in the morning." Josh said, standing and going below with Stephanie.

Sunrise in the Caribbean Comes Early

Morning came in without much of a fanfare; the sun came sliding over the horizon about 6 a.m. and found Davin and Josh getting the scuba gear ready for an early dive.

"Good morning ladies, did you sleep well?" Davin asked as Stephanie came up the steps to the main deck.

"Good morning, is the coffee ready?" Connie asked as she stuck her head out her cabin door. "Steph, can you turn on the water heater? I want a hot shower after the dive."

"Coffee's ready and the dive gear will be ready in a minute also. Are you ready for a dive into this crystal blue water?" Josh asked. The water was clear, flat and what people would call Nassau blue, a translucent color.

"Give me a of couple minutes to get my bathing suit on. Or do you want to dive naked?" Stephanie teased with a smile. Sipping a hot cup of coffee and still wearing her nightgown, she came up on deck.

"Naked is fine with me, us. " Davin said looking over at Josh and then to Stephanie. "What do you think, Josh?"

"Nah, you know there may be some fire coral down there and some stinging jellies. We should at least wear our diveskins." Josh commented with half a smile, like the one Han Solo of Star Wars fame would use when he was joking around but wanted to be serious.

"Ok, skins will do; get ready Stephanie. We should be ready in a few minutes. Would you throw mine up when you get down there?"

Twenty minutes later Davin, Stephanie and Josh were swimming over the reef sixty-five feet below the surface. Connie had elected to stay on board to fix breakfast and clean up their stateroom. The water was warm with visibility limited to about eighty feet, which is really not bad. While crossing over a reef, Josh saw something out of place for a reef; it looked like a line of rocks, straight and about four feet high and six feet across and about twenty feet long. After getting the attention of Davin and Stephanie, they swam over to the wall. After a minute of examination, they swam a little further and saw a shape that looked like a cannon and with a bit of examination, they determined it was a cannon; and there were several others lying

on the ocean floor, encased in coral and teaming with colorful reef fish.

Twenty five minutes later when they had surfaced and were sitting on the

deck of the boat, Davin finally spoke. "Now, that was interesting! Did you know that

was here, Josh?"

"No way, man; what ship do you think it is? Maybe it's a pirate ship or

maybe a merchant with gold and silver on board. Do we have enough air to make

another dive and really check her out?" Josh chuckled as he took his regulator off the

used tank and started to put it on a new full tank that Davin pointed to, indicating it

was full and ready.

"We have six more full tanks and three nearly empty ones and you forgot

when I bought this tub, I added a compressor to fill the tanks when needed. It is small,

but will do the job. It just takes a little longer than the ones at a dive shop. So, do you

think that is enough?" Davin stated. He then tested his new full tank for air and to

make sure the regulator was flowing properly. "After a cup of coffee, I will be ready

for another dive; do you want a cup?"

"Sure, black if you please." Josh answered and continued to check his

equipment, "Stephanie, are you going back down with us?"

"Are you kidding? I wouldn't miss it for all the tea in Manhattan." Stephanie

said without batting an eye, zipping her dive skin back up.

Diving on the wreck, they discovered eight more cannons and several parts of

the hull. The bow sprit was buried about forty feet from the first cannon they found, but they could not find any indication of a name. Dusting off several layers of sand, they were able to locate an old cutlass heavily encrusted with sea growth. Checking their pressure gauges, they saw they were getting low on air and decided to mark the spot and head back to the surface taking the cutlass with them.

"Cool, let's see if we can clean it up after we get some lunch." Josh said as he switched to a new full tank and placed the empty in the rack. "Let's get some lunch and then another dive in a couple of hours; maybe we can locate something that will tell us her name." He placed the cutlass in the fish well and filled it with fresh water.

"Stephanie, that was way cool; do you think anyone else knows about this wreck?" Davin commented and sat down to dry off. He had changed his tank and had taken care of his gear, making sure everything was safe from sliding overboard.

"Yea, lunch; then I want to do the last dive with you." Connie said as she handed Stephanie, Josh and Davin a plate with a large sandwich and chips on it. "I will bring up the drinks in a minute. So we have a sunken old ship, with cannons. I saw you bring up something. What was it?"

"Connie you need to see that down there; it is great. I never dove on a ship that old before. But you go, I am going to catch some rays and watch the horizon for a while. Thanks for the lunch."

"Let's see, it is 11:40; how about 2 o'clock back in the water?" Josh asked while he munched on his sandwich.

"That would be great; I will get your drinks." Connie said as she turned to return to the galley, "Oh, what do you want to drink?"

"Water for me." Davin said, taking a bite from the sandwich.

"Same here for us." Stephanie responded and continued to eat.

The final dive did not turn up anything to determine the name of the ship and it was getting late. They had to be in Norfolk, Virginia in a couple of days and wanted to visit Fenwick Castle in South Carolina before going up to Norfolk. But the earlier dive enabled them to find one cutlass, two gold coins, a teapot and three silver spoons. A minor take but not bad for the first time on the wreck; they made plans for a return visit in a few weeks.

They planned a nice dinner that evening and then to bed early. Tomorrow morning they needed to head back to the coast. The weather was good, and if the forecast held, the weather would be the same tomorrow: smooth seas, no clouds and great boating weather. They could only ask for more time on the wreck but were not going to get it. They were headed to Fenwick Castle and then on to Norfolk to meet with Captain Henderson. He had something he wanted to show them and had asked for them to plan on spending a few days in Norfolk with him. He had reserved rooms at the Hyatt for them and would not take no for an answer; they were committed to be there by Friday.

The next morning Davin set the coordinates of the wreck in the GPS and also wrote them down in the boat's log. After checking the boat to ensure everything that was supposed to be tied down was and that all the cabinet doors, bunks and necessary items were put in their proper place, they finally cranked the twin engines, pulled up the anchor and turned the bow of the boat toward the United States. It would take most of a day to get to South Carolina. In fact, they needed a very long day to make the

trip. Even using the northerly current and twin powerful engines, they still would be

required to run at night for a short time although that was something they had not

wanted to do. The plan was to reach South Carolina, clear customs, dock the boat,

pick up a rental car and head for the hotel, preferably before dark, but leaving later

than planned changed their plans, slightly.

Chapter 2 Anne Bonny's Gold

It was a beautiful sunny South Carolina day to be visiting the historic Fenwick Castle. It was built around 1699 by Edward Fenwick, and constructed similar to his family's castle in England. Lord Ripon, also known as Edward Fenwick raised thoroughbred horses on the plantation with his daughter. He was a loyalist. When the Revolution started, he fled to New York where he died in 1775. His daughter stayed at the plantation till she died, but not before leading a very interesting life.

"This is a beautiful place, Davin. Why don't we buy a place like this and settle down?" Connie asked as she, Davin, Josh and Stephanie strolled down one of the long halls of Fenwick Castle, located on John's Island not far from Charleston, South Carolina.

"Sure, babe, we made enough from the *MaryJean* to cover the cost of buying a place like this, but what about the upkeep, and that lawn out there would take at least a week to cut." Davin shot back as he laughed and glanced back out the door at the acres of green well kept lawn that looked like it went on forever.

"Hell, Davin, this would be a nice place to settle down in, maybe Connie and I should buy it. Is there a realtor around?" Josh jokingly said laughing.

"Josh, babe, I don't think I would like this place, it is so old and cold. Let's just look, and then get on over to Norfolk and play with that Soviet sub they are bringing in tomorrow." Stephanie said, as she kissed Josh on the cheek. "I love history as much as you do, but I can't live in a castle."

"Look at this. It says that young Anne, daughter of old Fenwick, ran away with her lover only to be caught later by the old man, brought back home where she was forced by her father to watch him hang her lover. Damn, what an ass! She was never right after that day and kept calling for him till she died, supposedly, many years later. Apparently, she had never gotten over his hanging. Wow, that old man of hers was not a nice guy, was he?" Stephanie said as she read the caption below a picture of a young lady in a small curio cabinet. The cabinet was full of old jewelry, a gold watch, small dagger and two lace scarves, one light blue and the other white.

"No, he wasn't, but wasn't she known as Anne Bonny or do I have them confused?" Connie asked as she looked at a painting of old Fenwick on the wall, right next to another portrait of a young lady wearing the light blue scarf and the necklace that was on display in the cabinet. "That must be Anne; look she is wearing the blue scarf and that necklace in the cabinet."

"Connie, Anne Bonny was a nasty little girl pirate that also lived around 1700, give or take a few years. I don't think Fenwick's kid is the famous Anne Bonny; they both had interesting lives but not the same person. Bonny is the one you mentioned out on the boat but could not remember her name. There was a little comment about Miss Bonny in the tour guide we picked up at the entrance. Maybe we can take some time to look up their history and see if they ever met or their paths ever crossed?" Josh suggested as he took Stephanie's hand and guided her into the bed chambers of old Fenwick. "Hell, this is nice, isn't it?"

"A little too gaudy for me, hon. But let's try out the bed while we are here," she suggested and dragged Josh closer to the bed. "I do like this bed cover and wow, this canopy bed is beautiful; can we get a bed like this?"

"What about Davin and Connie?" Josh asked as he scanned around the room. "There is a great view from this window."

"They can get their own bed." Stephanie stated and walked over to close the door. "Come on honey, it is so quiet here and private."

Davin and Connie moved on down the hall as the door closed behind Josh and Stephanie. They continued looking into each room and at the fine art hanging on the walls. Forty minutes later Josh and Stephanie caught up with Davin and Connie in the gift shop. After browsing the shop, Connie decided to buy a book on pirates and early myths about them.

"What time do we need to be at Norfolk tomorrow?" Stephanie asked as they climbed into the rental car.

"Anytime after nine will do. The sub arrives sometime after midnight around one a.m. and it will take them the rest of the night to get it set in the dry dock and ready for inspection. The nuclear guys are going in first to check for radiation, then the scrubbers go in to get any bodies out, if there are any; and once they are done, we get to go on board. With any luck and if the scrubbers get the boat ready on time, we should be in and out, and then on the beach with margaritas by six." Josh said, as he pulled his door closed. Davin started the car, looked around, backed out of the parking lot, and headed north toward Norfolk.

As they headed out to the highway, Connie started reading the pirate book. There was a story about Anne Bonny and a guy who called himself Calico Jack. "This is fascinating; Anne Bonny was a very bad little girl. Just like Josh said, wow, this is good stuff. I will give you the Readers' Digest version in a little bit. Hey, what's for dinner guys?"

"Steak, lobster, Mexican, Italian, what's your pleasure, guys?" Davin asked as they zoomed north.

"Mexican and a margarita for me;" Connie said as she turned back to her reading.

"What about some pasta? Italian would work for me." Stephanie commented, licking her lips.

"Is there a place around here that serves Russian food? We are going to be on a Soviet boat tomorrow, why not some Russian?" Davin was kidding even though they thought he was serious.

"Russian, I do not believe there are any of those around here." Connie commented and then went back to her book.

"No Russian? Ok how about just some pizza and beer?" Stephanie asked.

"I don't want either of those. What about a pint of beer and Irish stew?" Josh said with a small grin.

"Hell, this isn't going to be easy, is it?" Davin said as he looked around the car and was hoping he would find a restaurant that would fit everyone's needs. As they approached the corner, the light turned yellow and he slowed the car to a stop as the light turned red. "Look, there is a little café on the corner, why don't we try it?"

"I'm game." Connie said without looking up from her book.

"Sure, why not?" Josh replied while he looked over to Stephanie and winked.

Twenty minutes later, with food and drinks on the table, they sat quietly sipping their drinks and munching on some very tasty onion rings.

"These are the best onion rings I have had ever." Josh commented as he picked up another. "Hey, guys, how about a bottle of wine? It would go good with that steak we ordered?"

"Sure," then to the waitress, "Miss, what do you have in a nice red wine?"

"We just got in some 'Yellow Tail Merlot' from Australia. I like it; smooth and a nice smooth finish."

"Sure, bring a bottle and," paused as he looked around the table. "Four glasses." he finished after getting acknowledgements from his companions. "Bring two bottles to start with."

Minutes later the waitress returned and poured Davin a glass. He picked it up and looked, "Nice legs."

"Thank you," the waitress commented as she stood there in her near micro mini of a waitress outfit.

"Yea, I meant the wine but," Davin said then looked at her legs, "Oh, yea, yours too, miss."

"Davin," Connie said as she punched Davin from across the table. "Hey, bozo, we have not been married long enough for you to be scoping out the local talent."

"I meant yours babe, yours." Davin defended himself, as he looked up to the waitress again and winked, and said to her; "Thank you; you do have nice legs too."

"Yea, they are great rings and the wine is super. But what about that sub tomorrow? What do you expect to find, Davin, Josh?" Stephanie asked biting into an onion ring after the waitress left, smiling. "What does the Navy want with you guys? What do you know about that boat that they don't know?"

"I don't really know. But from the preliminary report we got, we expect that there is nothing unusual. However, you never know what little secrets we may find. This is the same boat we had encountered in the Bahamas. The sub captain did fire a torpedo at an American sub and he did kill an American President, and yes, now we know that our good old President was more crooked than any other and maybe as bad as Sadam Hussein. Connie's office is still putting the pieces together and may never find out everything he was into. Hell, maybe our good captain was paid to kill the president and then decided to; well, maybe he decided the only way to make sure nobody followed him was to kill his crew and disappear into the sunset." Davin commented.

"Good thought, Davin, but what did he do with his crew? And the report said that some warheads were missing. Where are they now? And how did that sub get that close to the coast without detection. A lot of questions and we have no answers."

Connie commented.

"We shall see tomorrow, won't we?" Stephanie said as she dove into her rib eye steak. "Good choice for a restaurant; this steak is great!"

Chapter 3 Old Friends

Norfolk Naval Yard, Virginia

"Passes please," the gate guard asked as Davin, Connie, Josh and Stephanie walked up to the gate. Within minutes all four were cleared and walking toward the covered dock which housed the Soviet nuclear submarine.

"Davin, have you ever been to the Norfolk Naval Yard before?" Josh asked as they approached the gangway. A young sailor was walking down the gangway, and upon seeing the four walking toward the boat, stopped and pulled a small hand radio and spoke rapidly into it, then proceeded down the gang plank to greet the four as they approached.

"Good morning, Mr. Pierce, Mr. Randal and ladies. Welcome to the Soviet Typhoon Class nuclear submarine TK-17 known by the crew as the *Terminator*. Well, from what we can tell, that is what the crew called her. It will be just a few minutes before you can go on board. I'm Ensign Cheryl Kent," she said and held out her hand to greet them, not exactly smiling but an almost smile, with a concern on her face.

"Pleasure to finally meet you Ensign Kent. Is there a problem on board?" Josh asked and shook her hand when offered. "Oh, by the way, this is Stephanie Randel, my wife and Connie Pierce, Davin's wife."

"Is there a problem on board, Cheryl?" Davin asked, looking over her shoulder at the boat.

"Just a small problem, but it should be cleared up in a few minutes. All will be explained." When her radio beeped twice, she paused and said, "One moment please." After unclipping the radio, she walked a short distance away from the four, spoke, and then listened. A frown formed on her face but then she composed herself as she re-clipped the radio and turned back toward the four waiting behind her.

"Problem?" Davin asked; "What kind of problem?"

"Yes. They have asked me to take you to the briefing room in the building behind you; shall we go? The Captain will be right over to brief you." she stated and started to walk to the closest building with four confused people following a short distance behind.

As with most military buildings; this one was no different. The building they entered was typical Navy, grey and with a bunch of windows that you could not see through because of the frosting. Upon entering, they were led into a large conference room with large over stuffed maroon chairs, a long conference table and not much else.

"Please take a seat, Captain Henderson will be here shortly. Would you like coffee or something to drink?" Ensign Kent asked and then when she did not get an answer, she poured a cup of coffee and took a seat in the back of the room.

"Did you say Captain Henderson?" Davin asked looking closely at Ensign Kent. "Big guy, dark hair, deep blue eyes?

"Yes I did! Do you know Captain Henderson?" Kent asked.

"Well, if he is the same Commander Henderson that was on that same boat last year trying to stay alive while in hostile territory with a mad boat Captain trying to kill us, then yes, I know him but not as a Captain. When I last saw him, he was not a Captain. He was a lowly Commander." Davin commented with a smile, taking a seat along with a hot cup of coffee.

"We do get promoted sometimes around here, especially when you are as good as Captain Henderson is with his men and women." Ensign Kent said with confidence and a smile. "I have had the pleasure of serving with him for the past six months and they have been the best six months I have had in the Navy."

"Well, can you believe that about old Bear; makes good in the Navy, and we thought he was getting out at the end of his past commitment. Now, what did you call that boat out there? Oh yeah, the *Terminator*?" Josh asked, as he walked over, poured himself some coffee, and added two sugars and a splash of cream.

"She is the latest in a Typhoon class nuclear boat, displacing about forty-eight thousand tons deployed in 1980 under Project 941. She was originally built as an Akula class boat which is Russian for "Shark", but, as you may know, Akula class is what NATO calls the boats built under Project 971 which are the smaller Shejuka-B class boats." Ensign Kent stated as she sipped her coffee, then got up, walked over to the coffee pot and refilled her cup.

"Is that it?" Connie asked; glancing up from her pirate book for a minute. "Wow, what else do you know about the *Terminator*?"

"Well, if you must know, the stats are that she is 574.5 feet in length, has a beam of 74.5 feet, drafts at 39.37 feet, and as I said earlier, she displaces about forty-eight thousand tons, that's submerged, really that is an estimate, it is about thirty-three thousand eight hundred to forty-eight thousand tons submerged. On the surface she is between twenty-three thousand and twenty-four thousand five hundred tons. She has two pressurized water cooled nuclear reactors, is driven by two propellers, has a complement of one hundred sixty-three men, four torpedo tubes for the 630mm torpedoes, two additional tubes for the 533mm torpedoes, and if she was like earlier models, she would carry twenty R5M-52 Ballistic missiles. She can run on the surface about twelve knots, submerged thirty-five knots and has a maximum depth of four hundred meters, one thousand two hundred feet. She is quieter and more maneuverable than earlier models. She is one of six built. TK-12 and 13 are in reserve back in Russia, TK-208, 17 and 20 are on active service, TK-202 was dismantled and, of course, the famous "Red October", well, never really existed. Our boat, the 17, was launched in August of 1986, commissioned November 6, 1987, and along with the other TK models, ours was designed to carry twenty R-39 (SS-N-20) missiles each equipped with ten nuclear warheads instead of the twenty R5M-52 missiles. The crew called her the *Terminator*. And now we know why. Is there anything else you need to know about her?"

"Wow, do you know the names of the crew, too?" Davin asked, amazed at Ensign Kent's knowledge of the boat.

"As a matter of fact, yes" Ensign Kent replied with a slight smile. "I have a complete file on all the crew, past and present; well, they would be present, if they were presently here."

At the same time about 100 miles away.

"Sir, do you know why I stopped you?" the motorcycle officer asked the red faced driver of the new Corvette ZO6, his hair tangled from the wind. He kept both hands on the steering wheel and looked down at his feet.

"Yes sir, I believe I do. What would you say if I told you that I am a Secret Service Agent and am on my way to meet with the President of the United States on a matter that could save the entire world?" the man at the wheel of the Corvette stated as he turned his head to look at the officer.

"Sir, if only I could believe that. Now, get out of the car and let me see your license, registration and insurance card. And sir, if you would be so kind as to move slowly." the officer stated.

"Didn't think you would believe me."

The driver opened the door and turned to get out, stopping with one leg on the ground and the other still in the car when the officer stepped back and pulled his weapon and aimed it at the driver. "Stop right there mister!"

After a couple of seconds; which seemed like hours to the driver, the officer continued, "Sir, please remove your weapon and place it on the ground, NOW!"

"If you would only let me explain, officer, and if you would please look at my credentials, you will see that I am not lying about that story I told you, and, if you want, you can call Camp David and speak to Daniel Drakes. He is the senior agent at the facility. He will verify my identification, but he will not know why I was speeding until I get there. Now, will you let me go, or better yet, just escort me there? It is only, what, about forty miles straight that way." The driver slowly removed his weapon and laid it on the floor. He then stood and stretched his six foot two inch frame over the much shorter police officer. Slowly he reached in his pocket, pulled out his wallet, and handed it to the officer.

The officer stepped back, glanced at the credentials and then placed the wallet on the hood of the Corvette. With his left hand, he removed his cell phone and called his chief. "Sir, I'm on the cell because I do not want this broadcast all over the world. I have just stopped a speeder that claims to be an agent for the government; his credentials look authentic but he was exceeding one hundred fifty miles per hour and accelerating in a Corvette. Could you call Camp David and get a Daniel Drakes on the line and find out if a Jerry Hancock is an agent of theirs and what I should do with him." After a long pause, he hung up the phone and looked at Jerry, "Mr. Hancock you are one very lucky man; my commander has just ordered me to escort you to Camp David and wait to assist you if needed. Is that acceptable to you Mr. Hancock?"

"Yes Officer, it is. Now can we get going? I am really going because of some information I have that is vital to the national security and the safety of the entire country. How fast is that bike of yours and are you willing to exceed the limit to get there?"

"The name is Mike Williams and I have pushed this machine to one hundred fifty-five mph, but that was for a short run and I do believe that vette of yours will exceed that. Maybe I will just follow at a safe distance and radio ahead to clear the roads. Now get going, I will be there shortly."

"Thanks Mike, I will see that the President knows of your commitment to safety and well, just drive safe."

Jerry reached over, grabbed his wallet, climbed in the car and started the powerful engine. After clipping on his safety belt, he slid the car in gear and accelerated to one hundred seventy-eight miles per hour, knowing that Mike was already on the radio clearing the way for him.

The Corvette sped on, accelerating to one hundred eighty five mph, and holding the road like it was glued there. The road was clear, enabling him to make the trip in record time.

"Jerry Hancock, Special Agent to the president." he stated to the gate guard as he slid to a stop at the front gate of Camp David. He had been here many times in the past, working with various presidents, but this was the first time he had to race up here with the type of information he carried. In all the years he had come up here, it had not changed much. The seasons each year did change the scene, but the security never changed. It was always non-compromising, no matter if he and the guard were best friends. He still had to show his identification and do the normal biometric scan. The type of scan varied from day to day, but all his information was in the system.

"The president is waiting for you on the front lawn. Park over there, agent!" the guard said pointing to a spot about one hundred feet down the driveway at a large parking area which was secured from view.

"Thanks, I know the way." Jerry said as he slipped his car into gear and headed to the parking lot.

Chapter 4 Life and Death on a Soviet Nuclear Submarine

After a short wait of about fifteen minutes, the door opened and in walked a short, slightly overweight captain. He instructed the Ensign with him to stand by the door and only let Captain Henderson enter when he arrived.

"Good morning, everyone, I am Captain Mike Morrow, the commander of Special Projects here at Norfolk and I have been assigned to assist you. Ensign Kent probably has told you that we have a rather curious problem to resolve."

"Ok, Captain, curious problems are what we do best." Josh commented and while setting his coffee down, spilled a few drops on the table. "Oops."

"Mr. Pierce and friends, our problem is a little more than curious, but when she met you that is what we thought too. That has now turned into a major problem on that boat out there. We have read the reports of your last trip aboard. Did you leave anything out that you would like to tell us about right now?" Captain Mike Morrow asked as he filled a cup with coffee and sat down across from Davin, Stephanie, Josh and Connie.

"What are you getting at, Captain? We were only on that boat for a short time and to answer your question, we saw nothing abnormal, except for the couple of dead bodies in the infirmary; which we stated in our report. So what is all the big mystery with that boat?" Davin stated being a bit annoyed with this new Captain. "Why are you involved? I thought Captain Henderson was in charge of this inspection?"

"I will get to that in a moment. We just need to wait a few more minutes until he arrives." Captain Morrow responded; he paused for a moment as the door opened and Captain Henderson entered the small conference room. "I believe you know the Captain."

"Hello guys, great to see you again; just wish it were under different circumstances. Is that coffee fresh?" Henderson said as he pointed to the pot of coffee on the table under the window. He poured himself a cup, turned, sat down and after a couple of sips, he set the cup down and looked at Captain Morrow, commander of Special Projects at Norfolk Naval Yard, and asked. "Mike, have you told them what we found?"

"No, I have not, sir. I wanted you to have the honor of that little task. I did not want to steal your thunder and I did not want you to miss the looks on their faces."

"What the heck are you talking about, guys? What is the big secret?" Josh asked looking at the two Captains.

"Well, guys, it seems that when they brought in that little boat out there we had several mysteries to deal with. One: the missing crew; two: the eight dead bodies on board; three: one missing nuclear missile and one missile without its warheads, as well as ten missing warheads, and three missing torpedoes, and lastly, there is the little box of gold. The missing missile was the one fired at London; the missing warheads, well, we don't know where they are." Captain Henderson said without cracking a smile. He just watched the changes in the expressions on the four of his guests.

"We know about the gold; the Soviet Captain was paid to fire a missile at London, which will explain one of the missing missiles. But then he decided to back out on the deal, fired a missile and exploded it before it turned toward the target. He just kept the gold and headed south and retired with his crew. At least, that is what we were told and we reported that also. So besides the dead, missing missile and missing crew, the gold was his payment."

"That gold is not on board; you reported he was paid in gold bars, which were stolen by the guys you helped put away last year. This is a small stack of gold and silver pieces of eight, and gold coins from the 17th century contained in a small chest. The kind of chest that looks like the ones used in pirate movies, but a lot smaller. Almost like one that would be used as a jewelry chest on a ladies dresser except that this one is very old. We had it and the gold date tested to see how old the stuff really is. And we have verified that the chest and gold are in fact from the 17th century, and from the date on the coins, it appears to be as old as 1696."

"Wow, where the hell did they get that?" Connie asked before anyone else could. "May we see the gold?"

"Yes, but not right now. According to the log book, they had surfaced and sent men ashore on an island not far off the coast of Bimini to get supplies." Henderson stated and then sipped his coffee. "They may have stopped at several other islands to relax and found it on one of them. We are researching the logs and the computer navigation system on board to determine their exact course."

"Ok, so they have some old pirate gold. Maybe they bought it on the black market or at some store in the islands somewhere. Maybe they just happened to find a guy with this little chest sitting on a corner who needed to get rid of it and well, there could be any number of reasons that could have gotten the gold on that boat."

Davin speculated, got up and headed for the coffee pot.

"Davin, a lot of good speculation, but there is something else. There was a letter in the bottom of the chest. The letter was addressed to a Captain Duncan and signed by Anne Bonny. The letter has been authenticated by carbon dating as being written around the turn of the century, the 18th century, more exactly about 1710 or 1720. We know from a little research that Anne Bonny was a notorious female pirate and she on occasion ran with a pirate going by the name of Calico Jack. I don't know his real name, but I'm sure we can find out. She also had a run in with a Captain Duncan, date and times unknown, but it looks as though she and this Duncan guy had something going and he got a little pay off, hence the chest of gold. This by today's standard would be quite large, say worth now about $250,000 and change. Back then it was still a large amount, maybe in U.S. dollars worth about $10,000."

"Damn, what could get him that kind of money? And do you think there's anymore?" Josh queried. "Here's a crazy thought, that wreck we dove on, do you think? Ah, no way; or maybe, nah, no way." he asked quietly to Davin.

"Josh, there is no way that that wreck has any connection with this gold. That would be such a long shot that I don't even want to think about it. But it would be kind of ironic if they were connected, wouldn't it?" Davin commented quietly back to Josh before returning his attention back to Bear Henderson. "Bear, what did the letter say?"

"Not much, just posting Captain Duncan as 1st Mate on Anne Bonny's ship and authorizing him this box of gold for his service and loyalty to her." Henderson commented, "This is a little contradictory from the stories we have heard about the two of them."

"Interesting, very interesting! Do you really think there is anymore hidden somewhere in the islands?" Connie asked and looked at Davin and Josh with some skepticism. Stephanie just sat there taking it all in without saying anything, just thinking and doing a little day dreaming.

"Look, let's call it a day, it's almost lunch anyway. Why don't you go get checked in at the hotel, relax a bit and we will contact you when the boat is safe to board. Call Ensign Kent when you get checked in and let her know how to reach you, or have you finally started to carry a cell phone?" Captain Henderson asked, looking at Davin.

"Yes, I do carry a cell now, here is the number." Davin said handing Henderson a business card.

"Finally, after all these years, you finally broke down and got one."

"I had to make sure they made one that I could not break, and finally they did."

"Ok, now get out of here, I will call you and maybe stop by later."

Chapter 5 Surprises

"Davin, this is really interesting. You should read some of this." Connie commented from across their hotel room in Norfolk. "Listen to this; it says here that nobody really knows when she was born, but most think she was the illegitimate child of William Cormac, a lawyer in County Cork, Ireland. Her mother was a maid by the name of Mary Brennen and born sometime between 1697 and 1700."

"Okay, what else did our little vixen do to become so famous?" Davin asked between washing his face and brushing his teeth.

"Well, if you must ask;" she kidded, smiling at the man she loved, standing at the sink in the bathroom wearing only a pair of shorts.

"I must insist, really, go on tell me more."

"Okay, if you insist. William was disgraced and forced to move, and can you guess where they moved?"

"Well, since there seems to be a lot of information floating around South Carolina about her, I would guess somewhere in the Carolinas" Davin surmised.

"Hey, pretty good for an old guy. Actually, it says they settled down in Charleston, South Carolina; back then the town was actually Charles Town. There he started another law business and introduced Mary Brennen, as his legitimate wife, and Anne as his daughter. Cool, huh? After a while, his business grew; he bought a plantation, and they became accepted members of high society. Rich kid turns bad, real bad; right?"

"Sounds like it; go on, Connie." Davin insisted as he lay down on the bed, bracing a pillow behind his head.

"Well, Anne was a little bitch from the get go. She demonstrated a fierce temper and a fiery disposition. Her mom died when Anne was a teenager and she had to take over all the responsibilities of running the plantation. It says here that when she was about fourteen, a young man tried to sexually assault her and he ended up injured to the point that he was bed ridden for several weeks. Whoa, it gets better; listen to this. At sixteen, she fell in love with a sea captain named James Bonny. He was a small time pirate and when daddy found out, he was really pissed. He wanted her to marry a respectable man in high society; this was obviously not going to happen."

"If she was living in a respectable home, how did she meet this Bonny guy?" Davin asked when he turned to face her while drying his face with a hand towel.

"Well, this does not get into a lot of detail, but it seems she was headstrong and longed for excitement and adventure, so she would hang out down at the port. That is where she met James Bonny. Wow, they got married and set up housekeeping, where she was the good wife and waited for him to return from sea. This did not last long. He quit pirating and became an informer to the governor, collecting a reward for turning in his pirate friends. I guess they were not good friends. She became restless and longed for adventure. She met a guy named Chidley Bayard, a wealthy man that traveled and she was able to travel with him and, of course, spend his money. But she did not fit in with his type of people. Well, she didn't stay out of trouble; it says here, she went to a ball with Bayard and proceeded to punch out the sister-in-law of the governor of Jamaica when the sister-in-law insulted her. Cool, she didn't take crap from anyone, did she?"

"Sounds like my kind of lady." Davin said jokingly as Connie removed her shorts and crawled onto the bed next to him. "So what else did this little lady do to become a piece of pirate history?"

"Well, up to now, she was just a young teenager getting into trouble. She left Bayard, and this is when she hooked up with a Captain Jack Rackham, known as Calico Jack. Great pirate name, don't you think?"

"Calico Jack, kind of strange name, why that, instead of Blackbeard or Captain Hook or something less feminine?" Davin asked just as the phone rang. After picking up the receiver to say "Hello", he paused for a moment before continuing with, "Oh! Hi Josh, what's up?" There was another pause and then Davin replied, "Yea, sure, come on over; we were just learning more about our famous sea witch and pirate." After a short pause, Davin continued. "Who? Well, the one and only Anne Bonny. Well, that is her pirate name. You two come on down, and yes, we have a frig full of stuff to drink, but you better bring your own glasses. The maid forgot to leave us clean ones this morning. Right, see you in a couple of minutes." Hanging up, Davin looked up at Connie, "Guess you heard, Josh and Stephanie are coming over; you might want to get dressed."

"Hell, they have seen me naked before, why dress now?" she teased.

"Cause they are not alone, for one."

"If you insist, I will slip on a robe," she replied. Connie stood up, and slowly strolled across the room to the closet before removing a robe. She took her time putting it on, so Davin would remember her beauty. "Better now, honey?"

"No, but for our guests, I guess I will have to endure you being clothed." Davin stated just as there was a knock on the door. Getting up he grabbed a tee shirt, slipped it over his head as he walked across the room, and opened the door to find Josh, Connie and Captain Henderson. "Come on in and pull up a sit down." Davin said waving them in. "What brings you up here this late, Bear?" Davin asked Captain Henderson, using the nickname he had acquired last year during their little trip on the Soviet sub that had brought them together again here at Norfolk Naval Station. Henderson was a big guy with very little fat on his six foot four inch frame, blonde hair, blue eyed, Navy Seal and Submariner. He was too tall for a World War II submarine, which were really surface ships that had the ability to run under water when needed, as opposed to the newer nuclear boats which were designed to run underwater with an occasional trip to the surface. They performed better underwater than on the surface. Henderson being as tall as he was had no trouble being in the nuclear navy and commanding a nuclear boat.

"Well, have you got anything to drink, and I will tell you. You may not like what you hear, but you need to know and I need to preface this with a little warning and disclaimer. YOU did not hear any of this from me. Understand? Let us call it professional courtesy and friendship between shipmates. But I could lose, well, might lose a lot, if anyone leaked what I am about to tell you."

"Whoa, sure you want to tell us?" Connie asked as she poured several drinks.

"Yes, you need to know because it affects you directly."

"Well, have a sit down and get on with it man. The drinks are getting warm and we are running out of time." Josh prompted, taking a drink from Connie when she handed it to him.

After a few minutes of passing out drinks and getting settled around the living room of the suite they were in, Connie and Josh were seated on the sofa with Bear across from them and Stephanie was standing by the wet bar and Davin in the over-stuffed leather Lazyboy, Bear stood up and looked around the room at his friends and raised his glass to take a sip, and then stopped.

"Well, get on with it big guy!" Connie encouraged, sipping her drink.

"Ok," Bear sat down, obviously very nervous about what and how he would say it, and then just blurted it out, "Well, I am getting married." He then let the silence fall.

"What's not to like about that Bear? Congratulations!" Davin said as he stood up and raised his glass.

"Well, I need you, Davin, to be the best man, and Josh, you are needed as my other best man. Well, I could not just leave out the two guys that damn near got me killed and then saved my life last year for the most important day of my, soon to be married, life. Now could I?" Bear stated and looked at his friends. "And I know you are going to love her, she is sweet, sexy and sweet, did I say sexy? And she just loves the Navy. Oh, she is a LT Commander stationed here in Norfolk, down at the Intel

center." Bear stopped talking just as there was as soft knock on the door. "That should

be her now." Bear said and got up to answer the door.

After opening the door, Bear stood back to let his soon to be wife enter the

room. Beaming he turned and announced "May I present the future Mrs. Todd

Henderson, LT Commander Anne Rackham. Anne, meet my best friends."

Davin and Connie looked at each other wondering if, no way. "Welcome to

the club, Anne, I am Davin Pierce. This is my wife Connie. That crazy looking guy

over there is Josh Randal and next to him, his wife Stephanie. You are joining a very

elite group of misfits. I hope you enjoy the ride, because it never ends with us. What

would you like to drink?"

Chapter 6 Family Tree

LT Commander Anne Rackham, a beautiful fiery red head with a can do attitude, was beyond sexy. In fact, saying she was sexy was not doing her any justice. She was beyond sexy. She was beautiful with a figure that any movie star would love to have, a smile to die for, and a personality that could melt butter; she was not only sweet and loveable, but also intelligent, witty, and a perfect match for Bear.

"How long has this been going on, Bear?" Davin asked reaching over to shake Bear's hand.

"Oh, about nine months, but we fell in love the day we met." Anne said before Bear had a chance to open his mouth.

"Anne, it is a pleasure to meet you. I guess it was easy to keep this a secret from us, since we haven't seen Bear in almost a year and he has a bad habit of not saying much in his emails or letters. But Bear, you should have told us; we would have come up sooner." Connie commented between sips of her wine.

"Connie, Bear was out on a sub a lot or on some classified mission somewhere, and when he would return, we would just escape to Maine or the mountains somewhere to renew our love."

"Anne, tell us a little about you." Connie asked, hoping to hear that she was not a descendent of the famous pirate Calico Jack, also known as Captain Jack Rackham.

"Well, I was born in Charleston, South Carolina not too many years ago and my parents were both Navy. Mom, a nurse, met dad, who was a Captain, pilot really, and was the air wing commander on a small carrier. I think it was the *Saratoga*."

she said smiling as she mentioned the *Saratoga*.

"The *Sara*, your dad was on the *Saratoga*?" "Wow! That is cool! I heard she was decommissioned and cut up; what a loss. She was a fine aircraft carrier and saw a lot of action." Josh responded and then asked, "What's he doing now, Anne?"

"He and mom are retired and still living in Charleston. They travel and enjoy retirement a lot. But I guess you really want to know the question that everyone asks?"

"Huh, what do you mean?" Stephanie asked, not knowing about the conversation that Connie and Davin were having about Anne Bonny and Calico Jack.

"Calico Jack, also known as Captain Jack Rackham is, well, somewhere up or down my family tree. Somewhere out there in the middle of the early 18th century, around 1716, he and a young woman, we believe was Anne Bonny, produced three children, a daughter and two sons that married and kept the family name going and going, until there was me. And we have it all documented with records, birth and death certificates. Dad even has a picture of Old Jack and a young, very pregnant woman. Well, it is a pencil drawing that is signed by some unknown artist. But it has been carbon dated to be around 1716, plus or minus a couple of years, not too long before he was captured and hung. I have not told anyone about my background till now. Even Bear has not heard this, but I have several family artifacts in a safe at my house. When we are done with this project, I will take you over and show them to you, if you are interested."

"What do you have?' Davin asked his curiosity peaked.

"Well, ok, I have two cutlasses, a box of gold and jewels and this ring." Anne said holding out her right hand to show a small but beautiful ring that had a half karat emerald with two small diamonds in a gold setting. "This ring has been passed down through the family since the birth of her children."

"Very nice, have you had it carbon dated?" Josh asked.

"Yes, dated to about 1715."

"We may need to come back to this later, but let's come up to date with our present situation." Davin said as he stood and walked over to the wet bar. While he refilled his glass, he asked "Anybody need a refill?"

"So what do you do for the Navy? No pirating or anything like that?" Stephanie asked, ignoring Davin's comment.

"Oh, not much, I am with Naval Intelligence. And if I tell you anything about my job I would have to kill you." Anne said laughing and then took a sip of her drink.

"Sure, Anne, just remember that Josh here is CIA, Connie is FBI, Stephanie is a Senior Chief with the Naval Reserve Intel out of Palm Beach and Davin is an ex-Army Intelligence First Sergeant and now with the CIA working with Josh." Bear commented indicating to her that her clearance level may not be as high as those in this room.

"Wow, sorry guys, I did not know. My soon to be husband sometimes neglects to inform me as to the company we are keeping. Bear, baby, next time let me know the level of company we will be keeping so I don't make a complete ass out of myself."

"Yes, dear, sorry, but I really did not want to bring up that side of my friend's lives until we needed to. But I guess now is as good a time as ever. So if you must know, this is the crew that I worked with on the Soviet submarine job last year and it is why they are here in Norfolk right now. I know you read the preliminary report on that sub out there; they helped me, or rather, I helped them recover that sub last year and now they are here to help me again to figure out why she is here and where the rest of the crew might be. We do have a few little snags, as you have read. But we are not here tonight to discuss that boat, are we?" Bear commented and then took a long sip from his beer.   "Ok, honey, I stand corrected. So I guess you want to know more about my background or more about Old Jack?" Anne asked as she looked around the room with a question in her eyes.

"Yes, as a matter of fact, we do. For more than one reason, most of which we cannot discuss in this room. But tomorrow, in the secure conference room, we can bring you up to speed quickly, if you like?" Davin stated as he settled back in his leather Lazyboy again.

"Sure, I can meet you there if you like." Anne agreed, "What time?

"Bear, let's say zero eight hundred, but how about breakfast at zero six thirty?"

"Sounds good with me; how about you Anne?" Bear agreed.

"Sure, there is a little café just outside the main gate, called the Control Tower, let's meet there at six thirty." Anne suggested.

"Works for us, six thirty it is." Josh agreed.

"So tell us more about old Jack." Connie queried settling back into her chair, very interested in learning about this old pirate.

Chapter 7 Who Let the Cat Out of the Bag?

The next morning Davin, Connie, Josh and Stephanie headed down to the naval yard to meet with Captain Todd "Bear" Henderson and his future wife LT Commander Anne Rackham. After breakfast at the Control Tower Café, they were off to the main gate and the conference room.

After being cleared at the gate and escorted to the conference room, they walked in to be surprised to receive some not so good news from Ensign Kent.

"Why so sad, Ensign Kent?" Davin asked as they entered the room and saw the look on her face.

"We have a problem. Come in and sit. Ensign Kent will fill you in." Captain Henderson said looking up as his friends entered the room. "And I don't know if it is a coincidence or not but did you see the newspaper this morning?"

"No, why?" Davin replied.

"A member of the Soviet Embassy was found dead last night in his car about six miles from the main gate. The FBI is looking into it, and from what I have found out through my sources indicates he had surveillance equipment in the trunk and several handguns and an AK-47 with enough ammo to start a small war." Ensign Kent said, handing a copy of the newspaper to Davin, opened to page two.

"Well, that is not good with us sitting here with a brand new Soviet Nuclear boat in our docks, and well, we have no reason to have it hidden." Connie stated to the room. "But, hell, let's get our work done and get that thing out of here. Good morning, Anne."

"Yea, good morning Anne, what have you got?" Davin asked.

"Good morning, not sure what to say, but maybe getting right to the point will make it easier." LT Commander Rackham stated as she stood and walked over to the white board, picking up a black marker as she went. Not removing the cap, she just started to roll it between her fingers, slowly looking around the room. "Well, it gets worse, we got word this morning that there is a small reactor leak on the main reactor on our sub. There is a team working on it as we speak; they hope to have it contained by lunch and then we should be able to go in. But there is another problem, one that we cannot control." She stopped and looked around the room again, as she picked up the newspaper, the Washington Post, turned it back to the cover page and placed it on the table face up.

The front page showed a picture of the Soviet submarine as it was being towed into Norfolk, Virginia. The caption stated that the sub was being towed to the naval yard for repairs and the crew would be visiting several historical sites while the ship was being repaired. Beside the picture of the boat, was a picture of the Captain of the boat and a short biography of him. The story went on to say that the submarine ran into some minor trouble off the coast and requested assistance from the US Navy.

"Now, understand, we were not trying to keep it a secret as to the sub being here, but this is a little overboard. Who took the picture, who leaked the story, and where did they get the Captain's photo? We don't know but would like to. I have some of my best agents over at NCIS working on it right now, but we do not expect to learn much."

"Do you think that dead soviet spy had anything to do with this?" Stephanie asked.

"That is quite possible; he would know who the Captain was and have access to a photo."

"Well, our little trip here has turned up some interesting things, hasn't it?" Connie stated to no one in particular. "So how does that change anything, really?"

"I guess thinking about it, changes nothing." Bear said as he got up and headed for the coffee pot. "The only thing that it has changed is that the world knows we have a Soviet submarine in our yard; and if they start to think about it, may question as to how it got so close to our coast without being detected."

"That, I guess, is the question of the day." Josh commented. "But the story does answer that, in part. It does say they had problems and asked for assistance. Doesn't that cover our backsides?"

"Yes it does for now, anyway." Bear stated then continued as he stood looking at the newspaper. "But it also says there will be Russian sailors visiting the town and if anybody sees them there may be questions."

"Yea, that's right," Davin stated, "Maybe we could find some Russian sailors somewhere."

"I may be able to help there." Anne said, "I have some Russian linguists that could pop around town and act as Russian sailors, only need a few and have them change clothes often to look like different sailors."

"That will work. Make it so, Commander," Bear ordered. "Ok that's it for now, get out of here."

Chapter 8 Decisions of Another Color

"Admiral, we have received word that one of our nuclear missile boats that has been missing for the past few months has been seen by satellite off the coast of South Carolina, U.S.A. The satellite photos show a tugboat in front of her, and all indications are she was being towed. They are a few days old but it confirms that our missing boat is in American waters and quite possibly in their hands. " Sergio Kuznetsov, head of Naval Intelligence, reported to Admiral Rostov, head of the Soviet Submarine Forces. They were sitting in the super secret naval intelligence headquarters underground briefing center outside of Moscow. Only a small handful of people even knew about the briefing center. Among them were the ten members of the special operations branch of the Soviet Submarine Navy, twenty members of the Naval Intelligence Service, and because of a small undetected monitoring device, an Intelligence Specialist at the National Security Agency (NSA) over four thousand miles away.

Henry Wilson was on duty in the basement monitoring center outside of Baltimore, Maryland listening to the conversation going on halfway around the world. Henry was smiling because he knew that the Soviet submarine was now located in the Norfolk Naval Yard under heavy guard and in a closed dock, so it could not be seen by Soviet satellites anymore. The words he was hearing were being recorded and transcribed at the same time. NSA needed to know what the Soviets were going to do about their missing boat. It was way above Henry's pay grade to decide what the

United States was going to do if the Soviets found out that they had their boat. But now he knew what they knew.

"Sergio, when did that report come in and where is it now?" Admiral Rostov asked between sips of his coffee.

"We are not sure. The satellite passed over the area two hours ago and we have not been able to get another satellite or ship to the area to confirm that it is still there. We have a task force heading to the area, but since it was almost in American waters we cannot enter without causing an incident. We believe it was being towed to their Naval Yard in Norfolk, Virginia."

"This is not good, Sergio. You do know we have recovered three members of the crew from that boat. Two were shot in the head and the other died from exposure." the admiral continued. "What is going on? No contact, three dead sailors, suspected firing on London. What else has this commander done? Or more importantly, what else is he going to do?" Admiral Rostov asked to no one in particular, as he just sat there worried and looking around the room.

There was a knock at the door to the secure room. Turning, the Admiral indicated to an intelligence agent at the end of the table to answer the door. After getting up, the agent pulled the door partway open and saw the Admiral's communication officer standing outside sweating and holding a newspaper. "This better be important, Commander."

"The Admiral needs to see this, now!" the communications officer stated as he handed the newspaper to the agent. The agent opened to the front page and almost screamed. "Admiral, this is real bad!" He raced over to the Admiral and handed him the paper, opened to the front page of the Washington Post.

"This is bad, real bad, gentlemen." Admiral Rostov said to no one in particular. "Do you believe the two American agents that were on that boat, ah, do you think they might be of help to us?"

"Don't know how! They were reported on board trying to stop our commander from firing a missile at London. They caused little damage and were put ashore as soon as possible, once captured." Sergio responded and then looked at the Admiral and other members in attendance.

"Admiral, sir, may I say something?" and after getting a nod from the Admiral, the young female commander continued. "Sir, what if those two Americans made a deal with our commander to defect and turn over one of our newest nuclear missile boats to the Americans for political asylum."

"That is a good assumption, Commander. What makes you think our boat commander wanted to defect?" Admiral Rostov asked as he was considering the possibilities.

"Sir, three dead sailors, two of which were shot in the head, and he has not made contact since the London incident. Our boat is sitting in Norfolk Naval Yard right now being taken apart and examined by all of their best intelligence people and ship designers. They will know everything about our newest missile boat."

"That is a very good point, Commander. Maybe we should investigate that assumption as quickly as possible." Pausing he looked over to Sergio and asked, "Sergio, do you have any operatives in the Norfolk area?"

"I believe we do sir, but not sure he will be helpful; read the article on page two. May I suggest that we do not use our normal courier service; the Americans have spies everywhere, and we do not want to compromise our agent."

"We know there is a nuclear specialist heading for Norfolk; we could replace her with one of our agents. That way we could gain access to the boat and maybe find out what happened," an intelligence officer suggested, as he read the document in front of him.

"I see that our man in Norfolk has been killed; by whom, we don't know and may never know," the Admiral commented as he read the articles.

"Commander Chekov, you need to replace this nuclear specialist and bring back the information we seek. Take a civilian transport to get there quickly. I do not want to use normal channels for any of this; the Americans do have our boat." Admiral Rostov ordered as he looked at Chekov. "Can you handle this commander?"

"Yes, sir! When do I leave?" Commander Chekov answered and agreed.

"Immediately, commander. Have you got a bag packed?"

"Yes sir."

"Sergio, give the commander as much help as possible and make sure she is armed with an American weapon, or one that is used by their military, not one of ours. Understood?"

"Do you want to bring the Americans back to Moscow or just observe?" Sergio asked.

"Observe, for now, anyway. I believe this meeting is over. Report as soon as you have any information. And issue Chekov a phone with encryption capabilities."

NSA, Ft. Meade, Maryland

Deep within NSA headquarters at Ft. Meade, Virginia, Henry Wilson smiled at his recent discovery. This might be just the break he needed to get out of the basement and up to one of those offices on the third floor, the ones with the windows; he had been down here way too long. Savoring his discovery, he slowly walked over to his secure telephone. This one connected his office to the Oval Office in the White House. He had used this line many times before, not to speak with the President, but to talk with his contact in the White House. Janie Kelsey was his girl friend, and a secret service agent stationed at the White House to protect the President. They often chatted on the secure phone when the President was travelling. Reaching for the phone, he pressed his personal code and then waited until the other end connected.

"Mr. President, this is Henry Wilson over at NSA. Sorry for the lateness of the call but this is extremely important. We have just intercepted some interesting information you need..." Henry started and then filled in the facts he had just heard. Henry was one of the few authorized to make this type of call. After the call to the President, he made three more calls, one each to the Director of Naval Intelligence at Norfolk Naval Station, another to the Director of the CIA and the third to his supervisor to inform her of the situation and his calls to all that had the need to

know. Each call was made on the red phone.

Chapter 9 In Search of Pirate Plunder (ISOPP)

It was a cool morning in Charleston, South Carolina but the temperature in the office was getting quite hot between Dennis Quaid and Natasha Haynes. The lights were turned down low and Natasha was pacing back and forth in front of Dennis' desk. They had recently heard that some tourists had been asking around about Anne Bonny and Calico Jack.

"Nat, now calm down a minute, they are just a bunch of treasure hunters and they don't know much about Anne. We have had a lot of tourists looking for pirate treasure and have they found any? No, they may have found a few bits of gold or silver on the coast down by Sebastian Inlet and south Florida. And even if they do, we have been searching those islands for, hell I don't remember how long, and we have not gotten any closer to her hidden stash. They will look and ask a lot of questions but will not get any closer than we do and besides, what if they do. We will just stay behind them all the way and if they do get lucky we will just take what is ours."

"What if they resist, Dennis, what then? Do we kill them too, like the others? I don't like doing that." she said shaking her head.

"Don't get cold feet on me now. You have done this before and you will do it again. Anne Bonny's gold will be ours and I am going to get it and nobody is going to stop me. Are you still with me or ...?" Dennis said in a low almost whisper of a voice almost too quiet to hear.

"Oh, I'm still in, and don't you think for one minute that I'm not. I have done your dirty work and will do whatever is needed, but I will not kill anyone. You know my policy on killing; I will not do it or be involved with any killing." Natasha stated. She then turned toward the window and looked out at the full scale mockup of a pirate ship down on the museum floor.

"I understand your concerns about killing, but if we have to take someone out then we will. If that bothers you, you may just get out now. But right now, we need that gold to keep this museum up and running. And I believe we have a show to get going, this place opens in twenty minutes. Why don't you get changed and I will unlock the front door."

"Okay, see you down on the floor in a few minutes." Natasha said as she started out of the office; but before going out the door, she turned and said, "No killing, I am only a pirate for fun and the show, not a pirate for real, and damn sure not a killer."

Dennis sat quietly for a few minutes listening to Natasha's footsteps grow quieter as she went down the steps to her office and dressing room. He reached over and picked up his cell phone and pressed star 59 star on the speed dialer. After three rings, a voice answered and Dennis said, "Hello, Rick, how's it going out there? Good, we have a little job to do. Are you available for the next couple of weeks? Yeah? Good!" After a short pause, Dennis provided further direction, "Round up the boys and get the boat ready. Make sure the dive gear is ready and the standard compliment of weapons, and bring enough charges to take down a large boat. We may need it; the team we are up against may have a lot of resources and we may need to do a little creative elimination of some unwanted guests." After listening to Rick's response, Dennis continued, "Okay, sounds good. Why don't you stop by later today and I will have a little cash for you to pick up what we need. Later." Dennis then pushed the end call button and looked at his cell phone for a few seconds before he put it down.

Ten minutes later, Dennis had changed into his pirate outfit, looking like a fierce Calico Jack, and was walking across the museum floor toward the bow of the pirate ship where Natasha was standing dressed as the famous female pirate Anne Bonny.

"Are you ready Nat?" Dennis asked as he approached.

"Ready as ever, Denny. Let's get this dog and pony show moving; we have a crowd forming outside. What did you change about your pirate garb?" Natasha commented, looking over his costume.

"Added the red belt, stole the idea from Johnny Depp, you know from *The Pirates of the Caribbean*." Dennis replied.

"Open her up, Manny." Dennis yelled over to the doorman, who looked and was dressed just like the famous Blackbeard the Pirate.

Manny just gave a thumbs up and unlocked the door to let in the small group of school children and their teachers, out for a field trip to learn about pirates and the early days of maritime history which was displayed within the Pirate Museum of Charleston.

The museum was located in an old Wal-Mart which they had acquired when the new Wal-Mart Superstore opened a mile down the road. The building was large enough to hold a full scale model of a pirate ship, many artifacts, both real and replicas. A complete history of the pirates of old and modern day pirates was depicted throughout the museum.

Weapons and log books were displayed and every staff member was required to dress as a pirate or one of their victims. A twenty minute show staged on the ship took place every hour and ran for about twenty minutes. Each show was a little different to show the attendees what it was like to be a pirate or have the unfortunate mishap of being captured by pirates. Depending on the group they had watching would dictate whether the show was toned down to a PG level or ramped up to a more dramatic and naughty version rated R or higher. Some partial nudity took place in the R rated show with Natasha or another actress performing as Anne Bonny and some of her more explicit exploits.

Chapter 10 What Else Is Missing?

"Mr. President, I raced up here because what I have to tell you and your staff may just change the course of your decisions over the next few weeks." Jerry Hancock stated as he and the president sat in the small conference room in the east wing of the main house at Camp David.

"Jerry, what is so important that you would risk driving up here at extreme speeds, when you could have just gone into the office and sent me a classified message with all the details and it would have gotten here quicker and with less danger."

"Sir, two reasons, the first being that we have discovered a mole in the office, one that has compromised several agents already and we do not know how many documents. And the second reason is this was too important to risk it being compromised."

"Ok, spill it, Jerry." the President ordered as he sipped his coffee.

"You should already know that we have a Soviet nuclear sub sitting in Norfolk right now!" pausing and getting a nod from the president, he continued. "Well, that sub was found two miles off the coast of Jacksonville, Florida, dead in the water, on the surface. We entered the boat and found eight bodies; the Captain was not among the dead. And, what we did not find was a complete complement of nuclear missiles. One was missing; well, just the warhead. And another missile was completely missing; we believed that was the one fired at London. Along with the warheads, we have not been able to locate the launch codes or keys. It seems that the Captain took them when he left the boat. Four life rafts are missing also."

"That is disturbing, Jerry. It looks like we have a group of Soviet military on our soil with a nuclear warhead, which, if I am not mistaken, contain up to ten separate nuclear devices. The R-39 missiles hold ten warheads each, am I correct?"

"That is correct, sir." Jerry answered.

"Damn, we don't know how long they have been in country or where they may have gone."

"Now you see why I raced up here." Jerry said, lowering his head as if to pray.

The phone rang in the other room. Moments later there was a light tap on the conference room door. "Yes." the president said, looking at the door as it slowly opened and a secret service agent entered.

"Sir, just wanted you to know there is a highway patrol officer at the gate saying he was instructed by Mr. Hancock to come up here." the secret service agent said, with a half smile on his face, "He is on a motorcycle, sir."

"Thank you; have one of the gate guards escort the officer up to the main house. I would like to meet him. See if he needs anything to drink." the president responded.

"Yes sir." the agent said as he closed the door and picked up the phone again. The agent instructed the gate guard to escort the officer up but to have him surrender his weapons before coming up. This was standard procedure for Camp David security.

Chapter 11 Departure

At 11:30 Commander Chekov arrived at the private hanger owned by the Soviet Naval Intelligence Division. Which housed an American built G4 corporate jet, capable of trans-Atlantic flight. Commander Chekov was dressed in a short leather mini-skirt, high heels, white silk blouse and a black overcoat to keep warm. She flashed her identification to the pilot and crew of the G4, and handed her luggage to a crew member who stored it in the aft luggage compartment.

"Be careful with that! It has some personal items in there that I do not want broken." she said to the crew member with a smile that could melt butter.

After being escorted aboard, she removed her coat, hung it in the closet, found the wet bar and fixed herself a vodka on the rocks, picked up her handbag, opened and removed her e-book pad and her Beretta 9mm pistol. She checked her weapon to see that she had a bullet in the barrel and removed the clip to ensure it was fully loaded. After ensuring it was properly loaded, she clicked on the safety and replaced it in her handbag, buckled her seatbelt, picked up her e-book pad and thumbed to the page where she had stopped reading. She leaned back in the overstuffed leather seat and began to read.

"Commander, we are cleared to taxi out, please take a seat and buckle up. We should be departing in about five minutes. Our clearance to Paris is on hold because of weather." the pilot reported over the intercom. "Please make yourself comfortable; there is food in the galley, and after we get to cruising altitude, I will be back to serve drinks. The co-pilot will be flying us to Paris; I will take the trans-Atlantic leg. We should arrive in Paris in a little over an hour. Sit back and enjoy the ride. After we leave Paris and get to cruising altitude, our steward, Janco, will come up to see you to get your dinner order. We have several excellent meals on board for your enjoyment. Once we arrive in the United States, we will remain available for you until the end of the operation. Now sit back and relax. The weather is not real good in Paris, but nothing we can't handle."

Fifteen minutes later they were pulling the gear handle to raise the landing gear as they headed to Paris.

"We will be climbing to thirty-eight thousand feet for our flight tonight and expect to arrive in Paris on time, around 12:30 in the morning. After refueling, we will depart around 1:45 for our nine hour flight to New York. We will refuel again and then continue to Norfolk, Virginia where there will be a car waiting for you. You are to pick it up at the Hertz counter; I believe they booked you a sports car." the pilot announced. The route had separate flight plans to divert attention from the United States Federal Aviation Administration (FAA).

Commander Chekov sat back and started to read the file on the missile submarine, her commander, the two Americans she was going after and Commander Harriet Lanstrom, the nuclear specialist. She did not want to sleep until after leaving Paris and consuming a couple of vodkas and dinner.

Her e-book pad held everything she needed; just hours before she left Moscow, files had been down-loaded with information about the boat, captain, Harriet

Lanstrom, and the two Americans that had caused the captain of the boat problems late last year. What had gone wrong with him? She was looking for a clue, but could not find one, but secretly she had her suspicions. The files were not complete, but everything that the intelligence unit had was included. Her pad was also loaded with some of the newest books being read in the states. One she especially wanted to read was written several years ago but had only recently become available as an e-book. This was the book by D.A. McIntosh, titled *Chain of Deceit*. She had heard of the book, but it had not been available in Moscow until it had become an e-book. After they left Paris, she planned on reading the two books she had on her pad, *Chain of Deceit* and *Retribution*, both by the same author.

One hour and ten minutes later, the pilot announced they were landing in Paris and to buckle up. She would not be able to leave the plane because of the weather, but the bar would remain open. Well, it was a private jet, so it would always be open.

"Commander, we are fueled and ready to leave. Are you strapped in and ready?" the pilot announced about forty-five minutes later as he looked over his shoulder into the rear cabin; he had not seen his passenger as she boarded, but got an eyeful of the lady in a short dress lounging in the back of his airplane. "The weather, as you can see outside your window, is still pretty nasty. So, stay buckled until we are clear of this stuff. It will be a little bumpy until we reach altitude." She signaled thumbs up to indicate she was ready. He turned and they started to taxi to the runway.

"Gulfstream 749, ready for departure." the pilot said to the control tower once they stopped at the end of the runway.

"Seven four niner, taxi onto runway and wait." the tower ordered.

"Taxi onto runway and wait, Gulfstream 749." the pilot repeated.

"Gulfstream 749, cleared for takeoff, maintain runway heading until passing the outer marker, turn left to 320 degrees, climb to twenty-five thousand, cleared as filed. Report passing outer marker, have a nice flight." the tower informed the pilot.

"It's been a pleasure, Paris." replied the pilot.

Twenty minutes later, the pilot announced they had reached cruising altitude and would start to serve dinner in a few minutes.

"Miss, good evening, we have several choice meals on board for your dining pleasure. You may select a rib-eye steak with fresh steamed veggies, baked potato and salad. Or we have roasted chicken with the same sides, or a couple of traditional Russian dinners that I do not recommend; we get that too much back in Moscow as it is. To go with any of those, we have a limited but very good wine selection."

"I will have the steak, medium rare and a bottle of your best red wine." Chekov replied and then went back to her reading. She had only two more files to read before dinner and then, finally, she would have time for the books she really wanted to read. It was 1:50 in the morning; the flight would take nine hours and it would only be about one in the morning when they arrived in New York. She had time to sleep between New York and Norfolk, a couple of hours would be all she needed.

Chapter 12 More Secrets

Later the same day at Norfolk Naval Yard

"Welcome aboard," Captain Henderson said as his friends climbed down the ladder to the control room where he was waiting. "Remember the last time we were here, Davin."

"Sure do, but I think this is a bit more comfortable and not as threatening." Davin commented as he and Josh started to look around the control room, "So, any theory as to what happened here, Bear?"

"Well, first off, the reactor leak was rigged to leak with a timer set to start a minor leak to slow unwanted visitors down but not stop them completely. We got that under control and have done the preliminary search. Other than what we told you yesterday, nothing new has turned up. The bodies were members of the crew for the most part; but two of them were not crew, and possibly the two you saw in the infirmary when you were here. Both have been dead longer than the other six. Well, they were killed by various means and have only been dead for about a week, but kept in the freezer where we found them. We will have the autopsy reports by tomorrow with the cause of death. All the damages you and I made when we were here, have been repaired, and not a bad job considering they did not go into port. Let's go to the Captain's cabin, we have one of our best lock pickers working on the safe. He should have it open by the time we get there."

"Lead on; Captain Bear." Josh said as they turned to head down the hall and down the stairwell. The captain's cabin was located just behind the control room and down one deck.

"This way; our safe cracker should have the safe open when we get there. He has been instructed to unlock but not open until we get there. We hope to find the ship's log and who knows what else." Bear said pointing down the corridor, "Second door on the left is his cabin, the one with the door open."

"This should be interesting." Josh commented and stopped in front of the door, waiting for his friends and then followed them in.

Minutes later they were standing behind the young seaman just as he turned the handle of the safe and stopped, looked over his shoulder at Captain Henderson and smiled, "Would you like the honors, sir. No booby traps or trip wires that I can find."

"No, Jeff, you did all the work; open her up, then let us see what we have." Captain Henderson said, obviously knowing the young seaman, "By the way, how long did it take you to crack it?"

Jeff turned the handle and pulled the door open and rolled back away from the safe to let Captain Henderson, Josh and Davin see what was in the safe.

"Eight minutes, sir. New record for me, but this safe was a piece of cake, only two locks." Jeff answered, smiling.

"Whoa, look at this, boys, we have hit pay dirt. The ship's log, a very nice 9mm Markarov and, ah, what's this?" Bear said as he pulled a small cloth bag from the back of the safe and looked inside. "This must be yours." Bear said as he tossed the small cloth bag to Davin.

Davin peered inside and then poured the contents into his left hand; out fell ten solid gold coins, all dating back to the 1700's. "This will buy someone a nice set of wheels, what do you think, Jeff?" He pitched one of the coins to the young sailor, who caught it with his left hand and then looked at it carefully.

"Pretty nice, pretty nice, sir;" Jeff said after he examined the coin and started to toss it back to Davin.

Davin held up his hand stopping him and said, "Keep it; you have earned it."

"Sir, I don't know if I should, all I did was open the safe." Jeff said refusing to keep the coin.

"Jeff, it is yours, no questions. Don't make me make it an order. You deserve something; you have been here for hours cracking that safe."

"Actually, I got here about ten minutes ago; this was an easy safe to crack. The one in the armory was a bit tougher, took me about fifteen minutes to crack it. This one took about eight minutes. I guess you did not hear me when I answered Captain Henderson, when he asked how long it took."

"Not bad, you don't work nights do you?" Josh asked quietly as he looked over at the 9mm pistol, gold and the ship's log. "Is there anything else in there that we should know about? Jeff, when do you finish your Navy hitch?"

"I have two more years, sir. Why?" Jeff replied and looked over at Josh, questioning his question.

"I may have a position for you, if you are interested. Here is my card. Call me." Josh said as he handed Jeff his card. Jeff took it and looked at it closely, reading that Josh was the Director of Special Operations for the CIA.

"Wow, sir; I will call you, for sure. Thank you." Jeff commented and put the card in his shirt pocket.

Captain Henderson then said, "I guess we should read the log and maybe this personal book here. Looks like a personal notebook. It may give us some clues as to what happened here. Josh, why don't you start with the notebook and I will review the ship's log. Davin, why don't you go to the armory with Jeff and see if there is anything down there we should know about."

"Sounds good to me, let's go Jeff." replied Davin.

All over the boat, technicians were downloading files, examining systems, taking photographs and generally dissecting the Soviet submarine to glean everything they could about where she had been, what she had done and why she had been off the coast of North Carolina without any crew, alive anyway.

Chapter 13 Executive Privileges

Jerry Hancock sat across from the President of the United States, Darrell Mitchell, and waited for him to decide on his next course of action. The room they were in was decorated with antiques, many from past presidents. Except for a few upgrades in the technology, the room was the same as it had been for the past twenty-five years.

"Mr. Hancock, we need to locate those warheads and the captain of TK-17, find out what the hell happened on his ship and why he and his crew are no longer doing what they were trained to do. We also need to find this mole, spy or whatever you want to call this enemy that is living under our noses. We cannot have this; we are the greatest nation on this planet with the most sophisticated intelligence system, and yet, we cannot find a spy in our own backyard."

"Yes sir, I understand but I cannot go back to the office to get help with that mole, and we cannot use an outside agency because he or she may go quiet on us. This gets us nowhere." Jerry was interrupted when the phone beside the President rang. "Go ahead, sir; I will step out if you need to speak privately."

"Yes," the President answered as he waved Jerry to remain seated. He stopped and listened before replying. "Bring him up to the den; have Henry run a quick background on him. I want to know everything about him that we can as quickly as possible." And then he hung up the receiver.

"I don't understand, sir." said Jerry.

"You will; let me do the talking." the President said smiling, "I think I have you some help; and if this works, he may be able to help with the mole problem too."

Minutes later there was a knock on the door.

"It's open." the president yelled at the door. The door opened and the Highway Patrol officer entered. "Hello, Officer. Yes, he is guilty; take him away!"

"If you say so sir," and the officer responded as he removed his handcuffs and walked over to Jerry Hancock.

"What?" Jerry asked, looking very confused, as he glanced at the President and then to the officer.

The President smiled and quickly stated, "I was just kidding, son; please, have a seat. We need to talk. But first, introductions and explanations are in order. Mr. Hancock is one of our best Secret Service agents and is a personal friend of mine. By the way, you know who I am, but would you tell us about yourself."

The officer responded with "Michael Olson, sir. I've been with the highway patrol for the past twelve years, spent four years in the Army, did one tour in country, eleven bullet stopper, oh I mean…"

"I know what you mean Mr. Olson, been there myself, 82nd Airborne, Military Intel, the oxy-moron world of intelligence, now go on." interrupted the President.

Officer Olson continued with "After the army, did the college thing, graduated with a Masters in Criminal Justice, went on to the academy, got on the Washington PD, then moved over to the Highway Patrol, got assigned to the motor squad, love riding bikes and having some fun, been a blast ever since. Not married, tried it once but it did not work out, no kids."

"What are your goals, Mike? You know, when you grow up." asked the President.

"Hang on a second." Darrell said as the phone rang, holding up one finger. "Yes." After a short pause he said, "OK, that's good." And after another short pause, he closed with "Good, now get me his Chief and let me talk to him. I don't care if it is after hours; call him at home if you have to. I need to speak to him now."

"Mike, what I am about to propose to you may seem a bit irregular and in most cases it is. But we have a problem and I think you can be of great assistance if you agree to what I am about to offer." stated the President.

"Sir, I will do whatever my country wants me to do. Just give me the word." Mike agreed before hearing what needed to be done.

"You may not be so ready once you hear what we have to do." Jerry Hancock stated while he stood and walked over to the coffee pot and poured a cup. He raised the pot toward Mike and after asking if he wanted some and getting a nod, he poured a second cup.

Seconds later the phone rang again. Darrell picked it up and waited, then spoke into the handset, "Good evening Chief Brewster, I assume you have been told that I wanted to talk with you by my aide. Yes? Good! I have one of your officers here with me, Mike Olson. No, nothing is wrong with him. He escorted one of my Secret Service Agents to Camp David for me and we need to keep him awhile for a special assignment. I would like for you to give me permission to retain him for an unlimited time to work with my office on a special project. I cannot say the nature of the project or how long it will take; I am not the kind of person that will order you or him to take on this project." After a short pause, Darrell continued, "The United States Secret Service will pick up his pay and benefits for the duration of the project.", and then after pausing for another moment stated, "Yes, he will return to you when this project is over; and no, he will not be able to discuss it with you or anyone else." After another pause, Darrell finally said "Thank you Chief; just mark him as on vacation or special assignment. My office will contact you when he has completed this assignment. I thank you and your country thanks you. Good night sir."

"Sir, was that my chief?" Mike asked, looking a bit puzzled as he glanced at Jerry and then back to the President.

"Yes, it was." replied the President. "Now you have to know what we are going to ask and then let me know for sure that you will be able to help us. Your chief has already agreed to release you for the duration of this project by placing you on special assignment with the Secret Service."

"Ok, sir, what do you want me to do?" Mike said, sweating a bit, as he sipped his drink.

Twenty minutes later, Mike Olson knew the extent of the assignment and agreed to help. He was granted an interim Secret Clearance and would receive a Top Secret Clearance within the next twenty-four hours; he had to complete a short form outlining his background which would be rushed through the system to make sure he was covered for anything he might overhear.

Within an hour, Jerry and Mike walked out of the office and were headed towards the parking lot when Jerry said "Mike, we can get the security guards to take care of your bike. You and I have a long way to go and very little time to get there."

"No problem, I can't believe what just happened. Am I dreaming? No, guess not, but can we stop somewhere so I can get a change of clothes; this uniform will make me stand out like Gumby in a banana parade." Mike quickly responded.

"That's a new one on me. Yea, I guess that an all black motorcycle cop uniform with side arm and all the accessories do make you stand out a bit. Since we are supposed to be working undercover, a change is probably in order. Where is your place?" Jerry said eyeing Mike's uniform, "But, hey, you do look pretty sharp in that outfit."

"Well, we have to be in Norfolk as fast as we can go without breaking too many speeding laws. But to answer your question, my new friend, I live just outside of Manassas." Mike commented; "But I think that is out of the way for our trip."

"Yea, we will stop at the first department store we see and get you a change of clothes. Government will buy. Let's check with the head guard and get a place to store your bike and then let's get out of here." continued Jerry.

"Right." Mike agreed.

Chapter 14 Pirates Code

At nine in the morning, Connie, Stephanie and LT Commander Anne Rackham were strolling around the Pirate Museum viewing the artifacts and mock ups of pirate ships, cutlasses, swords, canons and much more. Some of the artifacts were not fakes, but the real thing, gathered over the years and on display in the museum. After about an hour, Anne stopped in front of a display case to read several documents. All the items in the case were real and had some interesting history written on the plaques all around the items.

"Hey guys look at this. I had heard about a code from the family but really did not believe there was one, but look here." Anne called over to Connie and Stephanie and pointed at the cabinet. "According to this, pirates were pretty democratic. This says they had elections to determine who was to be Captain, split all booty equally, did not allow gambling on board ship or excessive drinking without severe punishment. And, I knew this one, no women on board because they felt there would be fights to determine who would have their way with them and they thought they would just bring bad luck. Cool. But my ancestor, our beloved Miss Bonny was on board, dressed as a man. Now we know why. And their luck was not always good when she was around."

"Yea, if they only knew that they had two women on board, all hell would have broken loose." Connie commented. "I guess someone knew; they both became pregnant by someone."

"Look at this. It confirms what Anne was saying about her linage. Anne Bonny was in jail and very pregnant and so was Mary Reade. Mary died giving birth and Anne just disappeared. Says she had given birth to two other children which were left with relatives in Ireland. And no record of what happened to Anne when she left jail or what happened to the children." Stephanie read from a display case that had a cutlass marked as one that was taken from Anne when she was arrested.

"This is all very interesting, but it just confirms what we already know." Anne stated and then stopped dead in her tracks as she looked at the case with the cutlass.

"Is something wrong, Anne?" Connie asked as she walked over to Anne and touched her on the arm. Anne just stood there looking at the case, eyes wide open, and starting to cry.

"What is it?" Stephanie questioned as she looked in the case to see what Anne was staring at. "Oh!" she said seeing the sash and two rings that had been taken off of Anne when she went to jail and kept in an English bank since taken. They are now on loan to the museum until the end of the year. The items were accompanied by a rough picture, a line drawing of Anne Bonny; the resemblance to Anne Rackham was uncanny. But what made Anne cry were the rings. They were identical with the one on her finger, making it a positive connection with her pirate past. She placed her hand over the ring, hiding it and feeling the history, actually hoping that no one would see it and then see its identical twin in the case. They might think she stole it.

"Let's get out of here, I have seen enough for now. We can talk about this later; I need to go, now." Anne said, continuing to cry as she headed for the exit.

Twenty minutes later, they were sitting at a café several miles away from the museum. They had not said anything until they had sat down and ordered coffee.

"What's wrong, Anne?" Stephanie asked after the waitress left to fill their order.

"That ring in the cabinet is a fake. Anne Bonny had only this ring, sash and cutlass. I know she may have had several different cutlasses but that ring and sash are both very good copies. It should not upset me but it does." explained Anne.

"So they made a copy; what's the problem with a copy?" asked Stephanie.

"The problem is that I have not had this ring off since my mother gave it to me. She never let it out of her sight and neither did my grandmother. Someone must have had this ring in the past to be able to make a copy. The sash is another story; my mother found it among other family heirlooms in a chest after granny passed away. In that chest was the sash, two cutlasses, two pistols and various other items along with a picture, very much like the one in the case back there, of Anne Bonny, Calico Jack, and another sailor standing in front of a ship I had assumed was one of their boats. The name on the boat was *Bonecrusher* and it had a date. I don't remember the date, but it was somewhere around 1700." continued Anne.

"Wow, ok, someone had possession of the ring around the time your grandmother had it, so they could make a copy. Is it possible that she had the copies made for some reason? Maybe to protect the family secret; but, I guess we will really never know." suggested Stephanie.

"No, we will know, because the answer is in that case and when this is over, we will reopen that chest and find out what else is in there." Anne commented and dried her tears. The coffee arrived and they passed the next half hour discussing possibilities of the chest.

Chapter 15 Capital Exposure

Arriving at the FBI Building in Washington DC is not an easy thing to do on a Monday morning. The traffic is heavy and with the rain and wet roads there were numerous accidents to get around. It took an extra forty minutes to get there, get to the parking garage and finally make it to his office, but Jerry was calm albeit a little wet from his trip across the court yard to his building. Mike had stayed at the hotel; since he was working undercover for the President, he did not have the proper credentials to get into the building and up to Jerry's office without a lot of hassle.

"Good morning Jerry, how's it going out there in the world of terrorists?" Judy Fredericks asked as he entered his office.

"Not good Judy, can you get me a cup of coffee and anything you have on the murder of Agent Gants down in Norfolk?" Jerry requested.

"Sure, not much is known yet, but I will get you what there is."

"Good, also could you ask Peterson to come to my office; I need to talk to him."

"Peterson is in Norfolk right now, investigating Gants murder. I will tell him to see you when he returns."

"I thought he was working the Henry Miller case over in Richmond."

"No, the chief reassigned him yesterday and sent him to Norfolk."

"Guess I need to be in the office a bit more often to see who is doing what." Jerry commented as Judy walked out of the office to get his coffee and the file he requested. Minutes later she returned, sat his coffee and file on his desk and then sat across from him, staring.

"Ok, Judy, I know that look, what's up?"

"Rumor has it that there are some very nasty things about to happen around Washington and we are going to be up to our necks in a lot of very hot stuff." Judy stated.

"Now, I don't know about any rumors, but, wait, close the door, please." He paused until the door closed, "I can tell you this. We have a mole in out mist; I am getting closer to finding out who he or she is, but not quite there. I have narrowed it down to which department and that is very scary. I can't tell you right now where, but will let you know that I am close and will expose this individual soon."

"A mole, damn, is there anything I can do to help?" Judy asked.

"Yes, keep your eyes and ears open; and if you see or hear of anyone being in a place where they do not belong, let me know."

"Will do, Jerry, how long are you in town?"

"I leave in a couple hours for Norfolk; we have a Soviet Nuclear Sub down there that Gants was inadvertently involved with and I need to follow up with Peterson and see where we are on that."

"When you get back long enough, you owe me dinner, remember."

"Yes, I do. I hate losing a bet, but this time it will be my pleasure. I should be in town for the weekend, so maybe Friday night." Jerry smiled at the thought of enjoying dinner with his partner. Judy was thirty-two years old, five foot six inches tall and could pass as a model. Her flaming red hair, green eyes and all the parts

in the right places were the envy of most of the women working in the FBI. Judy

always loved to mix business with pleasure and had on rare occasions shared Jerry's

bed.

"I will hold you to that, Jerry. Now don't get yourself killed or injured before

the weekend; let me do that for you." she kidded with him.

"Judy, you know I only kill on weekends and try my best not to get injured

during the week; I will let you hurt me this weekend. OK, now go, so I can get some

work done."

"See you Friday." Judy said as she left the office.

Two hours later Jerry picked up Mike and they were headed toward the

Norfolk Naval Yard.

Chapter 16 Changing Faces

Soviet spy Chekov arrived at 4 p.m. at the Norfolk airport. After retrieving her luggage from the baggage hold on the Gulfstream, Chekov used her diplomatic credentials to get through US Customs quickly, and then caught a cab to her dead contact's apartment. She wondered what had happened to her contact. Was he discovered by the FBI as a mole, or was it from just an unlucky encounter with a criminal element while working a case for the FBI? His cover was rock solid, so the FBI would not kill one of their own, and his death outside of the naval base was curious. Did the FBI send him there? Was he there doing his spying on the recent arrival of their missing missile boat? She would investigate that after she finished her current assignment. His file was full: trained in Moscow, on assignment in the United States for the past eighteen years, worked as a New York police officer, transferred to the FBI after six years on the force, got lucky and moved up the chain quickly, mostly because of his past training. The file did not say what his assignment was at the department.

She would go to his apartment and see what she could find out; besides, he had communicated to her where to find his weapons, to see if anything was missing. Hopefully, the FBI had not located them.

After retrieving a new Mustang convertible from the Hertz Rental car desk at the airport, she headed toward her dead contact's apartment. Within an hour after landing, she was picking the lock on the apartment of Robert Gants, her contact's undercover name. The lock clicked, and she stood and entered the apartment, ignoring the smell of stale cigarettes; she hated smoking. Slowly closing the door so she would not attract attention, she glanced around the room taking in every little piece of furniture, dust, books and litter that Robert had collected over the years he had been working undercover for the Soviet government.

Twenty minutes after entering the apartment, she had located the hidden panel with Robert's weapons and removed a small automatic 9mm with four magazines that were already loaded. Looking around, she located a small backpack into which she placed the pistol, magazines and an M-16 with collapsible stock and ten loaded magazines. Four extra boxes of ammo were also placed in the bag before she zipped it closed. Reaching back into the locker, she picked up another pistol, this time a 45 caliber Colt with six magazines and a holster which she slipped into her belt in the center of her back. She hoped she would not need any of these but took them anyway. Better safe than sorry later.

A click at the front door caused her to freeze, but only for a second. She closed the locker door quietly, stood and quickly looked for a way out. The apartment was on the first floor with a sliding glass door to a small patio, which she immediately slid open and exited to the patio and out the back fence to the street. Not knowing who was coming in the front door, she did not want to take any chances being caught. It couldn't be Gants; he was dead, but maybe his handler. Almost anyone, but she did not wait to find out. She would attempt to contact Gants handler later if she needed help.

She reached her car in a couple minutes, sat and watched the front of the apartment building for any sign of the unexpected guest. Not seeing anyone come out, she headed for her hotel and contemplated her next move. She needed to store the weapons in her room and head for the airport to meet Commander Harriet Lanstrom, the nuclear specialist that had been ordered from San Diego to Norfolk Naval Yard to help with the Soviet submarine. Only Harriet would not enjoy the encounter at all.

"Flight 143 from San Diego will be arriving at gate 26 in fifteen minutes." The announcer said as Chekov entered the airport terminal.

'That's her flight' Chekov thought to herself as she crossed the terminal heading toward the baggage claim area. She would have better luck meeting her there.

Commander Lanstrom came down to the baggage claim area a half hour later. Chekov was standing there waiting just as if she was really the driver for a Naval Commander.

"Commander Lanstrom, I am Chief Petty Officer Jackson. I have been sent to pick you up and take you to the Naval Yard."

"Chief, as soon as my luggage arrives we can be on our way." Lanstrom replied as she looked at the baggage starting to spill out on the conveyer belt. Minutes later, Lanstrom's bag slid down the belt, and after Chekov retrieved it, they headed for the car.

After driving out of the airport, they headed toward the Norfolk Naval Yard which was about an hour away.

"Commander it gives me great displeasure to tell you that things are not as they appear and I will be turning off the highway in a minute and we will be making a short stop." Chekov said quietly as she drove.

"I don't understand your meaning, Chief." Lanstrom questioned.

"You will understand in a few minutes. And I am truly sorry about this, Commander." Chekov continued.

Stopping the car on a secluded side road, Chekov pulled her small 9mm pistol and pointed it at Lanstrom. Without hesitation she said quietly, "Please get out of the car and go up to the house."

Lanstrom did as she was told. Once they entered the house Chekov continued, "Now remove your uniform and don't try anything stupid, I don't want to hurt you."

Lanstrom unbuttoned her jacket and slowly removed it. Minutes later she sat in her bra and panties, and slowly said, "You will not get away with this, young lady; the Navy will be looking for me if I don't show up at the base soon."

"Well, it may be a while before that happens. Now put these on." Chekov demanded, tossing a pair of slacks and shirt to Lanstrom. "They should fit; I looked up your size before picking you up."

"Are you going to kill me?" asked Lanstrom.

"No, I don't kill innocent people, not my style; I just need to use your identity for a while. So you are going to stay here; there is plenty of food in the refrigerator. There is no phone and no way out of here. Once I lock the door, this place is sealed solid. There are bars on the windows, the glass cannot be broken, and the doors do not have a way to open from the inside without a special key. And if you

do happen to get one open, the house will self destruct. There are explosives on all the

windows and doors. And don't think about going through the wall; it is concrete and

reinforced. We had this place built years ago as a safe house and no one has escaped

yet. Don't be stupid and try to be the first; you will not survive." stated Chekov.

"Why are you doing this?" Lanstrom demanded.

"As I said, I need to be you for a short time; and when I am done, I will come

back and let you go. If something happens and my schedule changes for some

unforeseen reason, after a set amount of time, someone will come out and release you.

If I don't return, I will probably be dead or in jail. Be smart and just relax for a few

days. All will be explained when I return. Oh, there is beer and liquor in the pantry,

the TV is hooked up to cable, and the stereo works. So be smart and take a little time

off from the Navy and just stay here. I will be back in a few days, or someone else will

come let you out within a week, I promise. Just enjoy the mini vacation while I go do

what I have to do." continued Chekov.

"OK, you have control now, but I will make sure you pay for this when I get

out of here." replied Lanstrom.

"Don't threaten me, Lanstrom. I can leave you to rot here. I am not going to

kill you, but if you cause trouble I will." declared Chekov.

"Ok, I will cooperate and I will stay here." replied Lanstrom.

"If I am not back in a week, someone else will release you, because I will probably be dead or have been arrested. So either way, you will be out of here in a week." stated Chekov.

Minutes later, Chekov checked all the doors and windows, and opened the front door. As she turned she said "See you soon or a friend of mine will. Enjoy the time off."

Chekov stepped out, locked the door and then opened a panel that looked like an electrical panel on the side of the house and flipped a couple of switches that armed the explosives and set several deadbolts on the doors and windows.

Within minutes, Chekov was heading toward the highway and her hotel. She needed to change into the uniform and then head to the Norfolk Naval Yard. After reaching the hotel and changing into the uniform, she signed onto her laptop computer to send a coded message to her contact in Moscow informing them about Commander Lanstrom and the status of her mission. She also requested more information about Lanstrom, which was sent to her almost before her request was received. Chekov was informed that the transition of Lanstrom's military record had been completed and she should proceed with the mission. Thirty minutes later, she was headed for the Norfolk Naval Yard.

Chapter 17 You Did What?

Later the same day at the Hilton Grand Hotel in downtown Charleston, South Carolina, the ex-Soviet Submarine Captain and thirteen of his surviving officers and crewmen were sipping vodka and watching the local news on the television and chatting about the previous week. The hotel suite was well appointed, complete with a wide screen fifty-five inch television, wet bar, living room, two bedrooms, and all the comforts that Chief Executive Officers of major companies would expect when they visited Charleston.

"Gentlemen, as you know, we have a problem. We have a very big problem that needs to be corrected quickly, before we go our separate ways. We can't sell those warheads as we had thought. We could let the United States government know where they are and just walk away, or give them back to our government. But that would mean we have to let them know we are still alive, which of course we do not want them to know;" their Captain commented between sips of vodka. He then wiped his mouth with his sleeve. "We do not have all the money we need to disappear as planned, yet we have a good start in that direction."

"If we divide the gold, we will only have about $500,000 each which may not be enough to survive on unless we take jobs and go to work. But we will not be able to work without new identities, so how much money does it take to get new identities?"

"I don't know what it costs, but we could buy some identities and start over, sir." a junior officer said. "I hear the identity theft problem is very big here and it is easy to purchase a new identity. To me, it is worth a few thousand dollars to buy identities and start over. I just want to live quietly away from the navy and other people; maybe buy a small piece of land in the west and fade into the countryside."

"Captain, we need the money you promised." the executive officer commented. "You promised we could sell all the gold and have at least a million dollars each, but we lost half of the gold when you tried to blow up London. We should not have let them take that gold. We should have killed them when we had the chance. London is a dump and we should have destroyed it when we had the chance and we would have been paid."

"Yes, yes, that was a big mistake. We should never have attempted that, but we did get paid for that. Well, most of the money anyway. My apologies, but we do have the warheads and the gold bars, so our choice now is that we can give the warheads to the United States or sell them. I wish you, Viktor, had not insisted on taking them in the first place. I don't know what you were thinking and why I let you talk me into that."

"Let us agree that selling to the United States is the best bet." the executive officer stated and glanced around the room, looking for acknowledgement to his commitment. "We need to make a decision, Captain. Are we, or are we not, going to sell these warheads?"

"We can ransom them." the weapons officer commented as he sipped his drink.

"Ransom?" queried the captain.

"Yes, ransom! We place the warheads in various cities and tell the President that if he does not pay us what we want, then we detonate one, then another, and another." the weapons officer stated without blinking. He looked at the executive officer and smiled.

"We have ten warheads; how do you propose we move them to the targets? I do not want to blow up innocent people." the captain commented, "And how can we detonate them. They are an air burst design. We would need timers and some sort of detonator. We do not have those types of things, or do we?"

"I can wire them to explode on command from a cell phone. Georgio and I can make it happen with a phone call." his weapons officer stated. "Pretty easy, kinda...." he started to say but stopped.

Four of the officers agreed, but the rest said they would not help ransom the warheads in the United States. The Captain did not agree at all with the plan; he just wanted to retire quietly and live in a small house by the ocean on Cape Cod or in the Hamptons. He felt he had enough money to do that, with his share of the gold and the stash he had been putting away for the past two years.

"We do not kill innocent people, but we must let them know that we really have the warheads. How do you propose we do that?" his dive officer asked.

"We just tell them where to find one, and let them know we have nine more. If they pay, we will tell them where to find the rest of them."

"That all sounds interesting, but I am not sure we should do this. What if they decide not to pay? We would have to destroy a city and kill millions of people. I cannot do that; we are not at war with this country. I do not want to kill innocent people in the country that I want to live in. I just can't do that. We would be at war with this country as soon as we destroy a city. They would hunt for us until they find and kill us all." the captain stated. "If they call our bluff, do we give up the rest or destroy a city? I cannot destroy a city. Let's try it; and if they refuse, we just give them up and disappear with the money we have."

All the officers looked around the room not sure of the correct answer. A young junior grade officer, normally in charge of their food and mess departments stood and walked over to the wet bar and got a cold beer. "I am with the Captain; if they call our bluff we just turn over the warheads and disappear."

"We need to decide now; or I will make the decision myself, which will be to give the warheads to the United States and ask for political asylum." Captain Viktorov stated without waiting for a reply.

"Why don't we sell them back to Moscow?" a junior officer asked, new to the crew and not understanding what was really happening.

"Not exactly a good idea. They right now think we are lost at sea and are all dead. Well, anyway, that is what we have tried to make them think. But as you know, that may be our downfall. They may have tracked us and right now have a bunch of agents heading over here to kill all of us." the Captain commented and then sipped his drink. "We cannot let them know we are alive or we for sure will be dead. Remember, we have committed a major crime and our government will not let us live for that. Stealing a nuclear submarine is punishable with a quick shot to the head; no trial, no pardon, just a bullet to the head and a large hole in the ground. Do you understand? We are dead men to our country! Now and forever, we are dead; just not physically, yet." Captain Viktorov explained.

"Kill us; they would not do that…. Would they?" a commander in the corner asked as he looked around the room for an answer.

"Yes, they would; we did steal a nuclear submarine, did we not?" the Captain queried and before getting an answer he continued. "Did we not steal ten nuclear warheads? Yes…. And, to top it off, did we not abandon our crew in the middle of the Atlantic Ocean? Yes we did, gentlemen; so you think they are not going to come after us?" After pausing for a moment to look around the room and refill his glass, the Captain continued, "Now gentlemen, we have created a real nightmare for ourselves. Our crew may have been rescued and told their stories. Stories that may have caused concern with our government, and now they are looking for us in Cuba, South America and even here in the United States. They suspect we are alive; and they will know we are when they find out that our boat is not sitting in pieces on the bottom of the ocean as the crew would have told them. And yes, they will find us, in time, unless we cover our tracks and do not let our government know we are alive and in hiding. This I am sure of. "

"Are you kidding, Captain?" was the question from across the room from his executive officer Viktor Mikhailovich.

"No Viktor, I kid you not. They are looking, and we need to make this happen quickly or not at all. This means we send a message to the U.S. government letting them know where to find the warheads. And, of course, we just go with the money we have and we live a lot longer. Or we try to sell them, and maybe get caught and are dead. It is your choice gentlemen, so it is all or nothing." After pausing for a moment to let his thoughts sink in; the Captain continued, "I say we give them to the United States and ask for asylum."

"Captain, your English has become very good over the past few weeks." his executive officer commented while getting tired of all this chatter.

"Yes, I have been working on my English for years, just waiting for today. Are you as ready as I am?" asked the Captain.

"Yes, sir;" his officers responded. "Which are we going to do, sell or give them back?"

"That my friends is the big question, isn't it? Now let's make a decision and get on with it." Captain Viktorov commented as he stood and walked toward the bathroom, "I will be right back, talk it over and when I get back we need to decide. My vote, and since I am the Captain you should take my decision into account, is we give the warheads as a sign of good faith to the United States and ask for new identities and asylum."

"Captain, do you have any regrets in what we have done?" his executive officer asked with a concerned look, thinking to himself that this man did not have it in him to blow up an American city.

"The only regret I have my friend is that we left the ship so fast that I left my favorite pistol and that small bag of pirate gold that we found in the Bahamas. And we don't know for sure that she sank or the charges went off as planned. I have no regrets and, well, I will be right back." replied Captain Viktorov.

The room became very quiet as each man thought about what had just been said and each needed to consider what their next move would be.

"Sir, I think we need to hold the United States ransom and have them pay us for each warhead." the executive officer Viktor Mikhailovich commented after the captain left.

Most of the room shook their heads in agreement; and a few had concerned looks on their faces as Captain Viktorov re-entered the room.

"Viktor, if we do that, we will be hunted down until caught or killed. I did not risk everything to become a fugitive in the country in which I have chosen to become a new citizen. Did you?" the Captain responded with conviction and determination not to let anyone stop him.

"I know how you feel, but we do not have enough money to get a new start, and well, I, for one, believe the United States will not bow down to us unless we blow up one of their cities." stated Viktor.

"What do you mean, Viktor?" asked Captain Viktorov.

"I mean that several of us have already decided to take the warheads and show the United States that we mean business." insisted Viktor.

"What have you done?" Captain Viktorov demanded.

"You will see. We have planned months for this and you cannot stop us." Viktor said as he pulled a gun from his waist and aimed at the Captain. "Georgio secure the Captain and anyone else that does not want to go with us."

"No, you can't do this." the young food service officer yelled as he stood up and charged at Viktor. He did not get three steps before being tackled by two of Viktor's men.

"Tie him up too; is there anyone else who does not want to become rich and live the American life?" Viktor asked waving the gun around the room but keeping a sharp eye on his ex-captain. The other two officers that were not sure about the plan decided they would go along with the executive officer, but looked over at the captain and winked. "Let's get moving; we have only two days to move the warheads and get to a secure location." said Viktor.

Chapter 18 Discovery

Three hours later Special Agent Jerry Hancock and Highway Patrol officer Mike Olson arrived at the gate to the Norfolk Naval Yard.

"Gentleman, may we help you?" the gate guard asked as Hancock rolled down his window and glanced at the Navy Seaman. He decided that this young sailor was going to be very professional in his job and would not take any bull from anyone especially a couple of midsized people dressed in jeans and polo shirts. The guard was the size of a horse and should have traded his uniform in for one that was at least a size or two larger. The one thing that most people believe is that big muscular men are dumb, but that was not always true and this sailor had intelligence written all over his face.

Handing the guard his identification, Hancock said, "I am Special Agent Jerry Hancock and this is my partner Mike Olson; we are special agents to the President and here to see an Ensign Kent."

"Yes, we have been expecting you, sir. Hang on for a minute while I run your cards through the system." the guard said as he looked at his partner and handed him the cards to run. "And do it quickly", he continued. The information he had received from his watch commander was that these two agents should not be delayed and given as much assistance as reasonably possible.

Minutes later the guard returned. "Mr. Hancock, you are cleared to enter. To get to Ensign Kent's location, just go straight down this road, turn right at the stop sign and go about a mile to the stop light. Make a left and go two blocks to the dock;

park on the east side of the street. You will find Ensign Kent in conference room 2 in building 197, first floor. There is a guard in the lobby. Show your IDs. They know you are coming. Have a good day, gentlemen." the large friendly guard said before he saluted the two agents.

Twenty minutes later, Hancock and Olson were standing in front of Ensign Kent holding out their identification. "Ensign Kent, I am Jerry Hancock with the Secret Service and this is Mike Olson from the Virginia Highway Patrol on temporary assignment with the United States Secret Service by order of the President. He has been granted a clearance level high enough to participate with this assignment."

"Gentleman, please take a seat. We have much to talk about. Would you like some coffee before we start?" Ensign Kent stated as they entered the room.

"Sure." Hancock responded.

"No thanks, Ensign." Mike replied as he looked around the conference room. It was bringing back memories of his time in the military and when he had sat in rooms just like this, planning operations and then taking his men out on missions that could very well have ended his and his men's lives.

"Ok, Ensign, what do we have?" Hancock questioned as he took a big gulp of his coffee.

"First off, Mr. Hancock, we have several serious problems and not much time to solve them."

"Call me Jerry, please;" he interrupted. He set his coffee down on the table and looked around the room.

"Ok, Jerry and Mike, is it.? Well, we have a Soviet nuclear submarine less than fifty yards from here and she was found adrift just off the coast of North Carolina. We have only had her for three days and are still going through her."

"Ok, sounds pretty simple at the moment. What about the crew?"

"Well, that is problem number one, no crew, just some bodies in the freezer, eight to be exact, died from gun shots. And we have some other mysteries to solve." Ensign Kent commented. "We have a team on board the sub right now that is taking pictures and inventory. We should know everything about that boat before the week is out. What do you need for the President?"

"The President just wants to know if she is safe being here and when we can return her to the Soviets, hopefully before they find out we have her. He knows we have had her for three days, that warheads are missing, and there are bodies." Jerry stated and continued to drink his coffee. "What he does not know is why she was abandoned, why the bodies are there, and why the warheads are missing. So he wants to know everything there is to know about that boat. We have the authority to get you anything you need to get those answers. Just name it."

"Well, Jerry, we don't know if that will be possible, returning her, I mean. How do we explain how we got her and why there were dead bodies left on board?" Ensign Kent asked but did not expect an answer.

A knock at the door interrupted their conversation; Ensign Kent looked up at the door as it swung open to let Davin, Josh, Connie and Stephanie enter. As Davin started to close the door, it was stopped by a large hand, the hand of Captain Henderson.

"Hold the door, Davin." Bear Henderson said as he pushed the door open. "Sorry, I am a little late."

"Come on in gentlemen and ladies. This is Special Agent Jerry Hancock and Mike Olson. They were sent down here by the President, and authorized by the President to give us anything we need." Kent said, introducing everyone. Then she took a seat at the side of the table with a fresh cup of coffee.

After introductions, everyone sat and just sipped coffee for a moment before continuing the conversation, letting everyone get relaxed in a very tense situation.

"Mr. Hancock," Captain Henderson started then paused and picked up his napkin to wipe coffee from his mouth. "Mr. Hancock, we have a serious problem and not sure where to start; but you can start by telling the President that there are two missing nuclear missiles."

"Captain, tell me something we don't know. We were messaged that two days ago, and the President already knows about the missiles. We need to know if that boat is safe to explore or if it is going to cause this nation regret having it. Are the other missiles safe? The President along with our office does not have a warm fuzzy feeling about any of this. Think of it this way. What is the easiest way to get nuclear weapons into this country?" After pausing for a moment for his question to sink in, he continued. "Yea, get a nuclear submarine drifting off the coast, let our boys snag it and bring it into one of our largest naval bases, then boom, set the damn thing off, destroying half of the east coast."

"Who sent the message?" Henderson asked Ensign Kent, looking at her with a little annoyance in his eye. He was ignoring what Hancock had said, at least for a minute.

"Sir, that was Admiral Compton, commander of Naval Intelligence here at the base."

"I want to see the base commander and Admiral Compton immediately." Henderson demanded, then looked back at Hancock, "Good scenario, and yes that could happen and we are looking at the possibility of that and do not have an answer yet. We are taking precautions and have a team ready to go in and disarm all those warheads if needed."

"Sir, he is also the base commander and should be here in about….." Ensign Kent started and then looked at the clock before continuing, "in about twenty minutes."

"Good. I hope he brings a padded ass, he is going to need it when I am done with him."

Minutes later there was a knock on the door. It opened and Admiral Compton entered the room; the naval officers stood as the Admiral entered. "Please take your seats ladies and gentlemen." Stopping just inside, he turned and said to his aid. "Ensign Phillips would you remain out in the hall and not let anyone except Captain Morrow enter." Then back to the officers and guests in the room he continued, "This meeting is now classified Top Secret and I have already checked everyone's clearance level, except yours, Mr. Olson. But by the order of the President, you have been given interim clearance to be here. You are not to discuss with anyone outside this room the nature of this meeting, the content of that submarine or any outcome of what we are about to discuss. Is that understood, Mr. Olson?"

"Yes, sir, I understand completely." Mike Olson agreed.

"Admiral, sir, we need to talk privately, before we go on with this." Henderson stated before the Admiral had a chance to start his briefing.

"Captain Henderson, I know what you are going to say. I did send the message to the President and I know you disagree, but it is done. We have a bigger problem. Mr. Olson, we all thank you for volunteering your time for this mission; you may wish you didn't. Now if I may, we have a serious problem here. We have just learned that the Soviets have discovered that we have their boat; they must have seen that newspaper article that got a picture of us retrieving her. But it could have been a lot of other sources; they have spies everywhere. Anyway, they know. We have also learned that the man killed several miles from the base was in fact an FBI agent that had been working on the base for about a year. He, right now, is no concern to us; his office is working that. Wait, Mrs. Pierce, you are with the FBI, am I correct?" She nodded and looked a bit worried. The Admiral continued, "You may want to check in with your office to see if they need your help on that one. Now on to the good news, a Soviet agent by the name of Chekov has been dispatched to investigate what we are doing with their boat and I suppose to get it back or destroy it. I would guess they plan on destroying it." Admiral Compton stated and then sat down at the head of the table.

"Do we know anything about this agent, what he looks like, to start with?" Henderson asked.

"Admiral Compton, Secret Service Agent Jerry Hancock," Jerry said as an introduction, then continued; "The President is worried that this is a trick to get a boat load of nuclear warheads on our soil with the intent to detonate them. Do you feel that is a possible scenario?"

"No, this boat was adrift, with dead on board; there is no indication that that scenario is one that is viable. As to the agent that is heading our way, no sir, we do not know what he or she, as the case may be, looks like or where he or she is right now. There are indications from NSA that the agent may be a woman. Their source could not be sure as to the identity of the agent, but has indicated that they believe the agent to be a woman. Do you have any other questions?"

"Yes sir, don't we have a Commander Lanstrom, from San Diego, some kind of nuclear specialist, on her way here?" Ensign Kent asked.

"Commander Lanstrom landed a couple of hours ago. She should be here shortly. She is in Naval Intelligence and is trained in Soviet nuclear submarines and systems." Admiral Compton replied. "Along with the men and women we have here at Norfolk, we will dissect that boat in three days and know everything there is to know about her. She is their newest and most sophisticated boat they have ever built, and we need to know what they have and quickly. The cold war may be over but that is only for the public, so they do not panic. The cold war is alive and well. The Soviets are ready to destroy us when the time is right and that boat out there is only one of six they have recently built. She is supposed to be the best equipped, most dangerous vessel on the high seas, or rather under the high seas."

"That's all well and good, Admiral, but what do we do after we dissect her? Give her back, sink her, or what?" Davin asked bluntly.

"We will cross that bridge once we get there, but we also have to deal with this Chekov when, and if, he or she arrives. That may change our time frame some, if Chekov shows up and causes us some problems."

"Ok, now what about the missing warhead? Aren't those things carrying up to ten individual warheads, each of which can destroy a city by itself? What are we doing about those?" Henderson asked the room, looking at the Admiral and then the rest of the room.

"Yes, each missile is designed with up to ten warheads. We have a team of specialists searching for them right now, assuming they actually made it to our shores. But really, those could have been off loaded with the crew at anyone of a thousand locations, including right here in the Carolinas. We are working on several scenarios and will hopefully come up with their location soon."

"So what you are saying is that you don't know where the hell they are." Connie stated looking at the Admiral.

"Yes, young lady, we have no freaking idea where they are." the Admiral commented; looking very disgusted with the whole situation. "We are not real happy about the whole situation, and I am sure the President is equally worried. We don't want an international incident and definitely do not want a nuclear explosion on our soil. The loss of life, destruction and future problems that would cause is beyond belief. We have a lot of work to do starting with dissecting that boat, removing all those warheads and other weapons, and then making a decision as to what to do with the remains. We have many serious problems here and very little time to solve them. Now, Captain Henderson, you have a crew that is out there now working on the boat?" After getting a nod, he continued, "Secret Service, you have been given a lot of authority by the President, I hope you are prepared to act on it." He got another nod to the affirmative from Hancock. "FBI Pierce and CIA Randel and Pierce, your involvement here is not really needed or required. I believe your assistance is best helping your respective departments in locating the warheads."

"Admiral Compton, Mr. Randel and I have specific knowledge about that boat and her captain. We were requested by Captain Henderson to assist. We, if you please, will continue with that request." Davin stated looking at the Admiral without batting an eye.

"Captain Henderson, I realize you are not part of my command, but keeping me informed would be greatly appreciated. They will stay with you till you have done your investigation." Admiral Compton stated, glaring at Captain Henderson.

"Yes sir, I will keep you informed, but formally request that you do not use standard channels to communicate any information off base. Secure channels may have been compromised."

"I do agree, Captain, and as of this moment, nobody will discuss or communicate anything about this project to anyone for any reason without clearing it through me personally. That goes for everyone except Agent Hancock, who will only communicate with the President using the direct line located in my office.

Chapter 19 Chekov's Quest

Chekov checked into the Hilton Downtown and took a long hot shower, dressed in the uniform she acquired from Commander Lanstrom, and after checking in the mirror, she turned and headed out the door. Twenty-five minutes later, she was pulling up to the gate at the Norfok Naval Yard.

Saluting, the guard at the gate asked. "May I help you Commander?"

"I am Commander Lanstrom, here to meet with Admiral Compton." she stated as she handed the guard her counterfeit ID card and a copy of her orders. Her orders were real since she had gotten them from the real Lanstrom. Her orders stated that she was on special assignment with no detail. They were just your normal orders, name, rank, and duration of assignment.

"One moment please, Commander," the gate guard said and then turned to the other guard and asked, "Johnson, check this for me," handing her orders and ID to Johnson, the junior sailor of the team on guard.

"They check out, Chief Douglas." Johnson stated after a few minutes on the phone. "Commander Jacobs, Officer of the Day has confirmed the Commander is expected. She needs to head straight to dock six and report to ah... report to Ensign Kent, who is in conference room 2 of building 197, along with Admiral Compton." Johnson said and handed her ID and orders back to her. He then asked. "Do you know the way to dock six?"

"No, first time here." she replied. Chief Douglas then proceeded to give her the directions to dock six, where to park and how to find building 197.

Twenty minutes later, she pulled into a vacant spot next to dock 6; she walked over to the dock where a guard was standing. After reviewing her orders and ID, the guard directed her to Building 197 across the parking lot. She was told Ensign Kent and Admiral Compton were in a meeting in conference room two.

Minutes later she approached the conference room. The guard stopped her and after checking her ID said. "Commander Lanstrom, welcome to Norfolk. The Admiral is expecting you." Then he knocked on the door and opened it. "Admiral Compton, Commander Lanstrom is here."

"Send her in." Admiral Compton said from across the room.

"Go on in, Commander."

"Thank you." Commander Lanstrom said as she entered the room.

"Welcome to our meeting, Commander Lanstrom. Please come in and take a seat; we have a lot to discuss," the Admiral said as he sat back down. "You can introduce yourselves after the meeting. Commander Lanstrom is a nuclear reactor specialist from San Diego, specializing in Soviet reactors."

Hancock and Olson looked over at each other, thinking that they knew the Soviets had sent a female agent over to find out about the sub and not knowing for sure that this Lanstrom was real or the agent. They did not know what Lanstrom looked like and this person did look very navy. She had the proper identification and orders to back it up, so, they assumed, she must be the real Lanstrom.

Commander Lanstrom was brought up to speed on the situation as she sat quietly absorbing everything around her. She studied everyone's face, mannerisms, uniform and every bit of the room they were in. Davin sat across from her and also watched her intently. His mind was constantly running with different scenarios.

"Commander Lanstrom, your accent is, is that southern?"

"Yes, is it Mr. Pierce, I am from Mobile, Alabama. Born and raised." She commented as she looked intently at Davin Pierce and wondered if he knew or suspected she was an imposter.

"Mr. Pierce, we can chit chat after this meeting. We have some more serious problems to cover; Commander Lanstrom's accent is not one of them."

"Sorry sir, I will keep quiet unless asked to speak." Davin said, still curious about Lanstrom. Something did not seem quite right with Commander Lanstrom. Call it instinct or just coincidence, a female Soviet agent and Commander Lanstrom reported to show up at the same time.

"OK, ladies and gentlemen, we can make a final decision about the fate of that boat after we know more about her. For now, no one will discuss anything about her outside of this conference room and on or around the boat itself. I have stated this before and hope to not have to make that statement again. Do not under any circumstances go against that order, civilian or military. We are all here for one thing and that is to discover everything we can about that boat."

"What is our next move?" Captain Henderson asked.

"Commander Lanstrom, you are to work with Captain Henderson on the boat; he will report to me. Understood?"

"Yes sir, no problem." Commander Lanstrom agreed.

"Everyone knows what they have to do, except Commander Lanstrom. I will bring her up to speed and send her over to the boat in about an hour." Admiral Compton continued. He stood and as he walked over to the coffee pot said "I think we are done here. Let's get to work. We will meet back here tomorrow at 0800 to discuss progress. See you tomorrow, dismissed."

"Before we go sir, may I ask a question?" Commander Lanstrom asked with a slow southern drawl.

"Go ahead, Commander."

"Sir, I know I just got here and do not know what has taken place up to now and I am sure I will understand better after your briefing. But why don't we just send it back now? We don't really have the right to inspect that boat. We have better technology than the Soviets and there is nothing to be learned from her. I have been studying Soviet technology for years and I have learned they are at least ten years behind us in aspects of nuclear technology. I don't believe we can learn much from her and we are wasting our time."

"Commander, this is our boat right now, under international laws of salvage. We found it abandoned and claim salvage rights. With that in mind Commander, you will follow orders. You have been sent here to explore that boat and document everything you find. And I expect nothing but a perfect report from you. Understand, Commander?" sounding a bit disturbed with her comment. "You will understand more in the next hour. Now, everyone else, please leave us. Ensign Kent, please make sure they have what they need out there. Inform the Watch Commander that they will be taking charge of the boat, effective now."

"Yes sir, no problem, sir." Commander Lanstrom agreed, obviously not real happy about her orders. She looked around the room at the others, hoping her performance was convincing.

"Good, now go to work." Admiral Compton ordered. "See you at 0800 tomorrow."

Ten minutes later, all, except the admiral and Lanstrom, were standing on the deck of the Soviet submarine being briefed on the status.

"Captain Henderson and invited guests, the boat has been deemed safe to board and your tour will start in the main control room. The bodies have been removed; autopsies will be completed soon. We should have a complete inventory by tomorrow noon." Ensign Kent stated as they gathered around the front of the submarines sail. Ensign Kent had gone below to check with the Watch Commander and get their radiation badges. "Captain Henderson, would you take Mr. Pierce and his team down the forward hatch to the control room. Here are your radiation badges; please wear them at all times while on or around the boat. I am going to the reactor room to let them know that Commander Lanstrom will be arriving in about an hour."

"Thank you Ensign, I would like everyone to meet in the mess hall in an hour for a short briefing and update. Would you inform the teams already on board?" Henderson ordered.

"Yes, Captain. We have several of our nuclear specialists already down there. They are just monitoring and keeping track of how the system is doing. It seems as though the previous owners did not turn off the lights or anything for that matter when they left home. There were still food and drinks on the table in the officers' dining room."

"That is very interesting, Ensign, ah Kent is it?" Josh commented.

"Yes sir, Ensign Cheryl Kent. OK, is everyone ready? Captain, please, after you." Ensign Kent said pointing toward the hatch.

"Let's get'er done!" Bear Henderson said and led the way down the hatch.

Chapter 20 Who Are the Bad Guys?

"Maid service," The floor maid yelled as she knocked on the door of Room 1096 of the Hilton Grand Hotel at 11:15 in the morning. Getting no answer when she knocked the second time, she used her pass key to enter. "Oh my!" she exclaimed seeing two men, one lying on the sofa fully clothed and the other on the floor beside the chair. Both looked dead. Both men had their hands tied behind their backs and a gag over their mouths, which she did not notice at first and said, "Excuse me, sirs." Then started to back out when she noticed the blood on the floor beside the one beside the chair and their hands being tied. Backing out, she turned and ran down the hall to the courtesy phone, immediately dialing the front desk, "Jeremy, call 911, request an ambulance and the police. We have two injured, possibly dead men in room 1096, tell them to hurry."

Meanwhile the crew was miles away heading for the warehouse to pick up the nuclear warheads, located at a private marina. Within an hour, two ocean going boats were heading toward a freighter about eight miles off shore. Each was carrying a single warhead. Several trucks and rental cars had been secured to transport the balance of the warheads, each heading for different locations with the intent to detonate if the government did not pay the ransom. Their plan was simple, distribution of the weapons was planned for one each in Miami, Los Angeles, New Orleans, New York, Philadelphia, San Francisco, Denver, St. Louis, and two in Washington D.C. Ten warheads, nine cities targeted, teams of two or three of his men would deliver the warheads, arm them and retreat to a safe house in North Dakota. Simple, the warheads were equipped with a remote detonator which could be detonated with a cell phone. In four days, they would be ready and then place their demands to the President of the United States. Either the United States would meet their demands or would lose several cities, quickly.

Two days later at a hospital in downtown Charleston, South Carolina, two unidentified men were being released after being rushed there from a hotel. Both men had sustained severe blows to the head, but not considered severe enough to keep them beyond a couple of days. They were declared healthy, but instructed to check in with their personal doctors for further observation and treatment. Neither one would do that, since they had no local doctor to check in with. They had other options, though.

"Hello, may I speak with Admiral Hamner?" the voice on the line said to the secretary in Admiral Hamner's office, located in the inner ring of the Pentagon. Admiral Scott Hamner was the Commander of the Atlantic Fleet. He was five foot ten inches tall, about one hundred eighty-five pounds and fifty-four years of age. He still ran four miles daily and followed an extensive regiment of exercise and diet. He was one of the youngest fleet admirals in the Navy and did not put up with the political BS that many in the Pentagon thought was required to just be there. He was always thinking outside the box or in this case the pentagon and had connections in many places. Today those connections were paying off. After a long time in waiting and hoping, his contact had finally called.

"Sir, may I tell him who is calling?" the sweet voice on the other end of the line asked politely.

"Tell him that Joseph Stalin is calling." he said not using his real name but the code phrase that had been agreed upon over a year ago.

"Just a moment, let me see if he is available, Mr. Stalin." She said, knowing full well that the user of that code name was in the process of defecting to the United States. She punched the 'Hold' button and pressed the intercom, "Sir, Mr. Stalin is on line one."

'I hope he is, I have been waiting for over a year for this day and now it is a matter of life and death to many of your people,' Joseph said quietly to himself sweating in the small phone booth in the lobby of the hospital.

"Stalin thought you would never call. How are you, old friend?" Hamner replied, using the correct response to the code.

"Not well, Admiral, Not well at all. I just got out of the hospital, seems we have a bigger problem now than when we first talked. Can we meet today?" Joseph Stalin asked firmly.

"Yes, where are you now?" Admiral Hamner asked, looking at his schedule, seeing what he needed to move to make this meeting happen. Upon seeing that he had nothing that could not be moved till later in the week or canceled altogether, he smiled, but it was a short lived smile.

"I just was released from Mercy General Hospital and am in the waiting room. Oh, we are in Charleston, South Carolina."

"Did you say we?" Admiral Hamner asked.

"Yes sir, I will explain in a moment."

"Ok, go to the airport, general aviation side; there will be a Gulfstream IV jet waiting for you. The tail number is N498WW. They will fly you to Andrews Air Force Base where I will meet you. See you in about an hour and half." stated Admiral Hamner.

"I have one of my trusted officers with me, he is just getting released. I will bring him also, that okay?"

"Does he know about the deal?" queried Admiral Hamner.

"I took him into my confidence; if he betrays me, then he knows he will not see the light of day for a long time and he will not like the accommodations."

"Good, bring him along."

"See you soon, old friend." With that the line went dead. Seeing his young officer approach he said to him, "Come, Eric, we have a plane to catch."

"Yes, sir;" Eric responded.

"No need for the sir anymore, Eric. You can call me Mikhail or Mike as our American would say. Yes, I like Mike so much better. Call me Mike from now on. We are going to be Americans and we need to take our American names. Yours, Eric, is already a well known name in this country. You are lucky, my young friend." he said as they exited the hospital and signaled for a cab.

"Mike, how are we going to pay for this transportation?" asked Eric.

"No worries, Eric. I exchanged some Rubles into American cash in the bank located in the lobby of the hospital. These Americans are very smart, providing a small bank inside a hospital." Mike commented as he climbed into the back seat of the cab, "Take us to the general aviation side of the airport, please, sir."

"Right away sir," the cabby responded. After waiting until both doors were closed, he pressed down on the accelerator and sped out of the hospital parking lot toward the general aviation side of the airport.

Chapter 21 Shots Fired

Officer Henry Banister was cruising north on Interstate 95 when he saw a dark sedan in the left lane ahead of him with a burned out tail light. Being the officer he was and very big on safety, he flipped on his lights and pressed down on his throttle to accelerate in pursuit. As he approached the car, it started to slow down and its right turn signal came on indicating the car was going to pull over. This is what Banister expected to happen. What happened next was not expected.

After the car stopped, Banister slowly approached the car and said, "Good evening sir, I just stopped you because your left tail light is burned out. Please get it fixed at your earliest chance."

"Yah, thank you;" came the reply in a very deep Slavic accent.

"I am required by the state of Virginia to see your driver's license and proof of insurance?" Banister asked, not suspecting anything but required to do so by the laws of Virginia.

"Yah," Was the reply he got and was handed a license and the insurance card.

Banister stepped back and said. "I will be right back, sir."

Back in his car, Banister pulled up a file and it showed the license number, address, date of birth and other pertinent information but the picture was of another man. *'Whoa, this is not good; I wonder what else they are hiding.'* He thought and then picked up his microphone and placed a call to dispatch to request assistance on a possible identity theft and car theft. "Dispatch, this is car 789, out on Emerson, we have a situation here, two men in a dark Chevy four door, Virginia license plate, Hotel

Papa Juliet 429, Avis rental car. I have two men, foreign nationals with fake identification. How do you want us to handle this?"

"Stand by, Banister." After pausing for a moment, the dispatcher came back, "We are sending backup, proceed carefully until they arrive. Should arrive in less than five minutes, location is four miles from you and heading your direction."

Slowly he got out of his car and pulled his pistol in case of trouble. Before he took two steps, the passenger door opened. "Stay in the car." he yelled at the passenger, just as the driver's door flew open. He raised his pistol and prepared to fire when both passenger and driver turned toward him and fired full automatic AK-47's at Banister, killing him instantly. Banister had gotten two shots off that had hit the driver in the chest and killed him too. Seconds later, the backup came flying down the road. Lights were blazing. After seeing Banister go down, Jacob Hawks and Linda Blazer immediately called 911 for an ambulance. The surviving shooter jumped behind the wheel and sped off.

Exceeding one hundred miles per hour, the chase was on. Picking up his cell phone, the shooter pressed speed dial to reach the XO. He informed him of the mistake and death of his partner. He weaved in and out of traffic and increased his speed. While going around a wide curve, the car started to skid, and moments later, he lost total control. The car flipped over and went off the road, down a small hill and came to an abrupt stop at the base of a very large old tree. The car was bent into a 'V' as if it were a pretzel and crushed the driver. His last words were in Russian, but translated to "Praise Allah." His cell phone connection died the moment he did.

Moments later, the patrol car skidded to a stop. Lights were blazing. Both officers jumped out of the car and ran to the wreck, only to find the body crushed inside. Upon inspection of the interior, they found one AK-47 and several hand guns. Linda walked to the back of the car where the trunk lid was popped open. She glanced inside and almost fainted.

"Jacob, come here, please." Linda said calmly to her partner.

"Just a sec," he replied.

"I think you need to come now. You have to see this." Linda said with a very nervous tone to her voice. "No, you really need to come now."

"See what," he said as he walked toward the back of the car and looked into the trunk, "What the hell is that?"

"If it is what I think it is, we have a very big problem." Linda commented, "I am calling this in. The FBI needs to get here, now."

"Right, do that. And tell them we need a bomb squad too. I am going to do a parameter search to ensure no other weapons flew out of the car." Jacobs said and then turned to do a search of the immediate area.

"Good idea." Linda agreed. She pulled her handheld radio, thought for a second, walked up the hill about one hundred feet away from the wreck, and called. "Dispatch, Sergeant Blazer, we need an immediate patch to the chief on a secure line. We have a serious problem."

"Stand by." A minute went by before she received a reply. "The chief is in a conference at the moment and has asked not to be disturbed."

"Dispatch, this is NOT a request, get the chief on the line, secure, NOW. I don't give a damn who he is meeting with."

"Yes, Sergeant Blazer, one moment." Within a minute, "Going secure now, you are on with the Chief."

"Thank you."

"Go ahead, Chief." Dispatch said after a few seconds.

"This had better be good, Sergeant, or you will be pounding a beat as a patrol man again. You dragged me out of a meeting with the mayor; what the hell is so, important?" demanded the Chief.

"Chief, we are out on I-95 just west of the Emerson exit, about forty miles north of Leesburg. We have a serious problem out here. The vehicle we were in pursuit of has crashed. The driver is dead. His partner was shot and killed by Officer Banister approximately fifteen miles south of our position. Ambulance and coroner need to be dispatched to both sites. We also need a bomb squad at our location immediately; we have a very large bomb in the trunk of the car that crashed. If I know my explosives, then this is not your normal run of the mill bomb; it is a nuclear warhead. My guess is it is Soviet, or, at least, not American. I also suggest bringing in the FBI; the driver is a foreign national, possibly Soviet."

"Damn, what the hell have you two stumbled onto?"

"Not sure, but one thing I am sure of, we do not want to touch that car without the bomb squad checking out that thing in the trunk."

"Understood; I will get the FBI and bomb squad on the way in the next few minutes. I will also contact the Department of Defense; they may want to get involved in this. What else do you need?"

"Well, since you are asking, send some sandwiches; this is going to be a long night." Linda asked, half smiling and trying to take the edge off the situation.

"You got it."

Within an hour, the highway had been blocked off and all traffic was diverted off and around the area. Lucky for them, it was late in the evening and traffic was light.

A helicopter landed at 10:15 p.m. and four men and one woman jumped out and walked over to Officer Jacob Hawks and Linda Blazer.

"Good evening. I am Special Agent Donald O'Neil from the FBI and this is Lamplighter, Douglas, Smith and Janet Day from the Washington office. We have been told you may have an international incident here." O'Neil said handing his identification to Officer Hawks. "State Department and DoD are sending a team out also. They should arrive in a few minutes."

"Mr. O'Neil, the bomb squad will be here in a few minutes; but if you can identify what we have here, it may help our boys out, just knowing what they have to deal with."

"Don't know if I can, but let's take a look." he said as he and Jacob walked to the back of the car and shined their flashlights into the trunk.

"Holy shit!" O'Neil exclaimed as he backed up. "I am not much of a bomb guy but that my new friend is no ordinary explosive device. What you have here is a dead terrorist and a Soviet nuclear warhead from an ICBM missile. Was he alone?"

"No, he was not alone; his partner is dead about fifteen miles down the road with one of our officers, also dead. So what do we do now?"

"We need to wait for your bomb disposal team to get here and see if we have a live one that is ready to blow or just the components. In the mean time, we wait."

"Right, they should be here in a few minutes."

Chapter 22 Getting Involved

FBI Headquarters, Washington DC

Senior Agent Doug Williams sat across from Director Carson in the executive conference room; everyone was quiet after listening to the recent phone call from their field agent in Virginia. O'Neil had called in his report about the warhead, and the two dead Soviet terrorists. After being informed that the warhead was not armed and deemed safe for the moment, he asked what to do with it. After a few questions about the dead officer, driver and his passenger, it was determined to keep this under wraps until they were able to determine if this was one of many or an isolated potential threat.

"Now what! I asked not to be disturbed." Director Carson growled. "Hello, Carson here." Pausing for a moment, he listened to the caller and then hung up without saying goodbye.

"Gentlemen this just got real nasty. That was the Secretary of the Navy and we are now involved with the Department of Defense, the US Navy, CIA, Nuclear Regulatory Commission and who the hell knows who else." Carson said to Agent Doug Williams and his two agents sitting in the conference room.

"Say again, sir." Williams asked, not understanding what was just said.

"This little international incident with two dead Russians and a nuclear warhead just got real nasty. It seems that the Navy has at this moment down in Norfolk a Soviet Nuclear Missile boat that is missing several warheads. I would say we have found one of them and we are being tasked to help locate the rest of them."

"How many are missing?" Williams asked.

"They said that each missile holds ten separate warheads; each is capable of destroying a medium sized city by itself. They cannot account for one missile warhead which means there are nine more missing."

"Damn, how do we handle this?"

"Stand by for a minute. I need to make a couple of quick calls. We will take it from there."

"Should we step out?" Williams asked.

"No, stay seated, help yourselves to some coffee, and just wait." Carson ordered, then stood and walked over to the window. He looked out for a moment and then went back to his desk where he opened the top left hand drawer of his desk; reaching in he picked up a handset that was red, pushed four buttons, and then spoke. "This is Director Carson, FBI Headquarters, authentication code, AC8738965. Thank you, I will hold."

"Good evening Director, how can I help you this evening?" Darrell Mitchell, President of the United States asked when he came online.

"Good evening Mr. President, we have a situation over in Virginia. Two of our officers have stopped a car with a nuclear warhead in the trunk; the driver is dead along with his partner and one of the Virginia Highway patrol officers. Yes, he was killed in the line of duty, sir."

"Director Carson, I have been expecting your call. We do have a serious problem and I was hoping I could keep your team out of it, but you are involved now and need to get fully briefed and soon. What have you done with the warhead?"

"It is secure and still in the trunk of the car. We have a bomb disposal team on site along with reps from the Nuclear Regulatory Commission; several members of the Navy are headed out there as well as DoD. It is as secure as we can make it out on the highway. This has just happened in the past hour, sir."

"Good, who is your man on site? OK, instruct him to let the Navy team and Nuke people take the warhead to secure storage." Mitchell stated. He paused for a moment after getting O'Neil's name from Carson and then continued. "Carson, I need you to meet with me in the morning for a full briefing; but in the meantime, send three of your agents to Norfolk Naval Yard and meet with Agent Hancock. Hancock is working with a Navy Captain by the name of Henderson. He will brief them on the operation. Have your team provide him and his team with any assistance he needs, including personnel, until this is finished. They need to be there first thing in the morning. You be at the White House at seven a.m. to meet with me."

As he was hanging up, Carson shook his head and then looked over at his agents. "We have a serious problem. The president wants to brief me in the morning and I need to send some agents to the Navy yard in Norfolk. Do you want to take on this assignment?"

"Sure, my team has nothing going at the moment."

"I was hoping you would say that. You take three of your best agents, ones that have experience in international affairs and explosives. Head down to Norfolk and meet with Agent Hancock from the Norfolk office, where he is working with a Navy Captain Henderson. Get with them and provide whatever assistance you can. They are in charge; we are to assist. And take whatever you need in equipment. Call back if you need anything; people, you know the drill. Now get going. They are expecting you and your team at six a.m. in the morning."

"I know a Henderson, maybe the same one. We will be on the road in an hour. I will call when we arrive and keep you posted. Enjoy your visit to the White House, sir."

"Yeah, thanks, now get out of here." Carson ordered with half a smile on his face. He had confidence in Doug and his team. They had been able to solve many cold cases over the years, but this one sounded pretty scary. He looked at his watch and thought he would only get a couple hours of sleep again tonight. When he got promoted to the position of Director of the FBI, he figured it would be a walk in the park, big office, same one that J. Edgar Hoover had used, same desk, but organized crime was down, most had turned legit and were not causing him the same problems J. Edgar had. All he wanted was a nice comfortable job till he retired with a pension that would keep him and his wife of forty years in beer and margaritas for many years. But no, that was not the case. Now, he had an active case that could very well be life and death for the entire country. Nuclear warheads on United States soil controlled by the enemy, Soviet's of all things; they were supposed to be our friends now. There had to be something deeper in this, and he hoped to learn that in the morning with his meeting with the President.

Since 9/11 the country had been in a state of alert, expecting another terrorist attack that never came. And since Bin Laden had been killed, Carson hoped the terrorists lost their desire to kill Americans. He hoped this was not another 9/11 on a larger scale.

He had met with the President many times, professionally and socially. They had been friends since Darrell was a junior senator and he was just an agent. What the hell had they gotten into now he thought?

Chapter 23 Deadly Nights

After he pulled into the garage of a vacant home on the north side of Alexandria, Virginia with three of his crew, executive officer Viktor Mikhailovich of the Soviet Nuclear boat smiled at the successes so far. It was 3 a.m. in the morning, yet he felt wide awake.

He had received a disturbing call earlier from one of his men driving north on I-95 north of Norfolk, Virginia. The crewmember said he was being chased by the police and his partner was dead. Before he heard more information, the line went dead with his final words, 'Praise Allah.' Mikhailovich figured the bomb was now in the hands of the FBI and that might be a good thing; the right people would know the warheads were in the country and that they were serious about using them.

"Brothers, we have the future to look forward to; if this works, we will be one step closer to world domination. Here's to a successful mission!" Mikhailovich stated lifting his glass to the other three loyal crew members with him. "I suggest you get some sleep. The next few days are going to be long and hard."

Within minutes, his men were headed for bed; the cargo was secure and all was quiet. Mikhailovich needed to check in with his other teams. He called each one to see where they were in their part of his plan. After hanging up with the last team, he poured vodka and smiled. He particularly enjoyed vodka, even though his religion forbid it. This was his only digression, but to be a true Soviet and to fit in, he and his men had to take on some of the infidels habits and he had grown to enjoy the taste of vodka.

The Denver van would arrive by late afternoon; the Los Angeles team would be in place in about a day, and already in place was one each in Philadelphia, St. Louis, Boston, New York, New Orleans, and San Francisco. Now he had only one warhead in Washington DC.

Each warhead had been modified to detonate with a sequence of commands from a cell phone that was in his possession. Two extra cell phones were with senior officers in LA and St. Louis.

Viktor Mikhailovich smiled as he sipped his drink. He was satisfied that he could take control and achieve his goal of holding the United States hostage. Many Americans would die at his hand; this mission had taken years to plan and many more years to get the right men in the right places to take over a nuclear submarine. He was only a young man of thirteen when given the assignment almost twenty years ago; he had trained in Iraq and then returned to his home in Russia, where he completed school, joined the Navy, moved into the Soviet Naval Academy, and up the chain of rank until he finally reached the level of Executive Officer of a nuclear submarine. The plan had been to become the commander, but that would have taken several more years. The time schedule had been moved up. It was already more than twelve years since the attack on the World Trade Centers on September 11. It was time to act and bring the United States to its knees.

He had been briefed to the names and positions of the other team members; several he had worked with over the years, gaining their trust and seeing the dedication in their tasks. He knew this mission would not fail. He and twelve men were committed to carrying out their life's mission and pleasing their god, Allah.

Taking one last sip, he set the glass down and went to bed.

Chapter 24 Complications of the Worst Kind

"Well, gentlemen, I just came up from the weapons locker and don't know if I should be worried or scared." LT Jerry Blair stated as he entered the control room. He stopped in his tracks as he saw two additional people he did not know. "Sorry to interrupt, sir."

"No problem, LT. What has you worried or scared?" Captain Henderson asked before introducing the two new players in their nuclear game.

"Sir, we were able to get into the weapons locker, and there are some empty racks in there. We were unable to determine if there were any weapons there and if there was any missing ammunition. We couldn't find the manifest to tell us the compliment of weapons that....."

"I can answer that." one of the new players stated, interrupting the young lieutenant.

"Ok, first, this is Captain Mikhail Petrovich Viktorov; he is the captain of this boat; he has defected and agreed to help us with our little challenge. Go ahead; tell the lieutenant what you just told us, sir." Captain Todd "Bear" Henderson said before Captain Viktorov continued.

"Lieutenant, along with the ten missing warheads; there are fourteen missing AK-forty-seven rifles, eight cases of ammunition, and six 9mm Markarov pistols with four magazines each. That traitor, Viktor Mikhailovich, who was my executive officer, is planning to hold the United States of America hostage until he gets what he wants.

If he does not get it, he is going to destroy several of your cities, one at a time, until he gets it."

"Damn, sir. May I ask why you are here? And what does he want?" LT Blair inquired as he walked over to the periscope and stopped looking at the Soviet Captain.

"I disagreed with what he and his team wanted to do and I was left to die along with one of my trusted junior officers, this young man here, Eric." the captain replied. "Once I recovered in a local hospital, he and I contacted a friend in your government and here we are, to help, and maybe save, some of your country. All I ask in return is to be left alone in my retirement along with my wife and daughter. Does that satisfy your interest, Lieutenant?" After a brief pause, Captain Viktorov continued. "What he wants is money, lots of money, and he does not care if he kills millions to get it. They want freedom in your country, but do not want to get it the same way I do. I just want to live the rest of my life with my wife and daughter, nothing more."

"Sir, I am truly sorry to be so blunt, but it is my job, and I am sure you did satisfy Captain Henderson, and now I am satisfied also."

"Captain Viktorov, Mr. Blair is with Naval Intelligence and it is his job to question things when they don't look right. LT, now you know about the weapons and the missiles; and as you can see, we do have a serious problem. We have help, but it may not be enough." He paused and continued, "Davin, how is the rest of the search going?"

"Not bad, the boat seems to be fully functional and ready to go to sea." Davin replied. He then looked across the control room to see Lanstrom entering from the far end, where she almost slipped on the knee knocker bulkhead. Davin was thinking she must not get on submarines too much to not know about the watertight bulkheads which provided many skinned knees on people not used to them.

'Damn, I will never get used to these hatches.' she said to herself in a soft mutter, barely loud enough but a few heard her. As she entered the control room, she spoke louder and said "Captain, we have another problem."

"Go ahead, what has gone wrong now, Lanstrom?"

"One of the techs has discovered what looks like a booby trap attached to one of the warheads. Would you care to join us in the aft area of the missile room?" Lanstrom asked and turned on her heels and started back to the missile room.

"Here sir," she said after they reached missile silo number 20. She pointed to the collection of wires and boxes attached to the side of the missile, and they peered through the open silo hatch.

"What the hell is that?" Davin asked as they looked at it.

"That is a timer and it is set to detonate in, ah, let's see, in thirty-six hours and eleven minutes and the clock is ticking." Lanstrom commented, and then added, "We don't know how to stop it. It may detonate if we attempt to stop it, or mess with it. My technicians, as you can see, are working on it right now, but I suggest we move this boat out of the harbor in case we are not successful in defusing it."

"Ok, we can move the boat, but that is a problem in itself. This is a nuclear boat and those are nuclear missiles, we will have to move the boat to the middle of the

Atlantic to prevent any damage to the coast when it explodes, if we can't disarm it. Can you disarm it?" Henderson asked, looking at Lanstrom with a questioned eye.

"That is the question I do not have an answer to and by the time we do," indicating her team, "it may be too late to get far enough away from the coast to prevent a major disaster."

"Captain, what is the max speed of this boat?" Henderson asked the soviet captain.

"She will do thirty knots submerged and twenty-one on the surface." he stated, looking worried.

"How many crewmembers do we need to run us out to sea, bare minimum?"

"Ten, fifteen would be best in case we have problems."

"Okay, Lanstrom, how long will it take to remove the remaining warheads so we do not have a simultaneous nuclear explosion?" He paused as he turned back to Captain Viktorov, "Sir, you said fifteen if we have any problems. Do you anticipate problems with this boat?"

"That, sir, is a problem also; we can't remove any warheads; they are also connected to that control detonator." Lanstrom commented before Captain Viktorov had a chance to say anything. She looked intently at both captains, not knowing what else to say.

"Captain Henderson, I cannot say by looking at that detonator that our traitor did not do other things to this boat to prevent it from moving. But I would suggest fifteen just in case we have other problems."

"Damn." Henderson almost yelled. "Mr. Randel and LT Blair, get all non-essential personnel off this boat in the next thirty minutes and both of you remain on shore also. I don't believe we will need a Naval Intel or company man on board. Josh, contact your people and get them to inform the President. Blair, I need you to contact Atlantic command and inform them of the problem and that we are going to run a Soviet Nuclear boat submerged at flank speed directly through their control area and we are NOT to be stopped. They need to clear the area immediately. All ships, civilian and military, need to leave the area. I don't know what damage we will cause if we are not successful and this thing blows. That's an order, LT. I see the look in your eyes saying you want to help, but I do not need any extra bodies here, just the people we need to run this boat to the bottom of the ocean and as quickly as possible. Now, move! You have your orders!" Henderson commanded. As he turned to Davin he quietly said "That means your ride ends here too, my friend; just naval personnel on this trip. But, as you leave, grab Ensign Kent and have her meet me in the control room immediately. We need a large seaplane, maybe two, for a ride home but we don't know where from just yet."

"Bear, I can be of service here. You know that. There may be clues on this boat somewhere telling us how to disarm that thing and I know this boat, possibly better than you. Remember, I crawled around this thing, too."

"I know, but I can't have a civilian running around getting in the way. Sorry. No ride this time. Now go find my future wife and get her off this boat. Tell her what is happening and keep her on shore. Under no circumstances is she to get back on this boat. If she does and I survive, I will have you shot."

"I will make sure she is on shore, Bear but…." Davin started but was stopped when Henderson held up his hand.

"NO, that is an order and I know with you being an Ex-Army Sergeant Major, you know how to take orders from a senior officer. Or do I have to have the Shore Patrol arrest you and drag you off this boat."

"Aye, sir."

"That's a navy response; at least respond properly."

"Yes, sir, three bags full." Davin responded and saluted his friend and quickly turned and headed out of the missile room at a quick pace.

"Now get out of here; all of you." Henderson yelled at the backs of his friends, and then turned to the soviet captain, who was conversing with Commander Lanstrom quietly over by the detonator, "Captain Viktorov, we may not survive this trip but it is your boat, are you with us?"

"If we have to scuttle her, I need to be the one to do it. Let's get this moving; we are wasting time." he said as he turned back toward Henderson. "I know Commander Lanstrom is qualified to disarm this mess but…." he said; he stopped short of finishing his statement when a hand touched him on his shoulder. Knowing that Lanstrom was going to protest his intention to leave her behind, he continued, "Never mind, she can do it."

"I don't understand, but we have no time to discuss it now. She's your boat; let's get her moving. You have the bridge Captain." Henderson stated. He headed to the bridge with the rest of the team while he asked for a crew list by which positions needed to be filled to run this boat.

"Ensign Kent, glad they found you; were you briefed on the situation?" Henderson asked and received a nod acknowledging that she had. "Good, here is a list of crew positions we need to fill immediately. It may be a one way mission; we don't have time to train anyone. We need experienced sailors in each area and we need them here in one hour. We are leaving the harbor in one and one-half hours so they need to hustle down here and be ready for work. The reactor is already coming on line. Now move it, Ensign, and I do not want you back on the boat after you get these positions filled and that is an order."

"Aye, sir" she yelled as she turned and ran up the stairway leading to the hatch and the main deck.

'Damn, these are good people; I really hope we can survive this adventure.' Henderson thought to himself as he looked around the control room. 'This boat is not completely unlike our own attack boats, but all the gauges are in an unfamiliar language and not in the same location, the controls are not in the same place. The first couple of hours are going to be real interesting. We may make it if we don't run aground or sink ourselves before we get out of the harbor. At least they would be on the surface and have the Soviet captain and one of his trusted crew on board to assist.

This was one large fast attack boat from a nation they were not at war with yet. A traitorous crew had put them in a situation that could easily start a war.'

While he walked over to the chart table, Captain 'Bear' Henderson started to plot a course that would take them far out into the ocean and away from any inhabited islands. Knowing the speed of the boat, he could estimate where they might end up and that was pretty close to the deepest part of the Atlantic Ocean. What kind of damage would be caused by the combined explosive power of over two hundred individual two megaton nuclear warheads? What kind of tidal wave would it cause? Could it stop the rotation of the earth? Would it change the direction of rotation or create a nuclear cloud so large that it would slowly kill off any remaining life on Earth? One war head, if detonated in Washington D.C. would destroy everything within a two mile radius immediately, cause severe damage for another two miles, kill everything within a five mile radius, and create a nuclear cloud that could kill slowly for an undetermined number of miles from ground zero depending on the wind speed and direction. This explosion, if even half of them detonated, could make the entire Atlantic Ocean a huge dead sea. Anyone within thousands of miles might die instantly and the rest a slow painful death, if a tidal wave did not kill them first or a potential earthquake that would be a result of the disruption to the Tectonic plates that helped keep the land above sea level.

'We have to prevent this,' Bear commented to himself, 'We have no choice, we have to stop this.'

"Sir, the reactor is up and fully functional." Lanstrom stated as she approached the plotting table. "And sir, I could not help but hear your comment. There is no option, here. We either prevent this or the world as we know it will not survive. I have been a nuclear engineer for many years and I have done the calculations too. This is not something any country would want; this is a no win situation if it blows. You have my total support in whatever you decide, and I will do whatever I can to help."

"Thank you, Commander. Your dedication may never be known if we fail, but I will know. So, tell me, how do they have this thing wired?"

"It looks like they had a programmer that not only understood explosives, but how to write a program that replicates and changes paths if we block one or more. What I mean is, if we find a way to stop the clock, it starts another one and reduces the time to detonation. If we cut a wire, it will detonate. It's like a dead man switch. If the power is turned off, it detonates. If the power is diverted or increased, it only speeds up the clock. That is just what we have been able to figure out so far. He or she is one smart programmer and has pretty much thought of everything to prevent us from stopping it. I don't know what salt water or water would do to the system. Probably detonate because the power would stop or cause a short circuit which in turn would detonate." Lanstrom stated as a matter of fact.

"You have discovered that in the last twenty minutes? I am impressed. Do you have any good news?" asked Bear.

"Well, yes. The galley is full of food and there is lots of vodka in the pantry." Lanstrom commented with a slight smile. "And, no, I did not discover that in the past twenty minutes. Actually I know this kind of set up. It is taught in a specialty school located in Iraq, or at least it was. The method was designed by a terrorist by the name of Al Jusualte, or something like that; he was trained at MIT and went home to become the Al Jihad's favorite computer geek. He designed spyware, Trojans, worms and viruses that he would release into the wild to cause major computer damage around the world. Of course, his target has always been the United States. I have studied his work over the years, hoping to find a way to cause him problems and design a way to stop his attacks. It is kind of a hobby of mine, computer geek at heart but nuclear physicist by trade. Anyway, this is one of his designs, I am almost positive."

"So we have a link to a major terrorist cell on board this boat. Commander, it looks like you have just gotten your hobby escalated to the top of your to do list and now have a crack at Al Jusu… or whatever's code. Are you up to the job? I hope so, because we do not have the time to find someone else."

"I am up to it, but would love to have a code writer if we can get one here quickly." Lanstrom replied.

"No problem, there are plenty of geeks on this base; I will have you the best here before we leave. We are burning daylight, let's get to work." Henderson said almost laughing because he used the same comment that John Wayne had used in one of his favorite movies. "And hell, we will eat our last meal in style and can be dead drunk when it hits zero. Great, we all go to our maker, stuffed and drunk."

There was silence for a couple of minutes as they both looked at the navigation chart. Hearing footsteps coming down the stairway, both Lanstrom and Henderson turned to see several officers and sailors coming into the control room.

"Captain Henderson," said Basil while saluting, "Commander Anthony Basil, diving officer, reporting for duty. This is Weapons officer Commander Tom Sanchez, Chief Sharp, and Seaman Sandia, Centrino, and Glasscock. They are your drivers, sonar and engine room operations crew. We have Crocket, Sims, Fletcher, Dominic, Hightower, Ring and Wagner heading this way. They should arrive in the next thirty minutes. They will round out the team. There may be a couple more before we leave to fill the empty spots, but I believe we can make this trip work with the men we have. What are your orders, sir?"

"Commander, this is Commander Lanstrom, nuclear operations, and she is in charge of everything nuclear and computer related, from the engine room to the warheads. Mr. Sanchez, you and ah, is it Glasscock, will work with her. The rest of you know your stations, so get familiar with your new boat. Are any of you computer programmers, geeks, hackers or anything in high level computer work?" Henderson asked and then paused and waited for a reply. Receiving none, he continued; "No, it was a shot. Commander Basil you know your job. I will be the acting exec. Soviet Captain Viktorov is in command. Here he is now." Henderson paused as Captain Viktorov re-entered the control room. "Captain Viktorov this is Commander Basil. He and his men have just reported in. He is your diving officer. His team is heading for their stations. We should be ready to leave in about forty minutes."

"Happy to meet you, sir! Wish it were under better circumstances." Captain Viktorov commented and stuck his hand out to shake the commander's hand. "Thank you."

Chapter 25 I.S.O.P.P.

About the same time over in the civilian side of Norfolk harbor, a one hundred twenty-five foot research ship was preparing to leave; her destination was Bimini, a small island about sixty miles due east of Palm Beach, Florida. The research ship, *Undersea Adventure* was equipped for a minimum of a thirty day voyage and had a small submersible submarine, scuba tanks, compressor and all the required equipment to search for and salvage a ship wreck short of raising the wreck itself. The *Undersea Adventure* was owned and operated by a small private organization known as "Sand and Sea International", but to the members of the team they were privately called "ISOPP" which was short for "In Search of Pirate Plunder". Their goal in life was to research and recover pirate treasure or ship wrecks and then place the knowledge and sometimes the treasure on display in one of their many museums located on the east coast of the United States and the Caribbean. They had six museums, four in the United States and two in the Caribbean. They had plans on starting two more, one in Hawaii and the other in San Diego, but this required money or finding another cache of treasure. They believed they were close to finding the lost treasure of Anne Bonny. They had narrowed it down to four islands south of Bimini, all just little spits of land, that had been ignored until recently when a small plane had crash landed in the water near one. While waiting for rescue, they had found several pieces of eight on the beach. This had sparked the interest of one of the survivors, a young woman named Natasha Haynes, who worked at the Pirate Museum in

Charleston, South Carolina. She had told her boss, Dennis Quaid. He owned the *Undersea Adventure* and was financing the trip they were about to take.

After a short stay in Bimini, they were headed to the eastern side of the Bahamas to continue a search they had started earlier in the year but for which they had run out of money and time. But now with new funding and almost all the time in the world, they were heading out again. They had planned a short visit to the four islands south of Bimini where Natasha had almost died in the plane crash. They planned to search those islands for a couple of days and then move on to the east side of the islands to pick up where they had left off the year before. Now, armed with new information and several new crew members, they felt they would succeed and return home rich.

The seas had been predicted to have four to six foot running swells and light showers for the first two days and then turn to clear and sunny. Their efforts had been stimulated because of the recent find of more treasure on the pirate ship *Whydah*, recently located off the coast of Cape Cod in just thirty feet of water about fifteen hundred feet from the shore. The treasure they sought was from the famous female pirate Anne Bonny. She had recovered this treasure after spending time in jail, escaping, and picking up a boat in Port Royal. She had retrieved all of hers and Calico Jack's booty; he would not need it since he was captured and hung two months prior to her escape. So she picked up their booty and supposedly headed to another island to divide it among her crew. An unexpected storm changed her destination and she never, supposedly, distributed anything. It was said her ship sank and most of the crew, including Ms. Bonny, died from the sinking. Some of this was speculation, some

fact, but all that was known for sure was that the treasure was in the Bahamas. They

were going to find it. This treasure was also reported to be twice the size of Sam

Bellamy's, which went down with the *Whydah* off the coast of Cape Cod.

Chapter 26 White House Blues

Within minutes of leaving the boat, Josh and LT Blair ran into Special Agent Hancock and his newly assigned assistant Olson.

"Hancock, where have you two been?" Josh asked as they approached the two officers.

"On the phone with the White House, why? Is there something we missed?"

"Well, yeah, we have a more serious problem than just the missing, ah, wait, let's go into the secure conference room and I will bring you two up to speed." Josh said and turned toward the building which housed the conference room. "Follow me."

"Actually no, we need to see Captain Henderson and relay the President's wishes." Hancock protested.

"Hancock, first the conference room, then you call the President, again; then if there is still time, you can talk to Henderson." Josh Randel demanded and pointed toward the building Olson and Hancock had just left.

"Ok, if you insist, let's make it quick; I have important information for Henderson. But I take it what you have to tell me supersedes the President's orders."

"To put it bluntly, yes! Now time is wasting and you need to talk to the President again and soon. Or you can call him and I will brief him and you can listen in." Josh stated as he stepped closer to Hancock and got right in his face.

"Let's go." Hancock said resigning to defeat and turned back toward the building. Once inside the conference room, Hancock picked up the secure hot line, punched in a couple of numbers and then recited several more to the operator on the other end. Within a few minutes, the President of the United States came on line.

"Hello, Hancock. I thought we were through and you were going to talk to Captain Henderson."

"Yes sir, but something has come up that needs your immediate attention. I am handing the phone over to CIA Special Operations Director Josh Randel. Mr. Randel." Hancock said and then handed the phone to Josh.

"Sorry to bother you again, Mr. President but some things just came to our attention that you need to understand and act on immediately."

"Go ahead Mr. Randel."

"Sir, we have not only discovered ten missing war heads but, along with that, fourteen AK-47 rifles, six pistols and related ammunition. But that is not the biggest problem. The remaining warheads, about two hundred, have been wired into a detonator set to go off in about thirty-six hours. We have not found a way to disarm the detonator without setting it off or anyway to shut it down. Captain Henderson is putting together a small crew, along with the Soviet Captain and one of his crew. They plan on running the boat to the middle of the Atlantic. He will try to disarm it before time runs out. If unable, he plans on scuttling the boat in the deepest part of the ocean, with time to be rescued, hopefully. The impending explosion has the potential of causing massive tidal waves and destruction up the entire Atlantic coast of North America, Europe, South America and Africa. He is planning on diving deep because the boat is faster at depth, which means he will not be able to make contact until he comes back up to the surface or returns to a depth for long wire communication."

Josh did not mention the fact that if all two hundred plus warheads exploded the damage that it would cause might not be a recoverable one, but he knew the President was a smart man and would soon figure that out himself.

"Why not use our underwater communication system?" The president asked, not knowing about the Soviet communication systems.

"Sir, that would be great if the Soviet boat was equipped with it, which it is not. And there is no time to install a system on board and still get far enough out to sea to minimize damage."

"Yea, I should have thought about that," responded the President feeling a little dumb for not knowing. "Ok, I will handle the situation here. How soon is he pulling out?"

"In about thirty minutes sir." Josh stated as he looked over at the three men standing in the room with him. Two were totally shocked and Blair was answering the unasked question. Do we tell the President the worst case scenario? He was saying yes.

"Mr. President there is one other thing you must know."

"Spit it out, Mr. Randel."

"Sir I really don't know how to say this, but, ok, here it is. If all those warheads detonate together or within a short time frame at the same location, somewhere in the middle of the Atlantic, I do not believe we are prepared for the resulting destruction."

"What do you mean, Randel?"

"Potentially the end of life as we know it; Armageddon to put it bluntly; the end of the world. That kind of explosive force could, in theory, shift the rotation of the earth, blow us out of orbit around the sun, cause a massive nuclear cloud which would slowly kill every living thing on Earth and/or shift the tectonic plates causing massive earthquakes, just to start. I am not a nuclear bomb expert but we have estimated that the simultaneous nuclear detonation of one hundred eighty warheads along with the nuclear reactor on that boat would be about two million times more powerful than the bomb dropped on Hiroshima at the end of the war. Now, that is only theory, sir. We really don't know what would happen; maybe nothing at all, but in theory we could all die. The entire planet would cease; life as we know it would be gone. We have to stop this or die. Make plans for a nuclear catastrophe of biblical proportions, sir. It will be like the moon slamming into our ocean, we all lose."

"Right, I did not think of that. OK, you say thirty minutes or less before departure. Is there anything I can do to help?"

"Yes, sir, order all shipping, Naval, civilian and private to get the hell out of the way and pray. All airlines are to be redirected and the Atlantic coast prepared to evacuate. To where I have no idea, but to head inland as far and as fast as possible, we only have, well, less than thirty-six hours before detonation."

"That will cause worldwide panic and maybe more destruction than the explosion by itself. What the hell are those terrorists thinking anyway? Are they terrorists or a group of insane Soviet crew members? Didn't they consider the outcome of an explosion of that size and magnitude?"

"Guess not, sir." Josh said and the line went dead.

Minutes after the conversation with Josh, the President's Chief advisor knocked on the door and entered without waiting for an answer.

"Mr. President, we have a problem."

"Bet mine is bigger than yours" was the comment made by the President without smiling. His chief advisor looked puzzled but continued into the Oval Office, closing and locking the door behind him.

"What, no wait this is serious, sir. The FBI just contacted us, a Director Carson, and wanted to talk to you directly but you were on the hot line so I took the call. We have an individual who just contacted the director over at FBI HQ and informed him that they have nine nuclear warheads taken from the Soviet nuclear submarine which we have at Norfolk Naval Yard. They are demanding ten million dollars per warhead or they will detonate them, one at a time, until they get what they want. They plan on detonating the first war head in a major U.S. city in twenty-four hours. The timer started at noon today and it is now about 2:15. Additionally; an FBI agent was killed outside the Norfolk Naval Yard. He had a camera with photographs of naval personnel and of the Soviet submarine before we got it covered."

"What the hell else can go wrong?" demanded the President. His chief security advisor was still unaware of the earlier call with Josh Randel. He briefed his chief advisor of the call from Josh Randel and then sat placing his head in his hands and slowly said to himself 'Why on my watch.' He was quoting to himself an old navy term for being the one on duty when disaster happens.

"We are also aware that the Soviets know we have their boat and they want it back, now."

"Tell them they can come and get it. No, better yet, tell them we are bringing it half way back."

"What?"

"You know we don't pay ransom to terrorists." the President stated, thinking to himself as sweat started to drip down his forehead, *'Not on my watch, not now, what are they thinking, taking America hostage. Those damn fools, they will never get away with it.'*

"We do not know what cities they are in. One could be sitting in a parking garage less than six hundred yards from here. Do you want to evacuate the government?"

"Where is the V.P.? And yes, get everyone out of the building. Tell them to head for their respective safe locations and continue operations as normal. We still have a country to run and no terrorist is going to threaten this country while I am still breathing."

"He is flying to Denver on Air Force 2 for a conference with the NRA."

"Good, at least he is not too close to me right now. Advise him of the situation and make sure he is not in the city at noon tomorrow."

"He is going to Cheyenne Mountain for an inspection tour tomorrow; I will make sure he has departed Denver early tomorrow."

"Did the terrorist say what time zone he was doing his countdown in?"

"No but he called at noon and said we had twenty-four hours. We assume at noon tomorrow we will lose a city."

"Make sure the V.P. leaves Denver tonight. I do not want to take a chance with the time; this terrorist may not know how to tell time or even read a clock."

"Right, sir!" replied the chief security advisor; as he turned to leave, there was a rapid pounding on the door. The chief advisor looked at the President. After getting a nod, he unlocked the door, and as he did, it burst open and the head of White House Secret Service John Polson rushed in, with a severe look of concern on his face.

"Mr. President, I am sorry for the interruption but there has been an accident. Air Force 2 is reported down about sixty miles southeast of Denver. There has been a nuclear explosion; it caused three airliners to crash into the mountains. Crash teams have been sent to each crash site but it does not look good for survivors. Luckily the explosion happened on I-70 and far enough from the city that very little damage was done. But there are many dead in the little towns around Denver just off I-70. As soon as we get more information, I will bring it in, sir."

"Get the National Guard activated and on site at each crash site and in any town that was close to ground zero. We need to contain this now, before it gets out of hand. This terrorist has just showed us they have the warheads and have no problem using them. I want all military leaves cancelled and every able soldier, sailor, marine and airman back on duty. We have just gone to war on our own soil. I want these terrorists stopped NOW! I want a shoot to kill order on them. They just declared war on us and we will retaliate with force."

"Sir, we can't shoot to kill, it's against the Geneva Convention. These are not soldiers."

"Yes, the hell they are. They are Soviet Naval and are soldiers. Shoot to kill; those are my orders and they will stand or I will replace you until I find someone with the balls to make it an order. Do you hear me Mister?"

"Yes sir, right away sir." the chief advisor responded without hesitation and then quickly turned and left the oval office passing John Polson as he departed. Polson looked at President Darrell Mitchell.

"Sir, now you are talking like a President should. Let's get these guys, Sir." Polson said and started to leave.

"Polson, assemble your teams and let's get this place ready to evacuate."

"Yes, sir." he replied and headed out of the office in a trot.

Chapter 27 Call to Action

Within minutes, the orders left the White House to every military unit, active and reserve, cancelling leaves and ordering everyone to report to their units to get their orders and weapons. We were in a state of war.

Homeland Security sent out their orders to shut down all airports, civilian and commercial. All aircraft except military aircraft assigned to patrol the country and for search and rescue were to be grounded until further notice. Road blocks were established to check all vehicles going into major cities. No road in or out of the cities was left unprotected. The Civil Defense system was dusted off and activated. The country was coming together in the name of national defense.

It did not take long for the media to pick up the news. Soon, every radio and television station had cancelled regular broadcasting and was up with Special Reports on the state of the nation. Rumors stated to run wild. By 4 p.m. East Coast time, there were very few people in North America that did not know we were at a state of war, the enemy were Russians with nuclear bombs to use against us, and one had been detonated near Denver, killing hundreds, maybe even thousands.

The National Rifle Association placed its own call to action, informing its members that we were at DEFCON 3, which meant we had the enemy on our soil and to prepare to defend our country. Most members took this to heart and opened up their gun safes and prepared. Others were a bit more extreme and reported to the local military bases to offer their assistance, bringing their own weapons. The military commanders, not being in that position for being stupid, accepted the offers and assigned each volunteer to a unit where they could assist and also be under

control. Military retirees of all ages reported, some in uniform, but all ready to assist.

Each was assigned to a unit and position commensurate to their rank and job specialty.

The retirees that were not in good physical shape were assigned positions that did not

require a lot of physical activity, such as command and control working closely with

active and reserve personnel.

By six o'clock, there were many questions by many people, but mostly the

media, such as how did this happen, where did the intelligence community go wrong,

how did the government allow nuclear weapons in the hands of terrorists especially on

our own soil. These questions and others were going to be answered over time.

At seven p.m. the Public Relations Officer from the White House commented

to a full room of reporters and was televised live by all stations. Somehow the media

had gotten wind of a bomb found in a car that crashed on I-95 late last night. It had

been removed, deemed safe, and was in a secure facility at Fort Lee, Virginia.

Within twelve hours, the nation was locked and loaded for war, but did not

know where or who the enemy was and were still looking and praying. Many people

were leaving the bigger cities, figuring that if the enemy was going to blow up a city

then it must be theirs. Packing all they could carry, many just locked their doors and

left. Denver was a target and the bomb exploded outside the city, so many figured that

they were safe in Denver; many others did not and were heading out of Denver fearing

the fallout from a nuclear explosion would eventually kill them. The highways were

packed; the road blocks were set to stop people from going in not out. But they were still worried. The terrorists could see that the country was prepared and might

leave and target another city, just to follow the crowds so they could kill as many

Americans as possible. Orders came down from each command to set road blocks on

both in and out roads. This started to slow the evacuation even more. People started to

panic and they started to look for other ways to leave the cities. Nobody had been shot

yet, but to say the least, the situation was becoming very tense. With luck, as the night

came, so would quiet.

Chapter 28 Don't Touch the Blue Wire

At 3:15 p.m. the Soviet Nuclear Submarine, *Terminator*, cleared the harbor and was heading on a course of 090 degrees at flank speed on the surface. While they were in contact with Command Atlantic Submarine in Norfolk, they could still listen to the news and send and receive messages.

Flash traffic was received of the crash of Air Force 2 with no survivors, including the Vice President, many of the cabinet and reporters, and three commercial airliners. The cause of the crash was a nuclear explosion on I-70 about sixty miles east of Denver International Airport.

There were only thirty-three hours and ten minutes left on the detonation clock. The bomb and computer experts were working as quickly as possible, taking no chance to accidently detonate prematurely. The program that had been downloaded into the computer system was as close to an Artificial Intelligence as any of the computer geeks ever saw. They rounded up not just get one super geek but three volunteers wanting to be the first to break this code. There was a little competition going between the three geeks and Commander Lanstrom, each knowing that failure was not an option; this was truly a life or death situation and not a computer game. No matter which one cracked it first, they all won. Each one of the three was an expert gamer and code cracker in their own right. Two were career Navy intelligence computer hounds and the third was a young female friend, named Jessica; they always enjoyed competing with each other. Now the race was on to save the world. She was asked to join in by the two of them when they learned of the situation. Captain

Henderson and Commander Lanstrom allowed her to come on board. Actually, it did not take much to get them to allow her on board when they learned she was the experts' expert, a master among masters, the best of the best, as they would say. She was here and competing with life itself. One of the four would solve this problem or literally die trying.

Ian "the dragon slayer" Souza was a Seaman third class, two years in the navy, graduate of MIT in computer engineering in the top of his class. His online user name was dragon slayer and for good reason; he loved playing Dungeons and Dragons on the computer and had gained worldwide recognition as a master. He also enjoyed building computer simulations for the same games he had mastered. Ian was twenty-two years old and worked in the Naval Intelligence branch in the computer department.

His best friend was William James Savage, four-year navy career, planning on twenty plus, if he survived this trip. William, aka Mr. Data, graduated second in his class gaining his Masters degree in Physics with a second Masters in Computer Science from Berkley. William was twenty-six years old and single; actually he was dating Jessica, off and on, right now it was off because she preferred her independence more than he did.

Jessica Angela Moore was a twenty-three year old blonde, blue eyed, five foot three inch, one hundred fifteen pounds of pure dynamite. She knew who she was and what she wanted out of life and she loved a challenge. When she heard from William that he was going to be working on a system to crack the code on a nuclear submarine, she wanted in. Jessica, aka JAM, dressed a little radical, and reminded everyone of Abby from the TV show NCIS. Jessica showed up to board the boat wearing a very short black pleaded mini skirt, black low cut blouse, a dog collar, high platform boots with red laces and a red bow on the back of the boots. Her hair was up in a pony tail tied with a red bow and she had a gold bracelet on her right wrist with the name of her father, MST Jeffrey K. Moore engraved on it along with US Army KIA Desert Storm February 25, 1992. She graduated number one in her class at Berkley, where she had met William, and her degrees were in Computer Engineering and Process Development. She was experienced in no less than ten different computer languages. She also read, wrote and spoke fluent Russian, Cantonese, Japanese, German and of course English. The race was on to crack the code and save the world and she wanted to be the one to do it.

Up in the control room, Captain Henderson and Captain Viktorov were looking over the charts and trying to find the best place to scuttle the ship, if need be, when they heard footsteps coming up the ladder.

"Captain, look what we found hiding in the galley." Seaman Glasscock announced as he escort Davin Pierce into the control room.

"Damn, Davin! I ordered you to stay on shore. If and when we get back home, I will court marshal you for not following...." This time Davin held up a hand to stop Henderson and was shaking his head indicating no you will not.

"Can't do that, Bear." Davin said and looked at the chart then back to Henderson.

"Why the hell not?" yelled Captain Henderson.

"I retired and am no longer under military law." Davin said smartly, "And, besides, it would not hold up in court if we survive, since I will be one of the ones that saved the world. Do you really think they will send me to jail? Think of it this way. When Admiral Kirk saved the world from its own stupid mistakes by killing off all the whales and he and his crew went to the future to bring one back, he broke more rules than I have and he only got a reduction in grade back to Captain of his favorite star ship. Now he did more than me, so saving the world is my saving grace, and if we don't, then, well, we will all be dead. Right?"

"Guess not, but…, keep Captain Kirk out of this! You are still in trouble for not following orders, and I will still have you punished if we survive. Understand?"

"Look, I know, but if we don't stop that ticker, then being on shore will not be any safer than being on this boat. Now I have several ideas and maybe can help divert a major shift in our world."

"Who is this Captain Kirk? Am I supposed to know him?" Captain Viktorov asked looking very puzzled at Davin and Henderson.

"I will explain in a minute Captain. Davin, since you are on a naval vessel and I am the exec you will follow my orders or I will put you off right now.'

"He can't do that. Can he? We are not near any land." Davin asked looking at Captain Viktorov and back to Henderson, after he got an affirmative nod from Captain Viktorov.

"Yes I can; remember how they did the XO on *Down Periscope*. But we don't have time to surface, so, I guess, we are stuck with you or shoot you out a torpedo tube. Now, what have you got in mind?" Henderson asked. "Captain Viktorov has the boat under control and we should be about here in the next twenty-eight hours, which leaves us five hours to scuttle or disarm that thing and go home." Henderson said pointing to an "X" on the map.

"Who is this Captain Kirk?" Viktorov asked again.

"He is a Captain of the Star Ship *Enterprise* on the movie and TV series *Star Trek*. You haven't seen them yet have you?"

"No, in my country we don't get a lot of western movies. They felt they were; well, not suitable for our people. I know they were wrong and they are slowly coming around to release those. Maybe I can see them soon. Can you get copies somewhere?"

"Yes, we have movie rental places, and they show a lot of them on television now. You might enjoy them. In fact, I will make sure you have copies of all of the *Star Trek* and *Star Wars* movies when we get home." Henderson offered.

"Captain Henderson, this is the missile room," crackled the boats internal communication system, disrupting the moment of quiet banter.

"Go ahead, Henderson here." he stated after he picked up a microphone and depressed the button.

"Sir, would you come down here? We have something you need to see, and bring Captain Viktorov with you. He may be of some help." Lanstrom asked over the intercom.

"We will be right down, Lanstrom; just don't touch the blue wire." he stated while he turned back to Davin, "You may as well come; maybe your ideas will help down there. Is your buddy, Josh, on the boat too?"

"No, Bear, he got tied up with Hancock and the President. He stayed on shore along with Anne, Stephanie, and Connie." replied Davin.

Meanwhile back in Norfolk

Back on shore, Ensign Kent was coordinating an aircrew and aircraft big enough and with the range to meet the sub and remove its crew if they were unable to disable the detonator and they scuttled the boat. Or to pick them up after they disabled the warheads and made the boat safe. Walking out of the building with the conference room that had been turned into a war room, she saw a large private research vessel heading out of the harbor and turning southeast.

"Where do you suppose they are going?" she asked of the team around her. "They should have received the notification for all vessels to remain in port. I will be right back." she said while turning. She ran back into the war room, picked up the phone, and placed a call to the local Coast Guard operations facility. "Hello, this is Ensign Kent over at Norfolk Naval Yard. May I speak to the commander or the duty officer?"

"Yes, can you hold for a moment?" replied the clerk.

"Sure," Kent said. After a moment's pause, a voice came on line.

"This is Commander Adams, Ensign Kent, it has been a long time, how are you?"

"Great, Sam! You know what has been happening? Well, I just saw a civilian vessel leave the harbor. Did we not put a restriction on travel until this is settled?"

"Yes we did. What size vessel and which direction was she heading?"

"Southeast and she is about one hundred twenty-five foot, moving fast, and looked loaded with underwater equipment."

"Possibly the '*Underwater Adventurer*'; she is a private research vessel with which we have had previous problems. They like playing by their own rules. I will send a cutter after her and bring her back. We have a cutter just south of them, and don't worry, we will stop them."

"Thanks Sam, if we survive this, maybe dinner?" Kent asked.

"Sure, just say when and where." replied Sam who waited for a second before placing the phone in the cradle.

"Bye for now, catch up to you later." Kent responded and then hung up.

Chapter 29 Sorry Mr. President

"Sir, there is a call on line one from one of the terrorists. We are tracing it as fast as we can and will have a location in a minute or two, but you need to pick up the line to complete the connection," the Security Advisor said as she entered the Oval Office.

"Hello, this is the President; to whom am I speaking?"

"Mr. President, I am Viktor Mikhailiovich, the ex-executive officer for the Soviet nuclear vessel you have in your Norfolk Naval Yard. You probably have already heard of me from my former commander. He wanted to give the weapons back to you, but I am sorry to say I should have killed him when I had the chance. Now I believe he is helping you. Well, that is fine. He can help, but it is too late. You may have noticed the explosion of one of the warheads outside of your Denver airport. We are truly sorry about that. I would like to say it was a mistake, but it was not. We were planning on detonating it in Denver, but from what I have heard on the news we were able to kill your Vice President and many of your people. With that, you see we are serious about our demands. We have eight more war heads all placed in strategic locations in some of your major cities. We will start to detonate them one at a time starting at noon East Coast time tomorrow and every twelve hours until you pay or we run out of war heads. Your choice, unless you pay us the ten million dollars per warhead, for a total of $80 million that will not even put a dent in your national budget. Your country sends more than that to Africa and other poor countries. I will call tomorrow at 8 a.m. to tell you where to take the money, and when I receive it, I will tell you where the warheads are. We know your government has it, so don't be so cheap. Save your cities and give us what we want. I have to go now; I know your intelligence team is trying to trace this call so I will make it easy. One more thing, our boat in Norfolk is also set to explode. We have a detonator set to explode at precisely 3 p.m. in two days. Do not attempt to disarm; it will detonate. We have it wired to all the warheads. Once we have our money, I will give you the code to disarm it. And I am right now calling from your Washington Monument. Come and get me, if you can. Goodbye Mr. President." And the line went dead.

"He is teasing us. Get some men over to the monument now and arrest everyone there. We will sort them out downtown," the President ordered. "No, wait. He will be gone before we get there and besides he may have been lying."

A knock on the Oval Office door resulted in the President giving a quick nod to his aide, who turned and opened it. In walked Agent John Polson. "Sir, we ran a check on this Viktor Mikhailovich. He is, or rather was, the executive officer of the nuclear boat we have in Norfolk. He was born in Moscow and raised in a farm town about one hundred miles south. His parents are Muslim and he was raised as a Muslim. The soviet government is cooperating with us and has sent over his complete military record along with those of ten other Muslims that were stationed on that boat. They were all in strategic positions, such as; missile control, computer operations, and weapons. Get the picture. This is sounding more like an Al Jihad operation that has been in the works for years. Is he doing this for the money or to kill Americans?"

"I do believe you just hit the nail on the head, Mr. Polson. They don't want the money; they want to kill Americans in mass. If, in fact, the Soviets are sending us correct information, which I truly believe they are; no reason not to. So, all indications are these guys are Muslim terrorists possibly under direction from one of the factions in hiding who saw an opportunity open in front of them and took the shot. Our country is vulnerable and open to attack thanks to the past administration. Oops! Did I say that? Sorry, guys. But seriously, we are vulnerable and need to act now. We need to find them before they destroy a city."

Chapter 30 Cruising on the High Seas

It had been ten hours and the boat was running at flank speed or thirty-three knots and seven hundred feet below the surface. All surface ships had moved further north or south to avoid being in the detonation zone with the exception of the *USS George H.W. Bush*, the newest, fastest super carrier in the Naval arsenal. She would remain one hundred twenty miles from the destination of the submarine with several fast rescue helicopters on standby to race out and pick up the crew. Ensign Kent opted for this as opposed to an aircraft, finding it easier and more efficient.

Within three hours of leaving the harbor, an automatic valve opened in the forward storage area and proceeded to flood the compartment. It almost flooded the adjoining compartments before the water tight bulkheads were sealed. Two hours later, one of the air circulators caught fire when one of the internal motors seized. This filled the compartment with smoke that took an hour to clear out, and now they only had five of the six available to recycle the air on board. They were lucky they only had a small crew and did not require all six. But, as a safety precaution, they ordered everyone to refrain from smoking. Finding out that there were no smokers on board to start with was a good sign. Almost, as if scheduled, two hours later all the lights went out in the crew quarters, galley and aft torpedo room. There was no explanation as to why and they were unable to restore the lights. More lights and systems started to shut down over the next few hours, leaving the boat in partial darkness with half the computer systems malfunctioning and the other half unstable.

Only twenty-three hours were left and they were still too close to occupied land to be safe. Carrying eighteen nuclear missiles with ten individual warheads each, they were betting their lives and the lives of millions that they could accomplish this without the loss of life. But the odds were against them, and time was running out. At a speed of thirty plus knots and a depth of seven hundred feet, they could not afford to lose any more systems and hope to maintain the speed and depth and life for that matter without having to surface. At exactly ten hours from leaving port, the second and third air circulators shut down along with the lights in the compartment that housed them.

"Captain Viktorov how many men do we need to scuttle this boat, if it comes to that?" Captain Henderson asked his counterpart in the control room with the emergency lights blaring and the crew fighting for their lives.

"I can do it with a minimum of six men, but once we start, we cannot stop and reverse the process. We should be able to escape through the pods in the forward torpedo room if we still have power up there. But that is not a promise; two may still have to stay to ensure it goes to the bottom and to manually launch the pods. And, if we have any more problems, we may not be able to escape at all." replied Captain Viktorov.

"Understood, what are these pods you are talking about? We don't have escape pods on our boats." asked Captain Henderson.

"It will be myself and my young commander, Eric, staying. We know the boat and can make her go down and she will implode long before we reach the bottom.

I believe the bottom is around eighteen thousand feet; am I correct, Captain?"

After pausing for a moment and taking a deep breath, Captain Viktorov continued,

"The pods are modified torpedoes; they are big enough for two people. We have

removed the warheads and placed a small air tank up there. All the fuel tanks and

motors were removed and replaced with a small electric motor. With some

modifications, we were able to add a depth gauge and some buoyancy tanks to control

our speed to the surface. There is a water tight hatch that can be released from the

inside and a small rubber raft. It is tight and not everyone can fit. But to be able to

place men on the beach it was our way of doing so without detection. They are

basically mini-subs which can be launched from our torpedo tubes. We have eight on

board. We are able to send up to sixteen troops to shore, or eight with special gear. I

believe they will be of use for this operation. Don't you agree, Captain?" Captain

Viktorov stated, smiling with this little secret about his boat.

"Yes, the bottom of the trench is about eighteen thousand feet, give or take a

few feet. If the boat implodes, do you think it will set off the detonator? And yes, I

agree those will come in use, possibly sooner than you think. With all the problems

with this boat, we may need them." Henderson concurred, shaking his head in

disbelief, and wondering what other surprises this boat might have.

"That is hard to say at this point, we are hoping that the people down there

can stop it before we sink her."

"Me too, sir. Me too." Henderson said. "There is still a very nasty storm up

there; with any luck it will pass and the crew can get off and be picked up. But even that is risky. The weather may prevent them from taking off and flying out this far.

But Ensign Kent may have had to take a different turn; maybe a carrier is not too far

and will send a chopper. I really don't know, but they do know the approximate

location for the pickup, at least if all goes well and we can get off this boat in time."

"Yes, Captain Henderson, it may be our last sea cruise. Let us hope it is not; I

would love to see my daughter go to college and become an American citizen."

replied Captain Viktorov.

"That is my wish too, sir. Let's get back to work. Maybe there is a way out of

this yet." Henderson stated as he looked around the control room.

"Let's take her up to fire off a message. We need to let them know our

status." Bear suggested.

"Good idea; Diving Officer, bring her up to periscope depth." Captain

Viktorov ordered.

"Aye, sir," he responded to the Captain. Then to the crew he ordered, "Five

degrees up, blow mains. Time to periscope depth approximately six minutes, sir."

"What's going on up there?" Lanstrom yelled into the intercom from the

missile room.

Picking up the microphone Bear asked, "What are you yelling about? We

need to surface to send a location report."

"STOP, DO NOT SURFACE!" she yelled with panic in her voice.

"STOP THE RISE!" Bear yelled at the crew driving the boat, bypassing the

diving officer.

"All Stop!" the diving officer yelled.

"Now what is the problem?" Bear asked as the boat slowed ascent.

"When we started up, the timers started to speed up."

"We have stopped the ascent, what are the timers doing now?"

"They have slowed; can you come down here for a minute, sir?"

"On my way," Bear exclaimed as he looked over at Captain Viktorov and received a nod.

Chapter 31 I.S.O.P.P. in the Bahamas

After using the bad weather to avoid the two Coast Guard cutters, the *Undersea Adventurer* ran for a day and a half to reach Bimini in the Bahamas. They pulled into Fisherman's Harbor on the southern side of the island and tied up. The storm had beat them up a bit and the boat required some repairs; nothing they could not handle, so they planned to lay over for a day or two to make repairs and take on more help.

Within an hour after securing the boat, her captain and crew were in the lounge having drinks and discussing world events. The news was on and each one sat there taking in the near riots and preparation the country was doing.

"Do you believe what is happening? Looks like World War Three starting back home!" one of the crew stated to nobody in particular. "Maybe we should call this off and go back and help. Captain, do you think that is why that cutter was trying to stop us?"

"Most likely, but he didn't, and we are here safe. So do not worry about it; we will get back in a few weeks and all should be back to normal." replied the captain.

"Nuclear weapons detonated on our soil. That is just not right. I hope they catch those Ruskies and hang'em." the crewman stated and then took a sip of his beer.

"What's the plan, Captain?" a young man asked as he walked up to the captain.

"Hey, Jimmy, we are laying over and doing some repairs. We'll then head out when the storm settles, probably in a day or so. Do you want to join us?" queried the captain.

"Sure, if you're buying the beer, then we are in." Jimmy answered and pointed to his buddy, "This is Al Motts; he is a good diver and wants in also. I told him a little about the job and, well, what else is there to say, he wants to join in the fun."

"Welcome Al, we will get you two a bunk in the morning and you can help with the repairs and be ready to leave in two days. Now let's have another round and get some sleep; it has been a long day. The rest of the crew will be up in a minute or two; they have some gear to store and then will secure the boat."

Minutes later, the rest of Dennis's crew walked into the lounge. They were all looking a little tired except for one very sexy female dressed in a very short pair of tight cut off jeans that looked as if they were spray painted on, a nearly shear light pink blouse hugging her ample breasts, and a pair of beat up deck shoes at which no one was looking in the entire lounge. The four others were in jeans, tee shirts, deck shoes and looking for liquid refreshment.

"Lady and gentlemen, may I present our two new crew members. This is Jimmy Summerland and Al Mott; they will be joining us on this little adventure. Jimmy, Al, this is Tony Sands, diver, mechanic and all around helpful in many areas, over here in the sexy little outfit is my girl, Natasha Haynes, just great to look at and she can dive, fix anything that has Scuba attached to it, and drive the boat when I am busy. Beside her is Harley Davidson. Yea, his parents were bikers and he got stuck with the name. His parents' last name is really Davidson. He's a good diver and welder and great drinker. Right, Harley? And last, but not least, this is Rick Jackson, the best deep diver I know. He is our cook and, well, he does other things for me that we don't talk about here. Now, drinks." Dennis paused for a moment to get the bartenders attention. "Barkeep, drinks for my friends and give me the tab."

The drinks flowed freely for several hours. Around midnight Natasha and Dennis slipped away and headed for the boat. Before they left, Dennis covered the bar tab up till that moment and added $50 more to cover several more drinks for his team, with a healthy tip for the bartender. "Ok guys, we need to be on the boat and up no later than 10 a.m.; we have a lot of work to get done before pulling out. See you in the morning."

"Right boss, no problemo, we will be there with bells on or at least ringing in our heads." Harley commented. "Hey do we have separate rooms at the inn?"

"Yes, you do. Just don't get arrested. I need all of you. And try to be a little bit sober." Dennis said as they left the bar.

"Now that the boss and his lady are gone, let's party. Barkeep, another round and when do the girls get here?" Harley yelled at the bartender.

"The girls are coming in at 1 p.m.; they usually are half toasted when they arrive." Harley said to the other drinkers at the table. Their plane lands at about 11:30, and as soon as they hit the ground, they start drinking and browsing. All high quality, hot and willing to play, but be careful. If you are not up to an all nighter then just

sit back and drink. Now let's party boys."

"How many are there?" Jimmy asked and sipped his beer.

"Well, the last two times we were here, there were six sexy stewardesses'.

All hot and ready. And since we are the only single guys in this bar, they should be

easy to take; and if Angel is with them, I will try to get them all over to see you guys."

Chapter 32 Running Deep

"Captains, we are running at thirty-three knots, depth seven hundred feet, course 130 degrees true." the diving officer announced as Captain Victorov and Henderson reentered the bridge.

"Thanks, Commander, we should be about here in the next twenty hours. That's if we do not run into problems and all runs true." Captain Henderson stated as he pointed to a location on the navigational map.

"Captain Henderson, do you think that will be far enough to protect the country from destruction?" Captain Viktorov asked. "My calculations say no, what do yours say?"

"No sir, I don't." Henderson replied, shaking his head in disbelief; they were running out of time.

"Bridge, this is the engine room." squawked the speaker box.

"Go ahead engine room." Captain Viktorov responded when he picked up the microphone and pressed the transmit button.

"Sir, can you and Captain Henderson come down here. We have a problem in the engine room." Chief Sharp yelled into the intercom.

"On our way, Chief." Captain Viktorov answered looking at Captain Henderson with a serious look. "What now?"

Arriving in the engine room ten minutes later, they found the chief with a very concerned look on his face. What could go wrong down here; they had some of the best engine operations crew the US Navy could offer.

"What's the problem, Chief?" Captain Henderson asked after they entered the engine room and he had scanned the area for obvious problems and saw none.

"Come over here and check this out." the chief said as he turned and walked to a panel above the control console. After opening the panel, he pointed to a small box.

"What's that?" Captain Viktorov asked as he looked at it closely. He reached out and almost touched the object, but thinking, he stopped.

"That, sir, is the problem. We have been in constant contact with the reactor room, standard procedure. Well, to make a long story short, when we vary our speed that thing starts to click. And seconds later, the reactor room calls us and tells us to stop whatever we are doing, quit speeding up and slowing down. We ask why? They say every time we slow down that damn thing starts to speed up. Almost like that silly movie a couple of years ago with Sandra Bullock. You know "*Speed*," where if the bus went below fifty-five miles per hour, it would explode. This is acting the same way. We slow down and the timer speeds up; we start to surface, it speeds up. I bet if we start to go down, it will speed up again. Do you think they modified this system the same way they did in that movie?"

"I hope not, Chief. That would mean that when we do slow down we die, and out here we just can't leave the boat on a small ramp like they did and let the bus explode. It does not work that way here. Are you sure that this is not something of an anomaly and you can slow us down without a problem?" Captain Viktorov commented. "Is this what caused us the problem a while ago. Remember when Lanstrom called us to stop our ascent to the surface. Maybe this is the same thing, so we can't go up and we can't speed up or slow down. This is not good, Captain."

"Let's experiment a little." Henderson stated. He picked up the microphone and called the reactor room and missile room. After getting them online, he briefed them as to the situation and explained that he wanted to do a minor experiment. They were going to cut their speed to twenty-seven knots and watch what happened.

"Bridge, we are reducing speed to twenty-seven knots; stand by, and maintain your depth and heading." Captain Viktorov informed the diving officer on the bridge.

"Aye, sir." responded the deck officer.

"We may have to accelerate quickly, so we will handle it from down here. Stand by."

"Aye, Sir."

"Bring it back, Chief." Henderson instructed the chief.

"Aye, sir. Captain, would you please watch that gauge? When it hits twenty-seven knots, yell out. Captain Viktorov, let me know if the reactor or missile room yell stop. I will not be able to hear you from back there at the control console." he said while pointing to the speed gauge.

Minutes later their speed was reducing slowly.

"Captain this is the missile room. The speed on the timer is increasing as our speed drops. I suggest we stop decreasing speed and quickly!" yelled Lanstrom from the missile room.

"Chief, take us back to thirty-three knots!" Captain Viktorov yelled down to the chief. Nothing happens fast on a submarine. "Chief, increase speed, now!"

There was no change in speed; it was still decreasing down to twenty-four knots.

Captain Henderson took off in a sprint, and headed toward the control console. Turning he found the Chief bent over the console. "What's wrong, Chief?"

"Damn control is stuck, grab that hammer over there." the chief yelled and pointed to the tool box.

After a hard whack with the hammer, the control started to move. The chief pushed the control lever to max and the engines responded instantly.

"Damn that was close." Captain Henderson said wiping the sweat from his brow.

"Look at this, it was rigged to jam; this lever was designed to drop in place when the throttle was pushed beyond a point which would increase our speed beyond thirty plus knots."

"What other surprises did they leave us?" Henderson said quietly to himself.

"Sir?" Chief asked looking at his captain questioning the remark.

He didn't need to ask, since he had been a captain of several U.S. nuclear boats, how long could they run at flank speed without running out of fuel. Since it was nuclear, that answer would be a long time; since they can run for years without refueling, they would be long dead from starvation before this boat ran out of fuel.

"Captain Viktorov do you think we could run close enough to the surface to maintain speed and maybe get….. No, that would never work; we cannot leave the boat going thirty plus knots. Impossible," Henderson answered himself. "What about your modified torpedoes?"

"Captain Henderson, maybe we could surface and get most of the crew off in the rescue rafts, even at speed we could do that." Chief Sharp suggested.

"It's worth a try." Henderson agreed.

"Bridge, this is the captain. Maintain speed and surface the boat." Captain Viktorov said into the microphone. "Let's get back to the bridge. We don't have enough modified torpedoes to get everyone off the boat."

"Chief, have you got it under control down here?" Henderson asked as he started to leave.

"Yes sir, I do now." the chief replied and looked over at his assistants and made a silent decision. He and his two men were going to go over this engine room with a fine tooth comb to see what and if there were any more surprises.

Minutes later the two captains entered the bridge. "Captains, we have another problem."

"Yes Commander."

"As we started to surface, we got an urgent response from the missile room." the diving officer started to say, "Well, Lanstrom said to stop immediately; the timer was speeding up as we started up again. Seems like we are stuck at seven hundred feet and thirty-three knots till…."

"We get the picture, Commander. Don't spread that around just yet. Let's see if we can find a cure for our problem before it becomes a bigger problem." Henderson said and then looked over at the clock; "We have nineteen hours till detonation, let's make those hours count."

"I need all department heads and civilians in the galley in five minutes." Captain Viktorov said over the internal communications system. "Bear, we have some decisions to make and new assignments to levy. Let's get down to the galley. Come on Commander." He indicated to the diving officer to go with them. His expertise was needed.

"Captain Viktorov, does your boat have a radio beacon?" Henderson asked as they headed for the galley.

"Yes, we do, but it cannot be launched safely at this speed. Maximum speed to safely launch is fifteen knots. But we can try, the worst that can happen is we lose the beacon; and, maybe, we can get a message off to your navy command."

"What about a torpedo launch with the beacon replacing the warhead or using one of your modified two man torpedoes?" Davin asked as he caught up with the two captains after overhearing their conversation.

"Good idea, maybe it will work. How many beacons do you have?" Henderson asked. "Maybe launch Davin out in one of those. He can surface and make sure the message is received."

"You wouldn't want me to go. Remember, I was Army and can't remember how to send a message." Davin shot back, with a half chuckle.

"Two, Bear, we have just two buoys and we have eight mini-subs; each will hold two people and survival gear or whatever you need to take." Captain Viktorov said as they entered the mess hall. Davin headed for the coffee pot and offered Bear and Captain Viktorov cups. Bear accepted and Viktorov declined.

"What's this all about, Bear." Davin asked as they entered and found most of the department heads waiting with coffee cups in hand and most chatting among themselves.

"Gentlemen, we have had several more minor problems arise and another serious problem, one that we may not be able to recover from...." Captain Viktorov started to brief the men; and when finished, he looked at Henderson. "We are open to ideas as to how we are going to rectify this set back."

Some discussions started at each table between the department heads but nobody came up with a solution.

"We need to launch a beacon to let command know what we are up against and then find a solution to the problem." the dive officer suggested finally.

"That is given, Commander. We need a volunteer to be launched with equipment that can transmit to command our situation and ask to be picked up. The volunteer will be shot out in a modified torpedo with a transmitter/receiver, life raft and rations. We cannot spare two people, so the chosen one needs to know how to operate the equipment and hope to survive being launched from our present depth. We are at seven hundred feet going thirty-three knots. We would prefer a navy person

or at least military trained." Captain Henderson requested this need over the ship

board intercom system. After pausing for a moment, he continued. "This is a one way

trip gentlemen and ladies; I need a volunteer in the next ten minutes. Think of it this

way, you will not be on this floating nuclear bomb anymore."

Chapter 33 Norfolk Naval Yard

"Admiral, we just received a communication from *CVN-77 George H.W.Bush*. She is in position and awaiting orders." Ensign Kent reported to the Admiral when entering his office.

"Tell them to stand by; the boat should be in position in the next eighteen hours."

"Aye, sir;" Ensign Kent answered as she pivoted on her heels and started out the door.

"Wait, Ensign. Please take a seat." the Admiral said as he pointed to a large overstuffed chair at the corner of his desk.

"Yes sir." replied Ensign Kent while looking very confused.

"This situation is only getting worse. What I am going to tell you only a few people know and it needs to stay that way. I feel you need to know the full situation before this gets worse. You may have to make decisions that your rank does not give you authority to make, but make them you must. If we survive this, I will see that you are promoted and receive your just rewards. But for now, I cannot. The President has informed me that Air Force 2 has crashed and there are no survivors; the dead include the Vice President and part of the cabinet. Three other commercial aircraft were also brought down by a nuclear explosion outside of Denver. It seems that the crew of that boat out there took the warheads and is using them to hold the United States hostage. They are demanding money and asylum. When the bomb exploded, it killed over eight thousand people, both civilian and government. They have threatened to use the balance of the warheads to destroy other cities.

"Sir, what would you like me to do?" Ensign Kent asked, just as there was a knock on his door.

"Come in, Lucy." The admiral yelled.

"Sir, we have another problem." Lucy said and then stepped aside to allow a young lady to enter the room wearing a short leather skirt and white blouse.

"May we help you miss?" the admiral asked.

"Sir, my name is Harriet Lanstrom, Commander United States Navy."

"You can't be; Commander Lanstrom is on board a submarine that left the harbor earlier today." the Admiral stated, as he looked at the young lady standing in the doorway of his office.

"Sir, I am Harriet Lanstrom, and the women onboard that Soviet Missile boat is a Soviet spy." she stated.

"Come in and sit down; we need to hear more of this. First, can you prove what you are saying, your ID card or drivers' license, something to prove who you are?" the admiral asked, indicating that she should take a seat, and then said to Lucy, "Do we still have communications with the boat?"

"No sir, she went silent two hours ago and we cannot reach her." Lucy said as she turned to leave again.

"Sir, the imposter was kind enough to not take my ID or anything with my picture on it, here is my ID." Harriet said and passed her ID over to the Admiral.

"Kent, take this out and verify it." he asked and handed the card over to Kent, who left immediately to verify the card. Since it was encoded with specific information that could not be duplicated, she was sure that in a few minutes she would know if the imposter was here or on board the submarine. "Hurry back, I have more to tell you."

At least her ID card said she was who she claimed to be, but only a DNA test would positively prove it. Luckily DNA was recently added to the magnetic strip on the ID cards and could verify true identity.

"Commander, may I have a quick swab, to test your DNA?" Ensign Kent asked, holding a cotton swab.

The commander leaned back and opened her mouth so Kent could get a good swab for the test. It would take thirty minutes to an hour to run the test in the dispensary located across the base. Luckily there was an emergency medical office located three buildings down on the dock. The medical office could run the test and have the results back in minutes. Kent ran the swab over to the medical office and was back in less than fifteen minutes, confirming her identity.

"Sir, she is real; the imposter is on the boat. DNA confirmed." Kent stated as soon as she returned and handed the ID back to Harriet. "I do believe we have a saboteur on board. What do you want to do?"

"First off, there is not much we can do. With no communication with the boat, we cannot warn them; and with you here, Commander, they have to find out for themselves. But, first, we need to encode a message to the commander of the *Bush* and let him know what is going on and tell him to let the boat know as soon as they get communication established again. Beyond that, not much, except let's get Commander Lanstrom settled in the BOQ and back in uniform. Then get her over to Intel for a complete debriefing." the Admiral ordered. He then asked, "Are you up to it Commander?"

"Yes, sir, anything I can do to help."

"Lucy, can you come back in?"

"Yes sir," Lucy said as she came back into the office.

"Take Commander Lanstrom over to the BOQ. Stop by supply and get her a new uniform with everything she needs. Then after she has cleaned up and changed, get her over to Intel for a debriefing. Explain to them the situation."

"Yes sir." Lucy replied and then said to Commander Lanstrom, "Come with me, Commander."

"Thank you, sir." Lanstrom said as she left the office.

The Admiral waited for a few minutes until he heard the outer door close. He then looked back at Ensign Kent and said "That has just put a real kink in this, hasn't it?"

"Yes sir. We need to let them know that they have a possible saboteur on board."

"As soon as we can; you will get that message off to the *Bush* as soon as we are done here. Now Ensign Kent, I understand you are a wiz with computers." the Admiral stated, getting a nod from her. "In a call to the President just over three hours ago, the terrorist informed him that the boat was wired to explode if they

attempted to speed up, slow down, surface or dive above or below a set depth. We

don't know the depth they are at or even if they know what could happen if they

change anything. We need to find a way to help those men out there. I want you to

pull up a complete schematic of that boat and find a way to disable that detonator. Run

scenarios to see what you can come up with. We only have eighteen hours left,

possibly only eighteen hours till the end of civilization as we know it. Use whatever

resources you need; pull anyone you need from any area. If you need civilians, then

get them. We will brief them and we will do whatever we can to bury their

involvement if we have to, but that is the least of our worries. Now, are you up to the

challenge?"

"Yes, sir! But how are we going to let them know out there if we develop a

way to help them?"

"I have some communications specialists working that right now. I have

instructed the intelligence section to provide you with the best computer system they

have and all the assistance you need. Now time is wasting, get moving."

"Thank you, sir." Ensign Kent said as she stood and saluted.

"No need to thank me. I have confidence in you. If we fail, so does the

human race. So, thank you, Kent."

Chapter 34 Soviet Nuclear Boat "The Terminator"

"Ok, let me get this straight, Bear;" Davin stated while still in the galley with all the department heads. "We are travelling at thirty-three knots at seven hundred feet below the surface while riding inside a nuclear bomb that is destined to explode if we surface, slow down or go deeper. The bomb is wired to about one hundred ninety nuclear warheads with the equivalent explosive power twenty thousand times greater than the Hiroshima Fat boy that exploded in 1945. This, by the way is coupled to a nuclear reactor that is very unstable and can by itself destroy all of New York City in a blink of an eye and slowly kill every living human, tree, plant, and animal on the entire eastern seaboard in a matter of weeks. Am I correct to assume this?" Davin finished, looking extremely frustrated.

"Well, not exactly, Mr. Pierce." Captain Viktorov stated. "We are travelling at thirty-three knots and we cannot surface or dive without setting off the explosives, that much is correct. But your assumption that the reactor is unstable is not quite true. Commander Lanstrom has assured us that the reactor is stable, but the computer system controlling it has been compromised and we do not know how stable it is."

"Ok, the computer that controls the running of a nuclear reactor is unstable. How does that make me and the rest of us feel? This sound like a no win situation. And you know; I love it." After a brief pause, he continued, "What do you want me to do?"

"Commander Lanstrom, is there a way to move the control of the reactor to a more stable computer system?"

"Possible, yes, but that may mean we have to shut down the reactor to move the system, or, no, maybe we can run them in tandem and slowly shut down the bad one. But that might also mean we could infect the stable system. Somehow we need to stabilize the reactor's computer. I have good people working on that as we speak. That one young lady is just about the best I have ever seen with a computer. With her and her buddies, we can do just about anything, if we have enough time."

"Ok, now what about those warheads? Any luck getting those computers to disengage that detonator before it hits zero. We do not want this boat to live up to its name '*Terminator*' and have it wipe out our entire world."

"Again, that is being worked as we speak;" Lanstrom commented. "Captain, if we are going to have any chance of surviving this, I need to get back down there. But I need to speak to you and Captain Henderson privately, if you please."

"Sure, Commander, my cabin when we finish here;" Captain Viktorov replied and then while looking around the galley, asked, "Anymore questions? No!"

Minutes later, Captain Henderson and Captain Viktorov were entering the captain's cabin. Once the door was closed, Lanstrom turned, locked the door and then looked at Captain Viktorov while smiling.

"What is on your mind, Commander?" Henderson asked as he sat down at the small desk.

"Father!" was all she said and hugged Captain Viktorov.

"Well, Captain Henderson, I am not really sure how to put this, so I will just say things are not what they seem. My name is Andrea Chekov; I am a commander with the Soviet Intelligence Command. I was sent here to infiltrate your command and gain access to our boat and report back to my nation what you have discovered. Most of this I have done successfully, as you can see. I, of course, have not reported back to my command because of our situation here." After pausing a moment, she continued, "The real Commander Lanstrom is alive and well; she was being held at a private secluded home outside of Norfolk. Before we sailed I sent a signal to my command to release her on Saturday. She has been released by now and most likely is at the Norfolk Naval Yard telling them exactly what happened. She will be attempting to warn you about me. The Commander was left unharmed and had plenty of food and water to last well beyond her release; and we do not kill like in the old days."

"What the hell! She is your daughter?" Captain Henderson exclaimed with surprise, completely ignoring everything she had said.

"I need to explain, Captain. Yes, she is my daughter. And I wish she had not come on this trip. But if we are to have a chance in surviving this, she is the best one to make that happen."

"She is your daughter?" Bear repeated, and then back to the fake commander. "I suspected something was not right with you when Davin told me his suspicions back at the base. He said something was just not right. But you had the proper papers and ID, so we were not going to push the subject. And now, wow! How the hell are we going to cover this?" pausing again, he finally continued as he paced around the small stateroom. "I think you need to enlighten me a bit more, sir."

"Well, that may be easy. Andrea married a civilian several years ago.
Well, she thought he was; he was actually working for the KGB as an operative and
was not ever supposed to marry. But he and Andrea met, fell in love and got married.
He did not tell his command, but instead got her transferred to work with him. That
was a fatal mistake.

"Miss Chekov, or may I call you Andrea for a moment? We suspected you
were not Lanstrom but had no way of proving it, which is why you are on board. Now
are you here to help us or...." Captain Henderson stated, letting his words trail off.

"I am here to help. I was not sent here to die. I was a nuclear specialist with
the Soviet Navy before I joined the Intelligence group. My knowledge is extensive,
but I am not a computer geek, as you call them, and need assistance there. I want to
make it home with my father and see my mother and younger sister again. They worry
a lot."

"Ok, now that I have confessed and will turn myself over to your authorities
when and if we return," Chekov continued. "do you want me back in the missile
room?"

"Yes, we need all the help we can get. Now, if there is nothing else, we will
keep your little secret to ourselves. Let's get this thing fixed."

"Aye, sir;" Commander Lanstrom replied and started for the door.

"Hold on a minute;" Henderson asked. "Ok, the real Lanstrom is safe and
may have been released safely already; this is good. Now this will be our little secret

forever if we can't stop this thing from blowing. What does your high command want to do with this boat?"

"I wish I could tell you, sir. They were a little vague as to what to do when I discovered what you had found out. Father and Captain Henderson, I have given this much thought and wish to become an American citizen with my father, so I am asking for political asylum. Your country is honorable and your team is the best I have ever had the pleasure of working with, I wish to continue with that, if at all possible, sir."

"Chekov, if we survive this; we will grant you your wish, at least the political asylum part. Not sure if we can get you in our Navy or not, but for now, don't let it worry you. Now, let's get back to work and save the world!" Captain Henderson said as he looked over at Captain Viktorov to get his agreement. He agreed. "Is there anything else you or your father wants to say?"

"Well, yes, there is." Andrea said as she looked at her father. Getting a nod of approval, she continued, "Well, my husband is a member of the crew; he is working undercover to discover what the crew had in mind. My superiors had some intel about the crew and wanted him to infiltrate the group. He was able to do that. Now we know the terrorists are Muslim and have been a sleeper cell in the Soviet Navy for years, planning on a scenario like this and the time was right to make it happen. But we don't know if he can stop it from within or not. If discovered before he can stop it, they will kill him, if he isn't already dead."

"I thought you said he made a fatal error? How did you know about that?" Henderson asked and then looked at Captain Viktorov. "Never mind, you two have been talking, haven't you?"

"We have not heard from him since they left my father and Dimetri, the man you know as Eric, at the hotel. My father already knew, but could not tell you till now, without giving away my identity. But now you know. The final thing is these men are Soviet sailors, but they are also Muslim. My government started getting information about several of the crew and their activities. With the information they had received, they started to watch each member of the crew, especially the Muslim's. Things did not look right, so they had my husband take many classes to learn the Muslim ways and then had him assigned to the crew with hopes to infiltrate their team. My father was not aware of my husband's assignment. Sorry father, it was their decision, not mine. We believed that whatever they were planning to do did not concern saving lives, but taking as many American lives as possible. We believed they were going to take over the boat and use the warheads to destroy American cities. We did not know this submarine was also set to explode in Norfolk to show the American government that they were serious. When my superiors found out that you had the boat, they sent me. My job was to get on board, find out why it was here and abandoned. My father was lucky they did not kill him and Eric at the hotel, but that may be part of their plan. Let them live, take the boat out and kill all on board. They also hoped that the boat would not get far enough away that it would cause a major tidal wave that would devastate the east coast."

"Yes, we have been talking ever since we left the harbor." Captain Viktorov disclosed.

"Not a concern right now. We do have bigger problems, so let's get back to work and see if we can survive this."

"Think positive Captain Henderson; we will survive. I would prefer to die as an American of old age and on dry land. I have never thought of myself as a sailor, like my father," Chekov stated as she started to head out of the stateroom and then began running toward the missile room.

Chapter 35 Norfolk Naval Yard

"Connie, have you contacted your department yet?" Stephanie asked as they drove toward the front gate to leave the base. She then turned to Josh and asked, "Hey, Josh, honey, what do we do now?"

"Yes, I contacted them and the boss wants me to work with Homeland Security for the next few days. Not exactly sure what they want me to do, but orders are orders." Connie stated, "My plane leaves in a couple of hours."

"Stephanie, we are going to meet with the Admiral and coordinate rescue operations with the carrier group *George H.W.Bush*. Has anyone seen Davin lately?" Josh responded and asked, just suspecting where he was.

"Josh, honey, you need to keep track of your buddies better. Didn't you see him go back on board? He said he had to speak with Bear." Connie said and then started to cry. "What if they don't get off that boat in time?"

"Connie, they have the best of the best on board that boat. They will get it done, or it will not matter to anyone of us on the east coast or for that matter, anywhere on this earth. That explosion will kill this planet. Maybe not immediately, but over the course of time, a very short time, all living creatures will be dead. Not to sound morbid or anything like that, but that is what we need to consider right now." Stephanie responded.

"I know Stephanie, I know, just don't want to think about it." Connie said.

"Hey, let's grab some lunch and get you over to the airport. Anne, what are you doing over the next couple of days?" Josh asked, looking around for a place to eat.

"I have been assigned to you, Josh, until this is over. Orders are to assist you in whatever you and Stephanie are doing." Anne commented not sounding real happy. "So I guess we go back to see the Admiral, right."

"Good, maybe you can tell us some more about your family while we eat." Connie said and then turned the car right to head for Bubba's BBQ located about a mile down the road. "It may help get our minds off the possibility of total destruction."

Twenty minutes later they were sitting in a booth at Bubba's, drinks and food ordered. The atmosphere was strictly south Georgia BBQ with wooden benches and tables.

"Ok, Anne, enlighten us a little on your family. From what I hear, your family has a long line of criminal activity, murder and better yet, piracy." Connie asked sipping her tea.

"Ok, just a little. Somewhere way back around the early 1700's, Anne Bonny was born and raised, supposedly not far from here, in Charleston, better known at the time as Charles Town. You know, she was bad from the get go, and ended up with Jack Rackham, aka Calico Jack. I won't go into her bad life; you can read books about her, some true some not, but she, Jack, and Mary Reade were captured. Anne and Mary were both pregnant and put in jail. Jack was hung and then put on display to show other pirates what would happen." After stopping to take a drink, she continued, "Not much is known from then on except Mary died giving birth, and Anne just disappeared from jail with both children. There are many theories as to where she ended up; nothing public is known. It is documented in our family diary and I know; the story has been passed down through generations in the family and now rests with me and me alone. But I guess I can tell my newest and closest friends. Right?" replied Anne smiling at her new friends and wishing the world was a safer place.

"Ok, so are you going to tell us?" Stephanie asked as her food was placed in front of her.

"Well, after Mary died, Anne took her son and Mary's son and was released. The reason, and how, was never told; she just left the jail with the boys. With some money she had acquired from friends, she was able to purchase passage on a ship to England and buy a small bit of land in northern England, and raised her sons as noble men. Nobody knew who she was, what she did or anything about her. They lived a good life, with Henry becoming a Duke and running their kingdom with an iron fist. Henry married and had three sons; Peter married and had two children, one son and a daughter. Hey, that's enough for now. I will tell you more later, but I will say now that we also had some of the more famous outlaws from the old west in our family. I will let you think about that one for a bit; I am hungry." explained Anne, looking up for the waiter or waitress.

"Wait a minute lady, do you mean to tell me that you are related to William Bonny?" Stephanie demanded as she picked up her iced tea to take a sip, but paused to ask.

"Well, yes, he was a distant relative and of course one of the more famous bad guys, Billy the Kid, aka William Bonny. And everyone knows about him, all around bad guy. But, hey, not all of my relatives were bad; there was a little known guy by the name of James Richard Ripple." answered Anne.

"Who was he?" Stephanie asked.

"He was a real nobody that lived in London as a small shop owner; well he died in London during the Second World War. He was a book seller and a British Underground commander. He was killed during an air raid but had managed to save over six hundred British citizens before he died." Anne commented and took a sip from her iced tea.

"Wow, and you say he is not a bad guy. He is a hero. You should be proud of him. Did the government honor him for his bravery?" asked Stephanie.

"Yes, there is a park named after him in south London, near where he died. They took the remainder of his family, my family, and relocated them to a safer location till the war ended. They kept the family going outside of the same town that Anne Bonny had taken her children to before she disappeared." explained Stephanie.

"Interesting, what has your family not done?" asked Josh.

"Well, we never became President or Queen of England, but we had a couple of monarchs and dukes; they were not well liked and two of them had an abrupt ending of life, one beheaded and the other, well we are still looking for the rest of his body; very gruesome death. Now can we eat?" asked Stephanie.

"Tell us a little more about William Bonny." requested Josh.

"Ok, between bites." Anne said and then took a big bite of her sandwich.

"William was born in 1859 but there is a little known secret that has recently come to light by some historians. They are saying that he was born not as William Bonney

but really as Willimina Bonney. He hated his father so much he ran away from home

at the age of fifteen. It is said that he was not a he but really a she. He, or she, had

small hands and wrists, on occasion would dress as a woman, and also enjoyed time

with paying clients as a prostitute. He/she took up the gun and became a gunfighter at

the age of fifteen and told people her name was William Bonney. William Bonney

also became known to many as Billy the Kid. Now it has never been actually proven

that he was a man or a woman, but there is some indication that he was a cross dresser.

He was a killer and he supposedly died by the gun in 1881 by Pat Garrett, a sheriff

who found him unarmed and supposedly shot him in the back, as the story goes

anyway. Now there is a little twist to that part of the story too." continued Anne.

"Wow, that is a story I had not heard before." Stephanie stated.

"Well, if you don't tell anyone, I will let you in on another family secret."

whispered Anne.

"We do have security clearances and must keep secrets, you can trust us."

said Josh and Stephanie, quietly.

"I guess so. Well, our family records and Willie's birth certificate indicates

that he was a she and like Anne Bonny hid her secret with the clothes she wore and

that she killed anyone that may have found out about her secret. Only Pat Garrett

knew her secret, and the supposed killing of Billy the Kid happened, but not the way

most people think. Pat Garrett had learned of Billy's secret years before and chased

her, not to kill her but to court her. And for about a year, they kept it a secret. Soon they had to make a decision and between the two of them, they decided that Billy

had to die. You see she was pregnant with Pat's child. They staged the killing, used

the body of a drifter dressed as Billy, and buried him on Boot Hill. With Billy's death,

Willimina could come out and the two of them moved to a small town in Arizona to

raise the child and live to a ripe old age. The child was named Bill and went on to

discover gold and become a wealthy land owner in southern California, more on

young Bill later. We have other things to consider." continued Anne between bites of

her sandwich.

"Wow! But tell us about Bonny, how did she become you?" asked Stephanie.

"I could go on for hours relating my family history but we are not here to

learn about who married who, had who and what became of them. In a nut shell, here

is the whole thing. In 1721, Anne Bonny disappeared from her cell with two children,

hers and Mary's, as I said earlier. Henry Rackham (1721 to 1786) became the duke of

Sherwood. He was Anne's son; his adopted brother was Peter Rackham (1721 to

1792), and their father was Jack Rackham who was hung as a pirate in November

1720. Peter had three sons: John (1738-1790), Harold Jr. (1740-1806), and one who

died before reaching his first birthday. Henry had four children that survived infancy,

but two died at the ages of ten and fourteen. Of the two that survived to adulthood, one

married in 1748 and produced three children (1759-1799, 1760-1804 and 1760-1810),

who married between 1781 and 1785. One of their sons, Morgan, moved to the new

world, America, in 1834; he married and had two sons Henry and William. William

Rackham, known as Willie, ran away from home, changed his name to William

Bonney after his great, great grandmother, Anne Bonny, and misspelled his last name, by adding an "e" when it should not have been there. He became known as "Billy the Kid. I just told you about that link. There are no records as to what happened to the other children." explained Anne.

"Son Henry married and settled down. In 1890, his son Matthew was born and became LT Matthew Rackham (1890 -1915) who was killed during World War I, flying as a pilot of a Spad aircraft. He was shot down over France in 1915, but took eight Germans with him resulting in his winning the Flying Cross for valor. The other three children never married and died of old age. Linda Rackham, (1915 to 1998) daughter of Matthew was born three days before Mat was killed in France. She and her older brother Zackary (1910 to 1985) ran a small printing business from 1929 to 1941 when he joined the Army as a pilot and flew B-17s over Germany. He was shot down but survived the war. Their main printing job was money, counterfeit money for the local mob. Linda ran the company. She married Jack Connelly, a business man, in 1942, just before he went to war. She worked in the airplane factory at night to help the war effort. Jack was killed on the *USS Saratoga* during the battle of Midway in WW II. Zackary had a son named William, who married Mary in 1960 which produced Anne Rackham in 1978. She became LT Commander Anne Rackham, who is about to marry Captain Bear Henderson." Anne finished and took the last bite of her BBQ sandwich.

"Now that is what I call a family history.' Stephanie commented with a stunned expression on her face. "How can you remember all that without notes?"

"I have been studying my family since I was a little girl; it has fascinated me and I just wanted to know more. I have learned so much in the past few years. When my mom passed away and left me all her stuff, I found it contained so much history which she never told me about and now I am just learning." Anne said as she finished her tea. "Ok, now what has all that got to do with that boat in the harbor?" Anne asked.

"To start with, you have a family history that may be useful in discovering why that boat had a small box of gold coins on it possibly from Anne Bonny's missing treasure." Josh answered.

"What?" Anne exclaimed, "Do you mean that besides having to worry about the whole world being vaporized by a nuclear explosion of biblical proportion, you are researching gold coins found on board."

"What else do we have to do, while we wait for our men to get back?" Connie said and then sipped her beer. "We had been looking at the life of Anne Bonny before you got here, and now, wow, we have a direct descendant that may be able to shed some light on how she lived and died."

"Hey what am I, a toad?" Josh commented, finally able to get a word or two in.

"Ok, sorry, honey. We only meant our men on board that boat; you are my man and don't forget it." Stephanie reassured him and then kissed Josh lightly on the cheek.

Chapter 36 Nine Hundred Miles from Norfolk and 700 Feet Deep

They were only a few hours away from total destruction and several of the men and women, along with Captain Henderson and Captain Viktorov were taking a short break in the galley.

"Captain Henderson, ah, I need to thank every one of you for being here, but you need to know what is actually happening. First, most of you know, we have a problem. A problem that may not end the way we want it to, unless we pull together and figure out how to disarm this boat." Captain Viktorov stood up and looked over the men and women in the mess hall before he stated, "Some of you already know part of our problem, but maybe not all. Captain Henderson would you take it from there, please."

"Ok, here is what we know: we are heading 260 degrees, at thirty-three knots, seven hundred feet below the surface with an unlimited amount of fuel. We could run for at least fifty years before we would deplete the fuel. But there is a problem. We do not have enough food to live that long; we have maybe eight months of food, unless the refrigeration goes out. But that is not the problem. The problem is this boat is wired to explode if we speed up, slow down, dive deeper, or attempt to surface. We are stuck right here until we die or blow up. At least we can steer without worry, at least for now. Oh, one other thing, we are riding in a nuclear device large enough to destroy most of the world as we know it. If it causes a chain reaction, as we expect, most of the world, as we left it, will be destroyed. But most of you already knew that, so I am just stating the obvious." Captain Henderson paused to take a breath before continuing. "Now we need to come up with some answers and quickly. Davin, you have been helping Commander Lanstrom in the missile room. I would like you to move over to the control room and help Ensign St. Johns and Chief Michelson to see if we can reroute the control system to allow us to surface and, well, you know, slow down without exploding. Commander Lanstrom, do you have any ideas as to how to disarm those warheads?"

"Sir, we are closer to understanding how they are wired and should be able to disarm them in a couple more hours. Wish us luck."

"Good, we may survive yet." Henderson said hopefully.

"Captain, the clock is still ticking down there. When I left, it said we had about ten hours before it hit zero and boom." Lanstrom stated throwing her hands up like something exploding.

"Well, I guess you need to disarm this thing before then." After a short pause, he continued, "The rest of you continue your job. If anyone has computer experience and speaks Russian, Commander Lanstrom could use some help, but I only want you to help if you consider yourself a professional hacker or have the ability to do that. We need to hack the system, but do nothing unless Commander Lanstrom approves it; I don't want to blow up this boat."

In the back of the room, a hand went up. "Yes, Seaman Harrelson."

"Sir, I would like to help Commander Lanstrom. I have a Computer Science degree and Masters in Computer Engineering, but I do not speak or read Russian."

"Ok, go with Lanstrom, thank you. She will translate for you. Any questions?" After a short pause, Henderson continued, "Good, now back to work; we have a world to save." And after another pause he added, "Oh, one other thing. This boat has been booby trapped. Things will quit when you need them or cause damage. Be careful. Also, I still haven't gotten a volunteer to take a ride to the surface in one of the torpedoes. Can you spare anyone? If not, I will have to pick someone that we can spare from the rest of the crew."

"Sir, I need everyone I have and could use a couple more if you can spare them." Lanstrom answered.

"Ok, I will see what I can do." Henderson replied.

Within a few minutes, the two captains were alone in the galley. At least they thought they were until they turned to leave and saw Davin at the door.

"What are you hanging around for, Davin?" Henderson asked.

"Well, I think since we have this almost unrecoverable situation, I should share this with my best friend." Davin said holding up a bottle of Dom Pérignon champagne. I found it in one of the officer's quarters."

"Don't you think we would be better waiting till we disarm this thing before we drink that?" Henderson asked.

"Well, yea, but I think we need to at least have a glass to toast our future success."

"Ok, one glass."

"OK, one glass," Davin agreed and poured three glasses.

"To our success," Henderson stated.

"Our success," Captain Viktorov repeated.

"Oh, yea, there are at least twenty more of these over there in the galley cabinet."

"Good, we will take care of them when we head back to Norfolk." Henderson agreed. "It will be party time then; we will stop the boat, surface and have a party on deck."

"That sounds good to me, gentlemen; now let's get back to work. Who brought this fine wine in here anyway?" Davin said, trying to be funny. The three headed out of the dining area and raced up to the bridge.

Chapter 37 Nine Hours and 48 Minutes

"Captain, we are maintaining thirty-three knots and seven hundred feet down." the dive officer acknowledged as the two captains entered the bridge.

"Maintain what you have, for the moment anyway." Captain Henderson answered. He walked over to the plotting table and started to examine the charts. "We are about here and we need to be here and unless we speed up we are not going to make it. What do you think, Captain Viktorov?"

"I believe you are correct, my friend. So what do you suggest?" replied Captain Viktorov.

"Maybe we should attempt to send up a message buoy first before sending a manned torpedo. And let Norfolk know what we are doing and that we have some problems down here." suggested Captain Henderson.

"Ok, I will get one of the techs to prep the buoy; maybe we can just release it and let it do its transmission. If we keep it cabled to communicate, then we take the chance of having it break the cable." Captain Viktorov said shaking his head, thinking that they might not get out of this alive.

"That may be the best way, but if they have anything to tell us, we will not have that chance. And your little boat does not have any way of communicating with our submerged communication system; if it did, we would not have this minor inconvenience." Henderson stated to no one in particular.

"Captain, I am sorry we are not as technologically up to date as your navy. We are a country that has been without much money for many years." Viktorov said and looked at Henderson with concern.

"Sorry, Captain Viktorov everyone is getting a little testy, me included. I am sorry." Henderson apologized.

"No problem Bear, I can call you Bear, right? If we make it out of this mess; we will celebrate."

"Yes, that's fine, sir. I would like that. Now let's get that buoy ready and one of your special torpedoes, we may still need to use it." Bear Henderson suggested.

Captain Viktorov picked up the microphone and called down to the missile room to get the only other Soviet crew member on board. He ordered him to ready the buoy for release and to bring up the recorder so Henderson could record the message.

Twenty minutes later, the Soviet crewmember, Eric, arrived on the bridge and reported, "Captain, the buoy is ready and here is the recorder."

"Thank you," Captain Viktorov said as he took the recorder from Eric and handed it to Henderson. "Captain Bear, here is the recorder, do you have any idea what we should tell them?"

"Not really, but I will make it up as we go." replied Bear.

Eight hours and forty-two minutes left before they reached the final destination. Things were not going well. The buoy was ready and the message had been recorded, frequency plugged in, and the system set to run continuously until the batteries failed, which should take about six hours.

"Ok, I think we are ready. Launch that thing." Henderson ordered.

"Opening number one torpedo tube outer door." the weapons officer announced, and flipped several switches, "Outer doors opened and firing now." He pressed the 'Fire' button, feeling the sudden surge of air push the torpedo out of the tube into the open ocean. "Torpedo away and heading for the surface."

On the bridge they watched its progress until it reached the surface and ran for fifteen minutes at fifty knots, when the engine shut down and the transmitter should have started to transmit its message.

"Launch successful, sir; the buoy has reached the surface and is running true. It will start transmitting in fifteen minutes, once it stops. And if we are lucky, which we could use a little more of, your people will hear it and know where we are and what to expect." Eric reported once the torpedo reached the surface. "Sir, the tube door will not close!"

"Torpedo room, this is the bridge."

"Go ahead bridge."

"Tube one outer door will not close, you will have to close it manually."

"Working on it already, Captain, will advise when it is closed." came the reply.

"Well, in less than nine hours, we will either be sitting on the surface with another bottle of that wine you have onboard or our atoms will be somewhere in the atmosphere. Let us hope for the wine." Bear responded to the report. "Is Seaman Jacobs ready for his ride?"

"Yes, sir, he is down in the torpedo room, going through his pre-launch checks now. He should be ready in a couple minutes." the dive officer responded.

"Good, we will hold on that for a couple minutes." Henderson ordered.

"We will drink to that when the time comes, Captain." Viktorov replied in response.

As they headed for the control room, two levels up, the collision alarm sounded. Both Captains immediately sprinted up the ladder and toward the control room, but stopped abruptly on the deck just below the control room when they saw smoke coming out of the electronics compartment about twenty feet in front of them.

"Holy crap!" Henderson yelled, "Fire control, fire in the electronics compartment." He yelled into the microphone that was at the top of the stairs. Continuing down the hall, they started to open the hatch. But when they touched it, they discovered it was red hot. Then he remembered that they had no fire control team on board. "Viktorov, grab that fire extinguisher."

Henderson grabbed another and a pair of utility gloves, while carefully opening the door. They started to spray into the compartment. Moments later, two seamen showed up to assist. It took almost an hour to put out the fire.

"Chief Sharp, find out what caused that and what systems it has just taken off line. We need to know now." Captain Viktorov ordered. They looked over to Henderson and Viktorov looked at Bear before he continued, "Bear, I do believe our problems are getting worse."

"You are so right. Let's get cleaned up and meet in the control room." Bear said and then turned back to Chief Sharp, "Chief, when you find out, come to the control room. We will be there. Send your guys to get refreshed. I wish I could say take a break, but we don't have time for breaks."

"Aye, sir." Chief Sharp said as he went back into the burned electronics compartment to help his men find out as much as they could as quickly as possible.

Back on the bridge, Captain Henderson and Viktorov looked tired and ready to throw in the proverbial towel but then after catching their breath Henderson looked over at the weapons officer standing at his control board and asked.

"Are you ready to launch Jacobs into the history books, Commander."

"Well sir, I would love to but we have another problem. The outer doors will not open and they have him loaded in the tube but cannot get the door open, either manually or electrically."

"Damn, if you haven't gotten him launched in the next ten minutes, pull him out and, well, we will try again if you can get the door opened on any of the other tubes."

"Aye sir. I will advise as soon as it is done."

"Thank you."

Norfolk Naval Yard; 1 hour later

"Admiral, we just got a message from the '*Terminator*'," Ensign Kent said as he entered his office.

"What is it, Kent?" the admiral asked.

Sir, she is about six hours from the termination point. They have some serious problems, running at seven hundred feet, thirty-three knots, cannot surface, dive, speed up or slow down without the possibility of setting off the missiles. They have not figured out how to disarm them yet, but are working as hard as possible to stop the clock. They have one more buoy and will use it to keep us posted but have no way to receive messages. They will attempt to launch a manned torpedo with more information soon. He said they are working as fast as they can to rectify that and also to disarm the boat."

"Kent, what is the status of Task Force 1?" the admiral asked.

"The *Bush* and her task force are three hundred miles north of our boat. They are maintaining a stationary position and running air operations, keeping the rescue choppers on standby. At last contact, they had four F/A 18's in the air at all times, covering the route of our boat and will continue to do so until one hour before detonation."

"Please don't use that word, Kent. Those people will find a way to stop the destruction of our planet or die trying. How much time do we have left?" the Admiral asked.

"As I said earlier, they have about six hours left. Either they surface, get rescued and let her blow, or, well, the third and only other option is not one we want to happen." replied Kent.

"Have you had any luck with your calculations?" the Admiral asked. After getting a no from Kent, he continued. "No way to let them know anyway. Why don't you drop that and let your technicians continue. You take up station in the communications room and keep me and the task force informed on any changes."

"Sir, Josh Randel and Connie Pierce have departed for Los Angeles to join the search for the Soviet crew; Commander Rackham and Stephanie Randel are in the reception area waiting to see you." said Kent.

"Bring them in, they need to be aware of the situation and maybe they will have some insight as to what we need to do here." the Admiral ordered.

"Yes sir." Kent replied. She then turned sharply and headed out the door to get Stephanie and Rackham.

"Thank you for seeing us, sir." Rackham said and saluted sharply.

"Take a seat Commander and Ms. Randel. You need to know the situation and time is running out for everyone." replied the Admiral.

Chapter 38 Treasure Hunters – Bimini Bahamas

"Get that gear tied down; we need to get moving." Captain Dennis barked orders to his motley crew; he then proceeded to review his charts as sweat dripped from his brow. It was going to be another hot and humid day, but at least they were in the Bahamas. It was another beautiful sunny day out here with crystal clear water, a gentle ocean breeze with incredible fishing, sexy ladies and stories of pirate treasure; what more could a guy want.

"Captain, we have the food and supplies stored. The ship will be ready in ten minutes." the self appointed 1st mate Natasha said as she entered the bridge, smiling and wearing her usual, very short, tight, cut off jeans and a loose fitting tank top with no bra. She was in the Bahamas where casual meant she only needed a bikini, shorts and a few t-shirts, nothing more, except a few cold beers.

"Natasha, we are this close to finding a treasure of unthinkable quality and quantity and you come up here dressed like that." Dennis said looking at her and could not help his thoughts running wild.

"Dennis, honey, I thought you might enjoy a sexy pirate onboard." Natasha said strutting around the bridge in her skin tight micro shorts and tank top, sporting a pirate hat and tiny sword.

"Well, if we were not getting ready to get underway, I would just take you down to my cabin and help you change your mind about that outfit. But since we are about to move out, I will just have to enjoy you up here. Lock the door." Dennis pointed to the door and then continued; "I figure it will take about three hours to get here." and he pointed to a small rock of an island. "That is where we have traced the treasure to be. With any luck, this time tomorrow we will be very rich or, well, I don't want to think about the alternative, dead."

"Dead, nobody said anything about being dead. What do you mean, dead?" Natasha asked with a stunned look. She did not like what he was saying.

"Well, there are pirates in these waters; we may have to fight our way to the island as well as to get away with the treasure." Dennis replied smiling. "Don't worry your pretty little head, we are well prepared."

"Pirates, I thought we were the only pirates in these waters." Natasha teased but still unsure of what Dennis was saying.

"No honey, there are more than us. There are the real modern day pirates that hi-jack boats and kill everyone, no witnesses. And then there are the US Coast Guard pirates and of course the Bahamian Coast Guard pirates. All of them will want to stop us from getting to and from our island." explained Dennis.

"The Bahamian pirates may be a problem; I don't think we will have much trouble with the U.S. pirates. I will just keep this outfit on, or maybe take this off, if we are boarded." said Natasha. She teased Dennis by untying the front of her top to show off her ample perfect breasts.

"Stop that, Natasha, before one of the crew comes up here." Dennis said eyeing her breasts like a high school boy.

"The door is locked. You like these, babe." Natasha teased.

"Yes, you know I do." Dennis quickly responded.

There was a knock on the door.

"Please cover those beautiful tits of yours and answer the door." Dennis ordered.

Natasha retied her top and opened the door.

"Sir, the ship is ready. Give the order." stated the man as he entered the bridge.

"Undo the lines and let's get going." Dennis ordered. He then turned the key to start the engines, first the left engine, and when it was running smoothly, he pushed the button to start number two. "Everything is looking good here."

"She's released sir." a voice over the walkie talkie that was strapped to his waist blared.

Engaging the propeller on the starboard side, Dennis eased the throttle forward and slowly inched the boat away from the dock. Once cleared, Dennis engaged the drive on the port side propeller and kept the boat at a slow no wake speed of three knots. They headed down the channel for the open ocean.

"Nice job, Dennis." Natasha commented looking out the bridge window at the beautiful Bahamian crystal clear blue water and sky. It was a perfect day to be on the water.

"Four hours to history." Dennis commented as he watched out the window. Once he cleared the harbor entrance, he pushed the throttles up to maintain a steady speed of fifteen knots. He reached over and turned on the air conditioner for the bridge. Minutes later they were in open water and heading southeast toward the island. The weather was near perfect for a cruise in the Bahamas. All hands were getting gear ready for the island expedition.

"Attention all hands" Dennis announced over the ship wide intercom. "We will be arriving at the island in about three hours and twelve minutes, give or take a minute or two, and barring no interruptions from the Coast Guard, both the Bahamian and U.S. boys. If the information we have is correct, we should find the largest most valuable pirate treasure ever recorded in history. The late female pirate Anne Bonny, may she rest peacefully knowing that new pirates will be uncovering her booty once again."

A cheer went up all over the boat and the men and woman on board went back to work, packing up shovels, axes, and other material to dig for the treasure.

One hour and ten minutes away from the dock, Dennis heard a loud horn, sort of like a fog horn, but they were not in a fog. The horn blared four long bursts and then was silent for a minute then four more blasts, then a voice that he did not want to hear.

"*Undersea Adventurer*, this is the United States Coast Guard, heave to immediately." The voice from the cutter boomed. "Heave to, now and prepare to be boarded."

"Damn, Natasha you better get some more clothes on. This may not be a social call." Dennis instructed her.

"Hey, maybe those boys over there have been at sea for a while and would love to see a little female skin." Natasha teased.

"Maybe so, but you still better change into something less revealing, please." Dennis commented, as he pulled the throttles back to full stop.

"Crew, we are about to be boarded by the Coast Guard, please cooperate with them. Do not give them any reason to suspect anything. Is that understood?"

Within a couple of minutes, a twenty-four foot Zodiac rubber raft powered by a large three hundred hp outboard motor pulled alongside of the *Undersea Adventurer*. After throwing a line to one of the crew on board, a boarding ladder dropped over the side and four armed seamen and an Ensign boarded.

"Take me to the Captain of this vessel." the young female ensign ordered the crewman that met them at the top of the ladder.

"Yes, sir, eh, miss. Follow me." he responded and turned sharply on his heel.

"Chief, you and your men take a quick look around, but don't touch anything without checking with me. And leave someone here at the ladder with a radio."

"Aye, sir." Chief Robert Kowalski answered.

Up on the bridge, Dennis and Natasha were waiting for his unexpected visitors. He was sitting in his captain's chair with a cup of coffee. Natasha had stepped out to the flying bridge to enjoy the sunshine and the view; she had put one of Dennis's shirts on over the tiny top, but did nothing to cover up the shorts. She looked sexier in the shirt which almost hid the shorts.

"Captain, I am Ensign Felicia Cortez from the Coast Guard Cutter *Intrepid*. We have orders to stop any and all vessels in these waters and you have the unfortunate misfortune to be in an area that is restricted. Only military vessels are allowed for the next couple of days. All commercial and private vessels have been ordered to stay in port. Did you not hear the order before you left dock?"

"Ensign Cortez, Dennis Quaid, captain of the *Undersea Adventurer*. We are on an expedition directed by National Geographic. Are you going to tell Nat Geo to go home and not complete our research? And, no, we did not get any such message." Dennis's lie was almost convincible, but even a non-trained intelligence officer could see through his story.

"Sir, we know that is not the truth. Are you going to stand there and lie to an agent of the U.S. government, or tell me the truth? Why are you here? We have been sending out warnings for the past eighteen hours on all bands and have posted on all islands throughout the area. You cannot tell me that you did not know this is a restricted area."

"Ok, ok, do not get upset; we are treasure hunters and are heading to a secluded area to recover what we feel is the largest treasure ever located in the islands and possibly the world."

"Now don't you feel better, telling the truth? Besides we already knew your mission and have been tracking you since you left Bimini. We wanted to be sure of the area where you were heading. Now we know, and we need you to turn around and go back to North Carolina as fast as this boat will take you. This area is not safe for you or your crew. You can get your treasure when our live fire exercise is over."

"OK, Ensign, when is that supposed to happen?"

"Sir, that is classified information, but I would suspect that it will be completely over in about a week. However, I would check with the local Coast Guard station before heading out again. We would not want your ship to be hit by a missile or misfired round, now would we?"

"Ensign Cortez, I am curious. There are many inhabited islands all around here. What are you doing with those people if you are firing live missiles over their heads?"

"That is not your problem, sir. Now we can do this the easy way or the hard way, Mister Quaid. There are naval operations going on, in and around the Bahamas, and you are presently in restricted waters and are required to leave immediately. That is not a request, sir."

"I guess we will depart and head for our home port immediately. If that is what we need to do to stay out of trouble with the United States Coast Guard. But we do this under protest. This is not U.S. territory, it is Bahamian. But I will not argue with you about that; you have a bigger ship and guns, which we cannot and will not go up against. Now Ensign you and your men have my permission to get the hell off my boat."

"My pleasure sir," Ensign Cortez acknowledged and turned on her heels and headed out the door and down the ladder to the deck below. "Chief, get the men and let's go." she said into the small radio she carried.

Up on the bridge Natasha asked, "Dennis, are we going home?"

"Not on your life, on to the island. Get Jackson to ready the weapon." Dennis replied.

"What, weapon, what weapon? You are not going to fire anything at that ship." Natasha yelled at him.

"Just do it, or get off my boat." Dennis yelled back.

Minutes later Natasha was standing with Jackson in the forward compartment with the secret weapon that they had installed months ago, just in case they had trouble. She had no idea what this thing was or why she came down to tell Jackson what Dennis had ordered her to do.

"What the hell is this thing?" Natasha asked looking over the strange tube in the forward compartment and then up at the open hatch above them.

"This little lady is the great equalizer. Now get out of here; it is ready to fire now. Once fired, it will take about twenty-six seconds to make contact with its target. Well, it may take a few seconds longer if the target is more than a mile away. They will not have time to react." Jackson responded as he worked on getting the missile ready.

"You know we will be killing U.S. citizens and military. Do you have a problem with that?" she asked.

"No, not really, they are stopping us from reaching our treasure." Jackson said and looked at his watch. He then picked up the microphone and keyed the bridge. "Dennis, we are ready down here. I just need to bring it up on deck. One minute to raise it up; going up now." There was a short pause till it reached the deck, "Ready for launch."

"Fire when ready, I have the engines hot and ready to run." Dennis said to Jackson and then stood and waited.

"Hatch opening, Natasha has left the compartment. Don't know where she is heading. I am in the fire control chamber; target acquired, and am firing in five, four, three, two, one." Jackson yelled in the microphone and hit the fire button.

A micro second later the missile flew off its launch cradle. After reaching one hundred feet, the missile turned over and sped toward its target. As soon as the missile left the bay, Dennis pushed the throttles full forward and the boat took off, gaining speed to its maximum of thirty-two knots.

Coast Guard Cutter *Intrepid*

"CAPTAIN, INCOMING MISSILE!" yelled the radar operator.

"WHAT?" pausing for a second "Incoming, man the Phalanx." the captain yelled to his crew.

A second later, the automatic missile suppressor started to fire at the now visible incoming missile. At one hundred ten yards, the weapon had completed its job and destroyed the incoming missile.

"Radar, where did that come from?"

"Captain, the trajectory indicates it came from the boat we just left. And they are hi-tailing at thirty-two knots heading 310 degrees." Radar replied.

"Helm, flank speed, heading 310 degrees;" the captain ordered, "Battle stations, this is not a drill;" Then he said to no one in particular, "So they want to play. Well, this is a game for professionals and they have just pissed off the most professional crew in the Coast Guard."

"What the hell was that, sir?" Ensign Cortez asked as she entered the bridge.

"Your friends over there just shot a missile at us. And now, we have to play police and go arrest them or kill them."

Chapter 39 Which Way Did They Go?

In Los Angeles, California, four men pulled up to a small self-service storage building located on the south side of Los Angeles International Airport (LAX). Within minutes of stopping in front of a fifteen by ten foot storage unit, they had exited the van and were looking around the area to ensure it was clear of any extra eyes. After a couple of minutes of scanning the area, the shortest of the group leaned over to the padlock and unlocked the door and raised it. At the same time, the other three opened the side door of the van and started to remove the large box.

"Take it easy with this; we don't want the same thing to happen to us that happened to Boris and Mickel outside of Denver. Be careful." the tallest of the four said in a whisper.

"Don't be silly, we have not even placed the detonator in the box."

"Ok, but still be careful, these things have never made me comfortable, even in the warhead. You know how bad our government is in building quality things. They used to be one of the best, but with all the budget cuts, this thing could just blow up on its own."

"As I said, don't be silly."

"Set it down gently."

"OK, OK, now let's set the timer and get the hell out of here."

Ten minutes later the detonator was set and the plutonium was in place. They were about to leave when a black van came through the gate and pulled up beside their van and stopped. The driver leaned out of the window and yelled. "You guys wouldn't happen to know where I could find some Soviet terrorists."

Startled, the four soviet crew men just looked briefly at each other, not knowing what to do or how to answer. Before they had a chance to answer, there were six armed men wearing FBI jackets and hats pointing automatic weapons at them.

"What is this?" yelled the tallest Soviet sailor, starting to reach for his pistol but stopping when he saw several heavily armed men approach him.

"You are under arrest for attempted murder, acts of terrorism and a few more crimes we have not documented yet." the man behind the wheel of the black van said as he stepped out of the van, holding up his badge to the tall Soviet. As he turned, he yelled at one of his men. "Jim, go in there and disarm that thing while we take care of these guys."

"How, how did you know we were here?" the Soviet asked.

"If you must know, we notified every possible storage facility in all the major cities to be on the lookout for any suspicious activities in their facilities; and when they did, no matter how simple, just call it in. You just happened to pick one that was very close to our location."

Minutes later the Soviet crew had been disarmed, cuffed and loaded into the back of the black van. Jim came out of the storage bay with the detonator in one hand and the plutonium in a box in the other. He was shaking his head with disbelief.

"What is it, Jim?"

"They had this thing wired all wrong, anything like a cell phone call nearby would have set it off. Even closing that sliding door might have set it off. Obviously the guy who wired it had a death wish, or maybe it was planned that way. We need to talk to him about this."

"And we will; load that back into their van and take it to 29 Palms for storage. And don't lose it, Jim. They are expecting you in two hours. Do you think you can make it by then?"

"Yea, even maintaining the speed limit; will we get a police escort?"

"They will meet you at the interstate. Now get going."

Chapter 40 FBI Headquarters Los Angeles

In the interrogation room were Josh Randel, Connie Pierce and Frank Robertson, senior interrogator in the LA division. They stared down at the tallest Soviet crewman and were about to start questioning him about his part in holding America hostage.

"We have one question we need answered right now, and you better tell the truth. We need to know where the rest of your crew is going." Josh stated, and then continued. "Your cooperation will be noted in your file which will make your trial go easier and you may only end up with life in prison instead of the death sentence. Or worse yet, we may just send you back to your country and let them kill you."

"You can't threaten me, I know I am a dead man and helping you is not going to stop that. So go away and find them yourselves."

"Connie, would you leave the room. This could get messy." Josh said and looked over at Frank and nodded.

"Josh, you cannot touch him, the law states that if we touch him or cause harm to a suspect, we could be sharing a cell with him." Frank commented.

"You know Frank, at this point he is not a suspect but a terrorist and I am not going to hurt him." After a short pause and a smile at Frank, Josh continued; "Well, not much, anyway."

"Josh, I cannot let you do it." Frank stated; "So let me do it. You sit over there. I don't want to get any of his blood on your Armani suit or shoes."

"Go for it Frank. I love it when an FBI agent gets down and dirty with a bad guy. This will be fun to watch."

"No wait, you guys can't do that, you have laws."

"Laws, laws! Man, you have broken so many of our laws that no matter what we do, you are a dead man; and we, well, we may just spend some time in the local resort jail for beating the shit out of you. But we actually may be given medals for saving millions of lives. So sit back and just take it like a man." Frank said as he looked at Josh and then back at the man sitting in the chair, who had started to sweat a little. "Look Josh, he has started to sweat; why do you think he is doing that?"

Frank walked around behind the sailor and put his hand on the back of the chair; starting to pull it back, as Josh watched the expression on his face.

"No, no wait. I will tell you where they are heading and as much as I know, but I want political asylum in your country, all charges dropped and a new life." the sailor said, almost yelling.

"No way, man; you will get political asylum, but spend most of your miserable life in one of our jails, if you are lucky. We will not drop the charges, but we will put in a good word for you with the District Attorney. That's the best we can do. Remember, we are just lowly Americans, someone you hate."

"Why do you say that, Mr. FBI man? Or are you just a low-life government man that follows orders like me. I was just following orders, Viktor told us what to do and we followed orders, nothing more. He had the plan to kill Americans. He planned it and we just followed what he said. He is my commander and like you I had to follow orders."

"Following orders is a cop out. Following orders that to most people would seem like they are at war when in fact they are not, is not the correct answer buddy." Frank said and then tilted the chair back even more.

"Why would you want to blow up Americans?" Josh asked, hoping to hear the answer he suspected.

"Why, you ask? Why? Why is because you are infidels. And all infidels must die."

"Infidels, we are infidels now. If we are infidels, then you must be more than what you seem. Where are you from, mister?" Frank asked. He pushed the chair upright and let it fall forward, then came around in front of the sailor and got up close to his face, almost nose to nose and asked loudly. "Where are you from? Only Muslim's talk that way; you may be from Russia but you talk like you are Muslim. Are you Muslim or Russian?

"I am Russian by birth, born in a Muslim family which is much better than you infidels. We are prepared to die, taking as many Americans with us as we can. Are you satisfied now, Mr. FBI man?"

"Now back to the question mister, where are they now and where are they going?" Josh asked again.

"I guess it will not hurt to tell you. It is too late now anyway. They are in place and will be detonated soon. Long before you get there, many will die tomorrow.

And many more in the weeks to come; you cannot stop us, we will win and you will die."

"You let us worry about that, just tell us, where are they?" Josh asked calmly again and then paused for a moment, "Now answer the question, where are they now?"

"Chicago, blue Ford minivan going to the parking garage at the airport, should be arriving in about two hours, set to go off at 9 a.m. tomorrow morning; white Chevy van in Washington DC parked in front of the Smithsonian Castle, set to explode at 10 a.m. tomorrow; another two are going to Seattle in a green Ford van to park at the south parking lot at the Carnival cruise lines terminal and set to go off at 11 a.m. tomorrow, when there are thousands of people boarding those big cruise liners. The fifth and final one is going to Boston; actually should already be there, just like the one in Washington D.C. It is in a blue Chevy Impala, in the trunk, set to blow at the same time as the Washington DC bomb. Now are you satisfied, gentlemen."

"Only when we have retrieved all of those and any others that you did not tell us about, so you need to come clean and fast. That accounts for five warheads, what about the other five?"

"Nice try, Mr. FBI man, but there are not five more, one was with us when you found us and one exploded in Denver. I told you where five are set to explode and the others are located in a warehouse outside of Norfolk Naval Yard, at a storage facility called ABS Self Storage, just off the highway, six miles from the main gate. We decided five were enough to do what we needed to do to convince your government that we meant business. The plan was to detonate those first, then, if needed, move the others into a city and blow them."

"Mass murder, well, that will really set well with the judge. Do you realize this could get you dead?"

"Yes, we were planning on going in with those last few, figuring the United States would not be livable after all those nuclear warheads destroyed your cities, so there was no escape for us."

Josh walked over to the door and opened it to signal the officer standing outside to come in. "Officer, take him to his cell."

Walking out of the interrogation room they came up to Connie, "Hey Connie, what did you get out of your sailor?"

"Well, he spilled the beans, Chicago, Washington D.C., Seattle and Boston, all set for tomorrow."

"Same as our guy." pausing as he saw another one of his interrogators come down the hall. "What did you get, Henry?"

"Chicago, Seattle, Boston and Washington D.C. and set for tomorrow morning" Henry replied.

"Same as us, Henry, go check with Mark and see what he got." Frank asked.

"No need, he finished a few minutes before me and told me the same thing."

"Assemble the team in the squad room, in ten minutes; Josh and Connie, notify the rest of the teams around the country, and then get back to the squad room." Frank ordered.

"Josh, can you get the plane ready to get us back to D.C.?" Connie asked as they headed down the hall.

"No problemo, sweetie, the plane is on the ramp and a quick call will get the engines warmed up so we can head out in about thirty minutes." Josh replied.

"Good, let's blow this popsicle stand." Connie responded and picked up the phone to inform her director of the situation, who in turn would pass it on to the President.

Forty-five minutes later, they were on board the Gulfstream 5 racing down the runway at LAX.

Chapter 41 The Terminator

"Captain this is the missile room" Lanstrom called over the ship wide intercom.

"This is Captain Henderson, go ahead." he responded.

"Will you and Captain Viktorov come down here; we have something to show you." Lanstrom asked.

"Can it wait a couple of minutes" Henderson asked.

"Well, yes, but make it a quick couple of minutes; we need to make a decision and soon." Lanstrom commented without hiding the tenseness in her voice.

"Ok, as soon as we get this little problem up here fixed, we will be there. Is it a decision we have to make or can you just do it?" Henderson queried.

"I don't want to make it myself; let's just say, if I make the wrong one, there will not be enough time left to grieve about it."

"Oh, I see; we will be there in a minute." Henderson said. He then looked over at Captain V and then to the helm. "Helm, maintain course, depth, and speed for now. That leak can wait for a couple of minutes. Commander, send anyone we can spare down to the torpedo room to see if they can stop that leak. How bad is it, anyway?"

"I just got back from down there. It is like a cold shower filling up the tub, about a foot of water deep." the commander replied as he toweled himself off.

"Ok, commander, get back there and stop the leak, somehow. Now go. We will be in the missile room for a few minutes." Captain Henderson said and then he and Captain Viktorov headed to the missile room.

Five minutes later they entered the missile room to find Lanstrom and her team standing around the missile console computer, literally scratching their heads and deep in thought.

"Ok, Lanstrom, what is the problem?" Captain Henderson asked as they approached the team.

"Sir, after many, many hours of sweat and broken nails, we have a solution." Lanstrom commented.

"A solution, wow that is great." Bear exclaimed and looked around the room again and at the techs.

"Well, you may not like it, and I am not sure it will work successfully, but it is all we have come up with." Lanstrom replied, not looking very happy, sweat dripping down her forehead.

"OK, so what is it." Bear asked.

"We need to launch the missiles!" Lanstrom said without blinking, being very serious, looking straight into his eyes.

"Didn't you say they are all connected together and removing one will set off the rest of them?" Bear asked and not looking real happy.

"Yes, but I said, we need to launch the missiles, all of them at one time. Captain Viktorov is it possible?" Lanstrom asked and then looked over at her father.

"Yes, it is possible, but I am not so sure at this speed. Opening the hatches may slow us down too much and cause an explosion. We would have to increase the air pressure in the storage tanks to push them out and with luck they will make it to the surface before exploding or running out of air and coming back down. Risky, very risky." Captain Viktorov commented.

"Did your super geeks figure out how to not detonate those missiles when launched?" Henderson asked as he looked over at the three young computer operators.

"Yes they have, but it is risky. But the only way to save ourselves and the world is to launch and let them sink to the bottom of the ocean, not get them to the surface."

"With or without the warheads?" Captain Viktorov asked worried that he would have to put some very dangerous nuclear capable missiles on the bottom of the ocean. They could degrade and explode which would only do what the terrorists wanted done.

"No warheads, well at least no plutonium, we started to remove the plutonium hours ago. We are about half done and running out of time." Lanstrom commented, and then continued. "Captain, I thought it would be prudent to do so; sorry, I did not ask permission."

"No problem, that was a good move, at least when we explode it will not be nuclear." Bear Henderson said with a little laugh. "Now how much more time do you need to remove the plutonium and be ready to launch the missiles."

"About three hours if we had four more crew to help. Otherwise we need six hours and we don't have six hours to work with." Lanstrom stated.

"Four more to help, no problem. As soon as we get the leaks fixed, I will send them down here."

"Captain, Bridge." squawked the speaker over Lanstrom's head.

"Henderson, here." he said into the microphone after removing it from its cradle.

"Sir, we have a problem up here."

"What is it, now?" Henderson asked looking back at Captain Viktorov.

"All hydraulics have gone off line, we have lost steering and dive control. The boat is five degrees bow down and speed is increasing. We just passed eight hundred fifty feet and thirty-five knots."

"Damn, what else is going to happen? Lanstrom, do whatever you need to lighten this boat and get those missiles out of here. Let's go Captain." Henderson said as he headed back toward the control room. "When ready to launch, let us know."

Chapter 42 Eight Miles from 29 Palms Marine Base

"They lied! Get those sons of bitches in here NOW!" Agent Frank yelled in the phone at the desk sergeant sitting at the desk in front of the holding cells located in the basement of the Los Angeles FBI Building.

"Who sir?" the desk sergeant asked.

"Those four terrorists you have down there. Bring them up here NOW!"

"No can do, sir. They are not here anymore."

"Where the Hell are they?" Frank yelled.

"Transferred down to 29 Palms Marine Base about an hour ago." the desk sergeant answered and started to sweat as he was being interrogated.

"By whose authority?" demanded Frank?

"Director Harrison, he said they needed to be under military protection. Sorry sir."

Without saying anything else, Frank slammed the phone down and ran out of his office heading directly to the Director's office. Barging in, without knocking, he stormed into the Director's office. "What the hell were you thinking John; we are not finished with those guys. And to top it off they lied to us. The bombs are NOT where they said they would be. And time is running out."

"Easy Frank, take it easy. We have them on the way to 29 Palms for their protection and ours too." Pausing when the phone rang and holding up one finger for Frank to hold up. "Yes,... Director Harrison, Yes,..... Holy crap, when did that happen? Are any of our guys, ok, two dead and three injured. Ok, we will be sending a team out. It'll be headed up by Agent Frank Murphy. Yes, he is leaving now."

"What the hell was that about?"

"Frank, someone hit the transport, killed all four Soviets, two of ours are dead, three injured. Now take your team and head out to I-10, about eight miles this side of the 29 Palms exit."

"On our way, John, but we have a bigger problem; only two of the locations they gave us had warheads. The ones in Boston and Seattle were there; the other two, Washington and Chicago, are missing, they have not shown up at the locations they told us and we have no idea where they are."

"And who killed them, is there another group in town that is about to blow us to hell and back?"

"That is a good question and I don't have a good answer. But, for now, get out to I-10 and meet with the Highway Patrol and get that site cleaned up. Send the bodies to 29 Palms."

"Did any of the Highway Patrol guys get killed?"

"Yes, four officers. Now go." Director Harrison ordered as he sat down and placed his head in his hands, feeling completely helpless.

"I am outa here." Frank said as he rushed out the door and yelled to his team, "Get your stuff together; we have a homicide."

An hour and forty minutes later, Frank and his team pulled up to the bullet riddled FBI van and two patrol cars. One was still burning. All the bodies were still where they fell, with a blanket over each one.

"What have you got, officer?" Frank asked when he walked up to the van. He then turned to his team and ordered, "You know the drill; get to work."

"Agent, ah, well anyway," getting no reply from Frank the officer continued, "according to one of your men, three black cars, all Chevy Impalas pulled up and just opened fire with automatic weapons. They shot the driver of each vehicle forcing them all to stop. One of the vehicles, as you can see, was also hit in the fuel tank which exploded and instantly killed both patrolmen. They were friends of mine. Your guys and the other patrolmen returned fire; they believe they hit several of the attackers, but are not positive. The cars stopped and opened up on the van killing most everyone in the van. Two of your men are critical but should live, the rest were not so lucky."

"Thank you, officer. Sorry about your friends; these guys were friends of mine too, so this is personal for both of us." responded Frank.

"Sir, if at all possible, I would like to join with you and help you find these killers." the officer requested.

"I will see what I can do; give your name and contact info to Joan, she is the one with the camera. Thanks again." Frank promised.

Chapter 43 The Terminator Missile Room

"Commander, what's our status?" Henderson yelled as he and Captain Viktorov ran into the control room.

"Hydraulics not functioning, diving planes at five degrees down angle, and speed is steady. We are taking on water in the forward torpedo room again. It is partially flooded. There are several other leaks around the boat, but those have been brought under control for the moment. I have Chief Sharp and two sailors working on the hydraulics. He thinks they can bypass the problem, but it will take time. We may not have much time." After pausing to glance over the dive controls and depth gauge, the commander continued, "Sir, we are passing through one thousand eight hundred feet."

"Damn, what is crush depth, Captain?" Henderson asked.

"Nine hundred fifty meters, oh, two thousand eight hundred fifty feet is our never descend below depth and her uncertified crush depth is one thousand meters, or about three thousand feet. That is what she was designed for, but that has never been tested. I would prefer not to test it now." Captain Viktorov commented, looking closely at the men in the control room.

"I don't want to either, sir, Commander." replied Bear.

"This boat is a nightmare, Captain; what the hell is going to happen next?" Henderson asked to anyone who would answer.

"Captains, the hydraulics are coming back online." the sailor at the number one dive station yelled across the control room.

"What hydraulics coming online?" Henderson replied immediately, running over to the operator. "What did you say?"

"Sir, the hydraulics are back online. We have control again."

"Stop the dive, level at, ah…." Pausing he looked at the depth gauge and read nine hundred ninety-nine meters, which meant they were at two thousand nine hundred eighty five feet, below design depth. "Level at two thousand nine hundred feet and hold speed and depth." Pausing again, "We need to fix those leaks and bring us up slowly, back to a depth we can control; maybe up to launch depth, but let's make it easy. The pressure is too great here; we will never get the hatches open."

"Captain Henderson, we are crippled here; this boat is not designed to cruise at this speed at this depth. If we come up too fast, we may expand some of the leaks that have stopped, bringing in more water. What do you propose, Captain?" Captain Viktorov stated, "May I take us up? I suggest you and your men search the boat for leaks that have stopped because of the pressure on the boat. The ones that are not leaking now may start again when we start going up and the boat expands again. This is not going to be easy, and remember we have to get rid of the missiles to lighten the boat, and at this depth, there is no way we can even open the missile hatches. Well, I don't think they will open, and if they did, I do not know what would happen."

"Noted, sir, we have to lighten the boat, so what can we do to lighten her and get us up to a safer depth?" asked Bear.

"Commander, can we hold this depth for a few minutes?" the dive officer asked, looking seriously at both captains.

"Yes sir, I just talked to Chief Sharp and he assured me that the problem has been fixed. They are looking for leaks; he will be up here in a few minutes." Viktorov commented.

"Good. Get Lanstrom up here too. We need to discuss our options and quickly." Henderson ordered.

"Captain, sonar!" the speaker box barked.

"Captain here, go ahead, sonar." Henderson spoke into the microphone after he picked it up and pressed the send button.

"Surface contacts, two destroyers and a large noisy frigate. Identified as Soviet." the sonar operator reported.

"Now what! Speed and direction?" Bear yelled back to sonar.

"Heading, two three zero, speed thirty knots, twelve thousand yards and closing." sonar responded, watching his scope closely.

"Crap, what the hell do they want?" Henderson said to himself. As he depressed the button again, he spoke into the microphone. "Sonar, keep us posted with any change in course or speed."

"Aye, sir." sonar responded.

A second later Lanstrom walked into the control room with a very puzzled look on her face.

"Lanstrom, why are we not dead?" Henderson asked as she approached.

"We got lucky, our little miss micro mini girl down there located a code and was able to disable the detonator to the missiles. Seems like just in time, too." Lanstrom commented and smiled for the first time since coming on board.

"Yea, we got lucky with that one. Are they going to explode if we launch them?" asked Bear.

"I don't think so. She and her two geeky friends down there have been able to crack a lot of the code and should have everything disarmed in a few more minutes. Along with some other nasty code they found, which may be causing some of our other problems." replied Lanstrom.

"That is great, Lanstrom. We now have another problem to go with the many we already have." Bear commented and walked over to the chart table.

He then explained that in addition to being stuck at eighteen hundred feet and unable to surface because they had taken on too much water and somehow needed to lighten the boat, they now had three Soviet ships closing in on them.

"The question still remains, will one or all of those missiles explode if we launch them?" Davin asked as he sat across the control room at the weapons control station. They were looking like over-tired friends. The fatigue and stress was catching up with all of them.

"Ok, say we attempt to launch all these flying bombs and one does not go, what, no don't tell me, we become one big hole in the water without the benefit of a titanium hull." Captain Henderson asked as he explored the room. His fatigue and stress were starting to really show on him. He looked over at Lanstrom and her

father, Captain Viktorov.

"Not exactly, sir, if we launch the first five, they should disconnect from the

computer which should stop the detonation of the rest. And with miss micro mini

down there, we have a great chance on surviving; she is one hell of a computer geek.

Those other two are complimenting her." explained Lanstrom.

"Well, then, why can't we just launch the first one that is connected to the

computer and have it disconnect the rest from the computer system that is controlling

the detonators?" Davin asked as he sipped his coffee, which everyone had been

practically living on since they left the harbor.

"Well damn, why don't we just launch it and find out." Lanstrom asked to no

one in particular. Looking at the people in the control room like she had never been

there before and wondering why the hell she came on this mini cruise.

"Ok, wait, why don't we just disconnect the missiles starting at the far end or

is it in a loop?" Henderson asked.

"It's a loop, sir." Lanstrom said and then added, "If we tamper with number

18 it may set off 1 to 17 or blow itself. We are not sure what will happen for sure, we

cannot be sure what will happen."

"So we are really back to square one." Henderson stated and looked closely

at Lanstrom.

"What, what is this square one?" she inquired with a very puzzled look on

her otherwise beautiful face.

"Back to where we started, and still without a clue as to how to keep from destroying the world." One of her techs replied as he entered the bridge and shook his head. "Commander, I have been over this system at least a dozen times and I think I can bypass the system and keep missiles 2 to 18 from exploding. But there is a problem with completely disarming the system, so I suggest that we disarm 2 to 18, fire number 1, and detonate it once it hits the apex of its flight."

"Ok, say we do that. How much time do you need to get missiles 2 to 18 disconnected from number 1?" Henderson asked.

"Actually sir, it is already done, I was disconnecting them as you were discussing the situation with Commander Lanstrom. Sorry for doing it without permission, but I saw the way in and just took it, before the system reset and I would have lost the door." replied Henry James, a young computer whiz who had been working with Lanstrom in the missile room. He had come up to this meeting at Lanstrom's request.

"Good work sailor, but how did you find it. No, don't answer that. I probably won't understand, but you said you found a door and did not want to lose it."

"Yes sir, the back door really is a way hackers use to re-enter a system once they have broken in. This person put one in, but every few minutes the system resets and at the same time it moves the backdoor, which made it very difficult to locate. But I got lucky, sir, actually while you were talking I got an idea and took a chance and there it was."

"What was the clue?" Lanstrom asked.

"Simple, Commander. When you were talking about the launch sequence, it just came to me to look at the code backwards and there it was, the backdoor. The programmer who did this system was damn good, but not as good as me, if I may be so modest. But I have not found a way to disarm number one. There has to be a way, but we may run out of time before I can find it." Henry James reported and looked down at the floor as if he was ashamed of what he did.

"Ok, so we launch number one; prepare it for launch. How much time do you need?" Bear stated.

"Ten minutes and we need to slow down to no more than twelve knots to safely launch." Captain Viktorov commented, "But I know we can't slow down at all, unless your man has found a way to slow us down."

"Sir, sorry I have not found that part of the programming, but give us an hour before you launch, and I think, now that I know the way he has written the code, that we may be able to slow us down safely. My partners down there are damn good and between us we can break it. If not, then we may have to launch at speed. Jessica is the best code cracker in the states. She has won many awards and written code you would not believe possible. Sir, can we do that?" Henry James responded.

"Supposedly, according to the engineers who built her, we can launch at max speed, but it never has been done." Captain Viktorov stated with a very worried look.

"Lanstrom, one hour, and then we launch." Henderson ordered as he looked at James and Lanstrom and hoped they, along with the micro mini girl and her friend, could do what was needed to allow the boat to slow down.

"And make sure all the plutonium is safely stored away from the missile

room. Not that that will help us if a missile explodes."

Chapter 44 Norfolk Naval Yard

"Admiral, have you heard anything from the *Terminator*?" Connie asked as she and Josh Randel entered the Admiral's office at 9 a.m. in the morning.

"No Agent Randel, nothing new." Admiral Compton answered, just as his phone rang, "Hang on a second." Picking up the receiver he spoke into the phone, "Yes, Angela, What? Ok, thanks." he said and then picked up the TV remote and turned it on. "Sorry, something terrible has happened."

"… few minutes ago a nuclear bomb exploded in downtown Boston, the damage has not yet been determined but initial estimates are over one hundred thousand dead with many unaccounted for. We will have continuous coverage throughout the day. Please stand by. Just in. With the detonation of a nuclear bomb in Boston, the President has ordered an immediate evacuation of all government personnel from Washington. He and White House staff have boarded Air Force One and have left Andrews Air Force Base for an undisclosed location. We have been told that the Senate and House were not in session and are ordered to report to their emergency site for protection of the government. An emergency meeting has been called at an undisclosed location for security purposes. More information will be provided as it comes in. Please do not leave this channel. We will also keep you posted on evacuation routes from major cities when we know them."

"Damn, who the hell are these guys? There are several more bombs out there, and we don't know where they are. Did they find the ones they said were not being used?" Josh asked the Admiral.

"Those were there, but no detonators; at least they can't do much damage. But Boston, the museums, the history, all gone." Connie said and started to cry. "We were told about one warhead in Boston, but did not know there were actually two.

"Connie, it's ok, we are here and alive, and we will find the other bombs and save this country, like we always do." Josh commented as he looked seriously at the Admiral. Josh started to say something, but then stopped.

"Agent Randel, what have you got for me? Is there anything the Navy can do to help locate these terrorists?" Admiral Compton asked, as he picked the phone up again and punched in his secretary's extension, "Angela, could you bring in some coffee, strong coffee and a box of tissues. Angela please come in, forget the coffee. We will get through this."

Angela came in crying, "Admiral, my parents live outside of Boston. What am I to do? I tried to call them but all the lines are busy or down."

"I will have someone check on them, please have a seat." Admiral Compton said as he turned in his chair, opened a small cabinet and pulled out a bottle of Tequila and another of Scotch, "What is your choice? I believe we need a drink."

"Tequila," Josh and Connie answered together.

"Scotch for me, Admiral." Angela said as she dried her tears.

"The fallout, depending on the winds could cause us major problems here, shouldn't we do something?" Connie asked after she shakily took the glass from the admiral, tipped it back and poured it down her throat.

"Yes, just a second." Admiral Compton said, picking up the phone again. "This is Admiral Compton, put on the staff duty officer." He waited until the officer came online. "Admiral Compton here, Commander, have you heard what happened in Boston and what is happening in Washington? Yes, Ok, put the base on high alert; issue protective gear and check the weather to see which way the winds are blowing. If they are heading this way, prepare for nuclear fallout and warn the population. If not, then alert all bases in the path of the fallout. We need to prepare for the worst. Understand commander? Good. Admiral Compton out."

"Admiral, Connie and I need to be going back to what is left of Washington, if we can safely enter the city, anyway." said Josh downing his Tequila and handing the glass back to the Admiral.

"We all have some things to do, let's get back to work, then. Keep me posted on your progress in DC; I will keep you posted on the *Terminator*." said Admiral Compton as he stood and took Josh's outstretched hand and shook it.

"Take care, best of luck; we all need it, now." Connie said as she stood and started to leave. She stopped as the phone rang.

As he picked up the receiver, Admiral Compton said, "Admiral Compton, here." After pausing for a moment to listen, his face showed even more shock, "I understand; has the *Bush* been notified? Good, keep me posted, Compton out."

"May we ask, Admiral?" queried Connie.

"Yes, you may, since you have a good friend and husband on board. We have just picked up satellite images showing three Soviet war ships in the area of our missing Soviet submarine. They look like they are on a mission. And I don't like

the idea of what they are going there for. I only hope they are not able to locate her. If

they do, then we have a bigger problem out there." replied Admiral Compton.

"What is this world coming to? Soviet terrorists are setting off nuclear bombs

in our cities, a Soviet nuclear sub is set to detonate and now three Soviet warships are

wanting to help detonate their missing boat." commented Josh.

"Yea, not a good day for us, is it?" Admiral Compton commented.

"We will stay in contact, Admiral." Connie said as they started for the door

again. Minutes later, Josh and Connie were walking over to their car, not saying

anything and just wondering how all this was going to work out. There was just so

much that had happened to include the destruction of Boston and many of the

buildings and lives close by. How many lives had been lost, how much history,

memorials, and who knows what else? Those who did not die in the explosion had

their lives changed forever, and no one really knew how long that forever would be.

Those Soviet terrorists had committed the ultimate mistake. An attack on the United

States would only bring one penalty, death. No matter when or where they were

caught, and they would be caught or killed attempting to escape. No court in this

country would let them go, if, of course, they even made it to a trial.

"Connie, I think we need to catch up to Anne and, well, see if she is ok."

Pausing, Josh looked over at Connie and asked "Are you ok?"

"No, Josh, many of my friends and co-workers are probably dead now and there is nothing I can do to help them." Connie stated and started to cry again. Josh put his arm around her to comfort her grief but she shrugged it off. "Please don't."

"Ok," Josh said as he pulled his arm back. "Do you know where Anne may be?" in an attempt to change the subject and her grief.

"Last I heard she was down at the battle room. But that was hours ago." replied Connie as she sat down in the car's front seat.

"Let's check there first; if not there, someone may know where she went." Josh suggested then started the car and started to back out, heading for the temporary battle room on the dock.

"Ok, stop the car, let's walk, I don't want to be cooped up in a car right now." Connie said. She opened the door as Josh pulled back into the parking spot, climbed out and turned to head toward the dock and the battle conference room.

Chapter 45 Dallas, Texas

"We have their attention now. Boston has a reported death toll of over one hundred twenty thousand and more to come with the fallout and injured." the Soviet Executive Officer vice Captain Viktor Mikhailovich said to the four other men with him.

"Did our guys get out of Boston before detonation?" After getting a negative from one of his men, he continued. "Good, they died heroes of the state. The Los Angeles team did what I asked; gave fake locations of the extra warheads allowing us time to place and detonate the extra one in Boston. Now we will not be so lucky. If caught, we will be accused of mass murder and destruction, and many lesser crimes. But I do not expect to be caught." continued Viktor, laughing as if this was all a joke to him.

"Viktor, it wasn't your fault. Boris and his boys had to go. They had been caught with their hands on a nuclear bomb near the airport. The plan is working and we will be rich men real soon. They don't know we are here. They would have told the federals everything; maybe they did and we don't know it. But they did not know we changed locations and that we were going to blow the bomb in Boston. But hey, they can't talk anymore anyway, you took care of that." his second in command responded.

"I know, but I really hated killing my own men. Water under the hull! Let's make another call to shorten the time frame now that they know we mean business." Viktor said as he reached in his pocket for his cell phone.

"OK, let's get these warheads ready and get the hell out of Texas. Time is money and we are running out of both."

An hour later, the five terrorists were heading west on Interstate 20. Their destination was unknown at the moment. They just needed to get away from Dallas. The bomb had been set for detonation in eight hours, which would give them enough time to get far, far away. But plans were made and sometimes just did not work the way they were supposed to.

"What the hell is that?" Viktor yelled as he looked out the front window and saw a major accident and traffic backed up for miles and no exit off the highway. "This can't be good."

"What do we do now, Viktor?"

"How far out of Dallas are we?" asked Viktor.

"Only about twenty-five miles, we are not far enough to escape the blast."

"Damn." Viktor said as he scanned the area around the highway. He didn't see anything that could help. There was just a service road down a steep embankment. However, it could provide a possible change of direction. "Ok, we don't want to attract attention, but we need to be moving now. Go down the embankment, not at an angle, straight down to the service road, and then turn back toward Dallas. There will be less traffic if we go back and then circle down south. Now do it." Viktor ordered. They still had time, but they didn't know it wasn't an accident. It was a road block, by the National Guard and State Police, checking every vehicle.

Chapter 46 Coast Guard Cutter Intrepid, Bahamas

"Put one over their bow, Chief." the captain of the *Intrepid* ordered. The *Intrepid* was a very fast one hundred twenty foot cutter. Actually, unknown to many, she was a hydrofoil and once up on its foils, there were very few ships that could outrun her. The one hundred forty foot research pirate ship just did not have the power to out run or out fight the Coast Guard Cutter, whether in speed or firepower. The *Intrepid* had her in its gun site and if the pirate ship continued to run, then she was going down. "Either she is going down or we are." the captain quoted James T. Kirk of Star Trek fame.

The *Intrepid* was a proud ship and equipped with the latest in high tech weaponry and electronics. Her captain was a veteran of Vietnam who had protected the United States coast ever since. A Viet Nam vet, running coastal watch for two tours of duty and having credit to his honor of saving several dozen downed airman and also sinking seven Viet Cong attack boats and one cruiser. He had no problem taking the life of a criminal or anyone who would shoot at him or one of his men or women. He was not vindictive, but extremely serious in doing his job and extremely efficient. One warning shot over the bow and if they did not stop, the second would be a non lethal shot to the engine room or rudder/stern area. Not exactly a kill shot, just a 'you will stop shot or the next one will be in the bridge or below the water line to sink immediately'.

Seconds after the command was given, the computer controlled 105 millimeter forward deck gun belched one shot which landed and exploded exactly fifty feet to the port side of the fleeing *'Underwater Adventurer'* sending a water spout over the bow and bridge that got Dennis's attention immediately. He slammed the wheel hard right in an attempt to keep from being hit by a second round, figuring the Coast Guard just missed. Dennis had never been in combat, being a draft dodger during Vietnam and choosing to run to Canada to escape being drafted. All he understood was gold and money.

"Dennis, what the hell are you doing? You cannot out run them and they did not miss. You were never in the military, were you? That was the classic 'one over the bow shot'. We lost baby, give it up; you should never have fired on that cutter. Those guys are professionals. We have lost, didn't you hear me. Pull the throttles to stop and give up." Natasha yelled as she stormed back on the bridge, soaking wet from the first shot, her now transparent top dripping with water, her hair dripping, and looking like she just stepped out of a shower, which in fact she had.

Dennis ignored her and turned hard left; he zigzagged his boat and pushed the throttles past full, hoping to get some more speed from his straining engines and looking for an escape route.

"Damn you, you're going to get us all killed." she yelled and ran out of the bridge and down the gangway to the lower deck. She was running toward the life boats. "Get out of my way, he is crazy. Move it…" Upon reaching the large Zodiac at the stern, she started to undo the cables to release it.

"What the hell are you doing, Natasha." yelled one of the crewmen.

"Getting off this boat before that Cutter over there fires again and blows us out of the water." she yelled back.

"Let me help. We may have to jump after we launch, because we are going too fast to ride her over."

"No problem now! Get that unhooked and let's go." Natasha yelled back unhooking the bow of the Zodiac.

Less than two minutes later, the yellow Zodiac was pushed over and they saw and heard the cutter fire another round.

"GO!" she yelled and then dove off the stern into the crisp blue Bahamian waters not waiting for the crewman to follow. But moments later, she popped up about one hundred yards behind the *Underwater Adventurer* and saw the crewman pop up about fifty feet away. The Zodiac was not too far off. She swam over, climbed on board and then turned to see the *'Underwater Adventurer'* burning and dead in the water. Smoke was billowing from the hole in the stern in the exact spot where the Zodiac and she had been standing. The crewman reached the Zodiac and started to climb on.

"Permission to come on board, Natasha." he asked as he clung on the side.

"Get up here, and you are?" inquired Natasha as she looked around for a way to start the engine.

"Oh, sorry, I guess we were not formally introduced, I am FBI agent Tony Sands, and miss, you just saved your ass from going to jail for the rest of your life. But you need to do something to help that. I will protect you, but you need to turn

states evidence and help us convict your ex-boyfriend."

"That works for me, Mr. Sands. Thanks for the help with the Zodiac. I did

not get into this to kill Americans; I just want the treasure." After pausing for a few

seconds while she looked for a way to start the engine, Natasha asked "Do you know

how to drive this thing?"

"No problem, Natasha. See if there are any towels in the storage

compartment; you may want to cover up. Your top is almost gone from our escape and

those navy boys have been at sea for a while. We don't want any accidental discharges,

if you get my drift." Tony Sands joked as he slid over to the outboard engine, and

checked for proper connections of the fuel line and steering cables. He then stood and

walked to the center console, and turned the key. After the engine turned over two

times, it burst into life. Tony moved the gear shift into engage. The small Zodiac

jumped and he turned it towards the Coast Guard Cutter. He used his right hand to

reach into his pocket to retrieve his badge and identification. Within a few minutes, he

would have to explain what he was doing and what other charges he would be placing

on the members of the pirate ship.

"Oh, yea, I guess I better cover these." Natasha commented as she looked

down at her almost bare breasts, figuring out what he had meant with his comment.

Chapter 47 Twenty-nine Palms Marine Base

"Colonel, we have delivered the bodies to the base morgue. I understand the nuclear device has been secured in the arsenal under heavy guard." General Barry Morgan stated to Colonel Russell, head of the Security Forces of 29 Palms Marine Base.

"We have the situation under control, sir. But I don't like having that unstable nuclear warhead anywhere near this base." replied Colonel Russell.

"Hugh, we don't have much choice. We are the most distant and safest place for that thing, and we will protect it and the base until the nuke boys from Washington can get here and take it." General Morgan commented as he picked up a small stack of papers off his desk.

"Sir, may I ask what is going on? We just heard Boston has had a nuclear bomb, like that one in storage, explode and destroy half the city. The reports are that there are over two hundred thousand dead and many missing. Have you heard anything from Washington?" asked Colonel Russell.

"Seems like four of those dead bodies we have over there in the morgue were Soviet crewmen from a, hold it, let's just say they were terrorists which from what it looks like, a plan that had gone bad, who were killed by their own men. How they found out, we don't know." Morgan said and looked up at Russell with a concerned look on his face.

"Terrorists, our country is under attack from unknown attackers. Should we put the base under high alert instead of the yellow?"

"Yes, do that, Hugh. Now we have some other things to discuss, but first please take a seat and would you care for a drink? I believe we need one, in light of what has been happening." offered the General.

"Sir, I prefer to stay sharp and will pass on the drink but would like some coffee." Russell answered.

"One moment." General Barry Morgan said as he picked up the phone and asked his secretary to bring in some coffee.

Minutes later the coffee had arrived, and both were sitting and sipping their cups of coffee.

"Colonel, we have another problem that you need to be aware of. This is classified information and you are not to discuss this with anyone other than me. Do you understand, Hugh?" General Morgan stated seriously.

"Yes sir, I understand completely, I do hold a Top Secret clearance and am cleared in the special access areas for nuclear and satellite information, but you know that already, sir. So, why all the cloak and dagger secrecy? My team and I are ready for anything you or the bad guys can throw at us, sir."

"Yes, I know, but you need to understand that what I am about to say is for your eyes and ears only." General Morgan commented as the sweat beaded on his forehead.

"I understand, sir." Colonel Russell said and sat up on the edge of his chair, while sipping his coffee.

"Hugh, we have known each other for a long time and besides becoming one of the best officers I know and a fine human being, I must say that in all the years I have known you, I can't say that I have ever seen you as out of uniform as you are today, Colonel. Now, would you kindly get in proper uniform and pin these on." General Morgan said as he tossed over a pair of stars to his friend.

"Sir, what are you saying?" asked Russell, not fully understanding as he caught the stars. He looked closely at the two silver stars, not understanding completely what had just happened. A promotion to Brigadier General had been his lifelong goal since he joined the Marines and graduated top of his class from the academy.

"I am saying that I am retiring when this terrorist stuff is cleared up. And you are now promoted to Brigadier General and are being assigned as the Commander of this base and all that comes along with it, including making you a new General. Congratulations General Hugh Russell." He extended his hand to congratulate his friend. "Now this is still a secret until next week, although the promotion is official now. We will have a promotion ceremony on Monday and the change of command will be announced on Tuesday. I will be here until all is cleared up or we are dead, acting as your advisor."

"I don't know what to say, sir. Thank you for the confidence." replied General Russell, shocked at the promotion, unexpected for at least another year or two. "Where are you heading, sir?" General Hugh Russell continued and sipped his coffee.

"I bought a small boat and house in Florida. I am heading for Fort Lauderdale to do a little fishing, maybe some scuba diving, play some golf and mostly be retired." answered General Morgan.

"Sounds a bit odd for you, sir. You don't strike me as the do nothing kind of guy." replied General Russell.

"I've been a Marine since I turned eighteen and have really enjoyed my career, but I just need a change." Morgan commented. "And when this is over, I will really need to slow down."

"Change is good. And sometimes we need a change. Best of luck, sir!" General Russell stated. As he stood, he stretched out his hand to thank Morgan.

"General, right now we all need some luck to catch these terrorists before they kill another American."

Chapter 48 The Terminator Launch Ready

"Missile room, are you ready to launch?" Captain Henderson asked over the intercom.

"Ready to go, sir! Seventeen missiles are disconnected, and deactivated. Missile one is primed and ready." Lanstrom responded and rechecked the firing board. "Ready, say the word."

"Lanstrom, how much time until the auto detonator fires?" asked Captain Henderson.

"Three hours eighteen minutes until the timer hits zero and she blows, sir. But I believe we have the detonator disarmed" Lanstrom replied. "More importantly, what are those Soviet ships up there doing?"

"Keep working on missile one, you have two hours." Henderson ordered. He then turned to the bridge crew and Captain Viktorov and said "I want to milk this as long as I can before we attempt to kill ourselves early. Do you agree? And those ships up there are looking....."

Henderson was stopped short when there was an explosion about one hundred yards off their port and quite a bit higher in the water column.

"What the hell was that?" Lanstrom yelled.

"That was an anti-submarine missile which was probably fired from one of those Soviet warships in hopes that we are close enough to feel it and then we would know they are serious about destroying their own boat and us with it." Henderson stated to Lanstrom and anyone close enough to hear his frustration.

"Are you kidding?" Davin yelled. "It's bad enough we are riding in a nuclear bomb, but now we have someone out to kill us."

"Hey, it was bound to happen. They probably have been tracking us from the time we left Norfolk. They're just not sure exactly where we are. That is because their shipboard sonar can't reach this depth." replied Captain Henderson. "Now, Lanstrom, get down there and get those missiles ready to launch." After pausing for a moment, he ordered, "Weapons, get four tubes loaded, no... make that all six tubes. We may have to fight a bit before we blow up."

"Yes, Captain, is that wise?" Lanstrom questioned.

"One way, or the other, this will be over in just over three hours, my friend. Let's hope she is as good as you believe she is." stated Captain Henderson as he turned back to the helm, "Helm, how is our trim?"

"Holding sir, but not sure how much longer." the young seaman responded from the helm. "We have been drifting down at about a foot every few minutes. At this rate, we will be below two thousand feet in about an hour." After a brief pause, he asked, "And sir is it getting hotter in here or is it just me?"

"Maintain the best you can, son. It will all be over in about three hours, one way or the other. And, no, it is not you; it is getting hotter in here." Henderson replied, and then turned to the dive officer and Captain Viktorov. "From what it looks like, the pumps are keeping the water at bay for now, but this could change quickly. Let's see; we have a partially filled torpedo room up front, the lower deck aft is partially flooded, computer problems all over the boat, and a multitude of failures. Your government sure didn't build a very good boat or that rebel crew of yours knew exactly how to sabotage this boat but good." Picking up the intercom mike he pushed the transmit button, "Chief, what's happening to the air in here?

"Trying to figure that out now, sir." was the quick response from the chief.

"I would say the crew did this; I have several suspects in mind that could have done this. What we don't know is what other surprises they have left for us. But I guess in, let's see." Captain Viktorov paused to look at the clock on the bulkhead, and then continued with the same thought. "I guess, in less than three hours, we will either be dead or drinking some wine to celebrate being alive, unless those boats up there find us first."

"I am all for that wine, sir." the helm piped in.

"Ok, speed and depth, please." commanded Henderson.

"Speed thirty-four knots, depth one thousand seven hundred nine feet from surface and nine thousand six hundred thirty-five feet under the keel, sir."

"Sonar, anything in the area, manmade?" Henderson asked.

"There is nothing but those three Soviet warships, sir. We are one thousand three hundred forty-four miles off the north end of the Bahamas. Closest land mass is the Bahamas."

"Good, ok Captain Viktorov, time is running out, and we are out of options and time. We have to make a decision, or just sit tight and wait. I will defer to your expert knowledge of this boat. What do you want to do, sir?" asked Henderson.

"I do believe we will wait the two hours you gave Lanstrom and then decide. But I would suggest we start doing some maneuvers. We can't change depth much, but we can maneuver some. Helm start some erratic turns and change your speed by no more than five knots every few minutes. That will confuse the sonar operators up there; they cannot penetrate below eight hundred feet from the boats, but if they start dropping sonar buoys, they will find us. And if, as I suspect, they have a hunter/killer submarine with them, our chances drop to nearly zero. Do you not agree?" replied Viktorov.

"Sounds like a plan. Keep working right up till we light that tube up, and maybe pray a little if that works for you." responded Henderson.

"Bear," Davin said as he walked onto the bridge, smiling and soaking wet.

"Where the hell have you been?" Bear Henderson asked.

"Been down below deck, trying to stop the many leaks this tub has. Do you know once we stopped one, another would start, almost like it was programmed to do so." Davin commented as he wiped his head with the towel he picked up as he passed the crew quarters.

"Yea, we figured that out a while ago. The saboteur of this boat really knew what he was doing. I would let it go; we only have, well, less than three hours until we become a very large radioactive hole in the water, anyway. Why not get ten bottles of that wine and bring it up here." said Henderson.

"Sure, what's the occasion?" asked Davin.

"It will soon be independence day, well, almost anyway. Just get the wine and well, eight glasses." Henderson ordered and turned back towards the chart table.

"Independence day?" questioned Davin.

"Yea, one big fire cracker. Now go!" Bear ordered.

"Right, sir." Davin responded and left the bridge, heading to the galley.

Two hours to lift off

With less than two hours before detonation and one hour before they decided to launch, tensions were running high. Davin, Bear, Captain Viktorov, the dive officer and helm were all sitting in the flying bridge quietly thinking of what they could do to survive this, when all of a sudden an alarm sang out.

"What the hell is that?" Davin yelled over the alarm.

"That my young friend is '*we are taking on water in another section alarm*'. Deck officer, would you check and see which deck is now flooding?" Bear asked over the alarm, "And shut it off, it is a bit loud."

"Aye, sir. Uh, we are taking in water in the missile room, sir," the deck officer reported to Henderson and Viktorov.

Henderson went over to the intercom and called the missile room. "Missile room, status please."

"We are taking on water down here, coming from silo four, six and ten." the tech replied.

"Is Lanstrom there?" Henderson asked.

"Yes, but under the console attempting to disconnect silo number one.'

"Ok, let us know if you need assistance with anything. Bridge out."

Twenty-five minutes later the missile room called, "Bridge, missile room, are you guys still awake?"

"Yes we are, go ahead, missile room." Bear replied after he walked over to the intercom and flipped the switch to talk.

"Well, we are thirty-five minutes from your requested launch time; we need fifteen to prep the missile. She is already fueled, but we have some other things to do to ensure she makes it to the surface and fires off and far enough up before exploding." Lanstrom replied, her voice tense and tinny over the small speaker.

"Prepare for launch." Bear ordered, "We launch in thirty-five minutes."

The tension on the boat was high. Water was leaking in many spots and many systems were already failed or failing. This boat was coming apart and there was nothing they could do to stop her from dying. The clock was ticking slowly.

Thirty-five minutes later

"Bridge, we are ready to launch. Say the word." Lanstrom said quietly over the intercom.

"Well, we have two choices, launch now and hope we don't blow ourselves up, or wait another hour and blow up ourselves. We may not be able to surface as it is, with as much water as we are taking on. We are taking on water in the missile room, torpedo room, aft lower decks and who knows where else soon. What do you say, Captain, now or wait a bit longer?" Viktorov asked.

"Assemble everyone in the galley, no exceptions. Now!" ordered Henderson.

"What about the helm, sir?" asked Davin.

"OK, get everyone to the control room, we will all fit. Get them here now." Henderson ordered.

Minutes later, everyone was assembled in the control room; Davin and two crew members had four bottles of wine sitting around the room, with glasses for everyone. Seconds later both Captains walked in.

"Here is the deal, lady and gentlemen. The situation is grim. We are taking on water. We have one missile ready to fire, but may blow ourselves up in doing so. The timer is almost to zero, which means it will blow itself up. We want to launch one of the manned torpedoes with Seaman Jacobs inside but the damn torpedo outer doors will not open. So, with that in mind, we have one hundred forty bottles of wine, which we do not want to go to complete waste; we brought out ten to take care of now, so drink up. You have fifteen minutes; then we launch. Enjoy. Oh, we also have three Soviet warships upstairs looking for us right now and they will find us shortly. And when they find us, they will try to kill us. So with that in mind, go ahead and have a drink, it may be our last." Henderson said grimly. He picked up his glass, and continued, "It has been a pleasure serving with you on this short cruise; it has been an honor serving with a group of men and women that have put others ahead of themselves. We may not survive much longer, but we did our best. Thank you!"

Fifteen minutes later

The crew had consumed all the bottles of wine and headed back to their stations, no one said a word, and it was so quiet you could hear that famous pin drop. Davin, Bear and Captain Viktorov stood in the control room wondering if they were going to be alive in the next few hours.

"Everything going ok, boys" Bear asked as he looked over at the helm and wondered why they had not touched their wine, but understanding why without asking.

"Well, not exactly, sirs. We are still taking on water and several more leaks have started. We have drifted down to one thousand seven hundred seventy-five feet and can't hold it much longer." the dive officer stated.

"We are going to fix that in a few minutes, Lieutenant. Thank you." Bear commented.

As he flipped the switch on the intercom, Bear ordered "Missile room, three minutes to launch."

"Missile room, ready."

"We will launch from here. Release control to the bridge. Time to detonation?" Captain Viktorov asked.

"Forty-five minutes and counting, sir." Lanstrom replied. "Control is yours, father."

There was another explosion about a mile away. The shock wave bounced off the boat without causing any damage. They were still a bit too far away, but sooner or later they would narrow it down and locate them. The next explosion was much closer, about eight hundred feet deep and four hundred yards off. The shock wave was a bit harder and blew out several lights and enabled more water to come in.

"Thank you my daughter," Captain Viktorov replied. "See you on the other side."

"Captain Henderson, do you want to do the honors?" asked Captain Viktorov.

"No, sir, this is your boat. Those buddies of yours upstairs are getting closer, and when we fire that missile, they will know exactly where we are when it breaks the surface." replied Captain Henderson.

"Yes. Standby." replied Captain Viktorov.

Captain Viktorov unlocked the firing button and handed a second key to Captain Henderson, "Turn that key when I say…. Now." Both keys were turned and locked in place. "All I have to do now is push that red button." he said as he held his finger over the button.

Henderson nodded and Viktorov pushed the button and waited. It seemed like forever before they felt the surge of the missile leaving the silo? Then there was silence, dead silence.

"Sonar, where is that missile?" Bear yelled.

"We are lucky that the sail on this boat is in front of the missile tubes, sir. She came out of the tube and hung just over the deck for a second as we passed under it, then started to sink behind us. The missile is at nineteen hundred below and behind us right now and continuing down."

"That isn't good." Captain Viktorov stated.

"No, but what choice do we have; we are running at thirty-four knots and going away from it. If it explodes, we will feel the concussion and hopefully be far enough away to not sink us." Bear stated. "Helm can we get more speed out of this thing? Captain, do you think we can surface safely yet? Why didn't that missile go to the surface?"

"I don't know." Viktorov said. He was confused as to why the missile did not go up, but instead sank.

"We have to risk it. Lanstrom, is it safe to surface?" Bear yelled into the intercom.

"As far as we can tell, yes," came her reply.

"EMERGENCY BLOW! Blow all ballast and engines ahead combat full." Bear ordered. "Sonar, where is the missile now, and where are those warships?"

"Two thousand one hundred twenty feet and still falling. The warships are two miles to the east and heading this way. They must have detected the missile launch."

"She should implode in another few feet." Captain Viktorov commented.

Ten seconds later the sonar operator yelled. "She is imploding sir."

"Hang on; this is going to be rough!" Bear yelled. "Depth and speed?"

"Twenty six knots and sixteen hundred feet, rising fast, almost too damn fast." the dive officer yelled, "We need to slow down, Sir! We will break her back if we break the surface too fast."

"Pull back the throttles to twenty knots; the concussion will push us up faster." Captain Viktorov ordered.

While slowing to twenty knots, they continued to rise fast, passing through fifteen hundred feet moments later.

"We will break the surface in thirteen minutes, sir. Slowing to twenty knots." reported the dive officer.

"Captain, Sonar, concussion wave heading our way at sixty knots, impact in about thirty seconds."

"Hang on, gentlemen." Bear yelled.

The concussion wave hit the boat in the stern, flipped it up rapidly, and caused the boat to abruptly start a nose dive down at over thirty-five knots.

"Trim, stabilize, stabilize!" shouted Captain Viktorov.

It seemed like forever before the boat began to respond, and it did, but real slow. They had descended back to nineteen hundred feet. The boat was very quiet again. You could hear the throb of the engines and hum of the electronic systems. No one wanted to take a breath for fear of causing a change in the attitude of the boat.

Chapter 49 Washington DC

The President was sitting in the Oval office when the word came in about Boston. His National Security Advisor had rushed in only moments earlier with the written report and was now sitting across from him looking over the written report on casualties and damage in Boston. The numbers were not good.

"Sir, we have to find the last two warheads before that idiot sets them off." his advisor stated as he pulled a handkerchief from his pocket to remove the sweat from his forehead.

"That is an understatement, son. We have just lost tens of thousands of people and history, far worse than 9/11. This will be treated more severely. These are terrorists and I expect them to be brought to justice. We don't have much time left. Get the money ready to pay them. We cannot negotiate with terrorists, but we also can't let them destroy another city and kill more Americans. I can't tell you what I want to say, but if I were to place an order, it would be to find the bombs and kill the terrorists. If I were to give an order, that is the order I would give, you get my meaning, Mr. Security Advisor."

"I understand sir."

"Is there any progress on finding where they are?" the President asked.

"No sir, we haven't gotten much from the field, or at least the Intel groups are not saying much."

"Ok, what else do we have? Middle east, how is the troop withdrawal doing?" the President queried.

"Actually we are not pulling out any more; there is a request on your desk to send thirty thousand more troops in. I know that is not the plan, but the General and Intel over there have discovered some interesting information and it is in your intelligence report that you have not been reading. That report is to help you decide how to direct the war effort, but with your refusal to read those reports...." The National Security Advisor was cut off by the President before he had finished. The Advisor was quite pissed off with the President who refused to listen to the reports or even read them.

"Listen to me, Mr. Advisor. I am the President; and if I choose not to read a damn report or listen to your ranting, then I will do that. And if I choose to paint the White House pink, I will do that. You work for me, I don't work for you!"

"Mr. President, with all respect for the office, I work for the people of this country and you do too. If you do not respect that, then I cannot do my job and neither can you." the Advisor stated, and stood to make a point of his anger.

"Point taken, Mr. Advisor; but if you ever try to tell me how to run this office, I will replace you quicker than you can bat an eye. Do you understand me?" the President threatened.

"Yes sir," he replied, but he thought that this president was not considering the safety of our nation and needed to be removed. He did not know how, but he needed to be replaced. The people of this country deserved better and in the next election which was coming up soon, they would, hopefully, get one that cared more than this pompous ass.

Chapter 50 Prepare to Surface Again

"Is everyone ok?" Bear Henderson asked, looking around the bridge at his crew and thanking them quietly. "Helm, status?"

"We are holding at nine hundred fifty feet, speed twenty-nine knots, sir." the helm responded.

"Good, Sonar, status?" Henderson yelled at sonar.

"Sonar, sir, nothing in the water to worry about at the moment, except those three Soviet warships and they are eleven thousand yards heading 280, running at twenty-four knots, running active sonar. They know we are here and….." stopping short, "Torpedo in the water, bearing 195, speed forty-five knots, ten thousand yards and closing." Sonar responded.

"Weapons, prepare decoys, fire on my command." Henderson ordered.

"Decoy's ready."

"Missile room, status?" Bear asked over the intercom.

"Missile room, we are a little wet, but holding, water about six inches, sir. The other missiles are stable. The computer system is holding, beyond that only a few cuts and bruises, sir." Lanstrom stated and then said. "Sir, we are still here, thank you. Ms. Micro mini got a bad cut on her head but will be fine. She is back at the computer, never missed a beat."

"Save the congrats till we get this boat back on the surface. We are not out of the woods yet. We have reports all over the boat of more water coming in, and the pumps are not keeping up." After a quick pause, Henderson ordered the helm.

"Surface now, not too fast, we are riding in a cracked egg; just get us up there."

After another quick pause, he continued, "Sonar, where is that torpedo?"

"Eight thousand yards and closing, sir." Sonar reported.

"Aye sir." the helm responded and pulled back on the control wheel, as the dive officer ordered to blow ballast again. They had taken on an equal amount of water, forcing them back down with more flooding, as they had ejected by blowing ballast during the first ascent. The boat started to inch up slowly, very slow. "Sir, we are going up but not very fast, as ordered, and maybe not fast enough to get us there. The extra flooding is preventing a normal ascent."

"Captain Viktorov, is there a way we can stop the flooding, and maybe get this cracked egg to the surface?" asked Captain Henderson.

"All the pumps are at maximum, and the bulkheads are secured between compartments; there is not much we can do except take the slow rise to the surface and pray that we make it." replied Viktorov.

"Ok, Davin it may be an hour before we reach the surface. Take a couple of techs and head back to the galley and get that wine ready." Henderson ordered, not because he wanted wine, but to get Davin off the bridge. And, he was hoping, they would be able to enjoy a bit of wine to celebrate being alive.

"My pleasure, Bear. On my way. On my way!" Davin yelled as he turned and left the bridge, tagging two sailors that were just standing in the corner and waiting for something to do.

"Ok, now that the civilian is off the bridge, give it to me. Are we going to make it to the surface, alive?" Bear asked his team.

"We have a less than twenty per cent chance of making it, sir. We are too heavy and not getting any lighter. We need to dump some water or a lot of something to get this tub light; otherwise, we will start sinking back to, well, let's see, crush depth on this tub is about thirty-five hundred feet. We will not make it that deep. We are broken and will implode before that, sir. Unless, of course, that torpedo gets us first." the dive officer commented. "You asked for the real story; sir, that is it."

"Roger that, LT." Bear responded. "Ok, missile room, prep the rest of the missiles for immediate discharge, not to the surface but just off the boat. Sonar, torpedo?"

"Seven thousand yards and closing, fifty-five knots." Sonar replied.

"Aye, sir, they will be ready in ten minutes." Lanstrom responded.

"We don't have ten minutes, do it in five or don't bother." ordered Bear as he turned to the dive officer and helm, "Helm, turn toward the torpedo and increase speed. Let's play chicken with that thing and maybe reach it before it arms itself. Little chance, but we'll give it a smaller target anyway."

"Aye, sir, turning." Helm responded.

"Yes, Sir! Five minutes till launch." Lanstrom yelled into the intercom.

"Is there anyone capable of firing the torpedoes?" Bear asked.

"Firing yes, loading, no; you forgot the outer doors will not open. My officer is an engineer, runs the engine room and is trying to get the doors to open. We do have a torpedo in tube 2 ready, when the door can be opened."

"Ok, let's hope the missiles will lighten us up enough." Bear commented. "Missile room; are you ready yet?"

"If you stop calling us, we will be ready in two minutes." Lanstrom yelled back.

"Two minutes then. When ready, just fire them. Do not wait for my command; just launch them" ordered Bear.

"Aye, sir." the missile room replied.

One minute later, they felt the surge of the first missile leaving the silo. A moment later, they heard two more leave the boat.

"Any change, helm?" Bear asked.

"A little sir, she is responding a little better. We have increased our ascent. Sir, it is getting better as each missile leaves the boat."

"Great, we may just make it." Bear commented, "Missile room, did you fuel those missiles? Do we have to worry about massive implosions?"

"No sir, no fuel and no possible implosion like before." Lanstrom replied.

"Good, how many more?" Bear asked.

"Six more to unload, sir." the diving officer replied, "I've been counting."

"We are rising better now sir, thank you." the helm commented. "Six hundred feet sir, six minutes to the surface."

"Good, we may just make it, sir." Bear Henderson said and continued to look around the bridge, hoping nothing else would go wrong with this boat. "Sonar, where is that torpedo?

"Three thousand yards and closing." Sonar yelled back.

"Four minutes to the surface, sir." Helm called out.

Tension was high. Sweat poured off each member of the crew; the air conditioner still did not work. Several of the crew had already removed their shirts. The minutes seemed like hours, and the leaking continued, but slowed as they rose higher in the water. They were still very heavy, but they had a chance now that they had dumped eighteen non-nuclear missile casings over the side. It was tricky, but they were doing it. They would know in the next three minutes if they would be alive to see sunrise in a couple of hours.

"Two thousand yards, sir." sonar responded.

"Fire decoy 1." Bear ordered and they heard the first decoy leave the boat at a ninety degree angle. After waiting twenty seconds, he yelled "Fire decoy two!"

Moments later, the second decoy left the boat in the other direction.

"Sonar" Bear yelled.

"Torpedo tracking decoy one, detonation in fifteen seconds. Ten, nine, eight, seven, six, five, four, three, two, one and the torpedo struck the decoy at fifty-four knots detonating in a large underwater fireball. The concussion wave would reach the boat in about twenty-five seconds.

"Hold on everyone." Bear yelled and reached out to grab the hand rail around the periscope, but his hand was slippery with sweat and he did not hold on. He fell to the deck when the concussion hit the boat. Seconds later, the concussion wave slammed into the side of the boat rolling her over to the side, almost completely over. Light bulbs exploded, pipes broke, and the men and women on board were thrown to the deck. Several broke bones on impact. Immediately the collision lights turned red and water started to fill more compartments.

"Helm, status?" Bear yelled over the noise.

"Seven hundred and fifty feet, sir, she is not responding, we are diving again, speed thirty-four knots and five degrees down. I am trying to pull us back up." the helm yelled.

"Get us level and holding as quickly as you can." Bear ordered. After picking himself off the deck, he reached for the microphone and depressed the button, "Casualty report, all departments."

"Captain, Sonar. Surface ships are at full stop, active sonar pinging away. They know we are here."

"Thanks, Sonar. Keep an eye on them. We are going to the surface, and I do not want to come up under one of them." Bear stated and then turned to Captain Viktorov, "Sir, we need you to get on the radio as soon as we start to break the surface and talk to your ex-comrades and get them to stop shooting at us. We are defenseless here; we cannot fire a torpedo at them, nor do I want to. We have no way to stop them from blowing us out of the water unless you are able to convince them to stop.

Can you do that?"

"That I can do, Bear; just get us to the surface and I will stop them." Captain

Viktorov agreed. "But you know everyone will be taken prisoner and I will probably

be shot as a traitor, I can live with that, I guess. Would you please ensure my daughter

is safe?"

"Yes, sir, you have my word. But I think we may be able to talk our way out

of becoming prisoners of a non-war. While you are talking to them, I will be on the

radio to my command. Now let's get this boat to the surface. Take us up, Helm."

It was a slow climb from seven hundred and fifty feet with water still pouring

in on many decks; but with the missiles gone, the boat was a lot lighter and was able

to climb out of her watery grave.

There were only ten minutes to go, then five, then one and finally only

seconds remained prior to surfacing. Everyone felt the tension slip away as the boat

finally broke the surface and settled into a slow cruise at eighteen knots. Captain

Viktorov was on the radio attempting to communicate with the commander of the

Soviet destroyer. It seemed they knew each other, both having gone to the Naval

Institute together. Captain Henderson was in the communications room on the only

other operational communication device, an antiquated teletype machine. But it was

working, and he was able to send a flash message to Norfolk, who in turn sent a flash

message to the *George H.W.Bush*. The *Bush* immediately launched six F/A 18 Super

Hornets, fully armed and ready to take on anything. Additionally, they launched four helicopters.

"Cut the engines, stabilize the boat, open the hatches, and get some fresh air in here." As he flicked the switch on the intercom, Bear shouted "Davin are you down there?"

"Yes, and ready." Davin replied.

"How is the weather outside?" Bear yelled up the ladder to the lookout who had just climbed up and opened the hatch.

"Great, sir, not a cloud in the sky and the surface is calm. Whoa, sir, you need to see what is coming over the horizon."

"What is it, son?" Captain Henderson asked.

"A formation of F/A 18 Super Hornets and three Soviet warships, about ten thousand yards off our port side."

'Cool, at least they are not shooting at us anymore.' Bear said to himself, and then yelled down to Davin, "Davin, bring the wine and glasses to the deck, we are going to have a party." Captain Henderson switched to ship wide intercom and announced "All hands, we are on the surface. The weather is great! Come up and let's celebrate ours and the world's survival." Then he commanded his radio man, "Send another message to Norfolk that we have succeeded in disarming the missiles and are sitting on the surface with a very leaky boat and waiting instructions. And tell them, thanks for the reception committee."

"Aye, sir, I will be on deck as soon as I send the message, encoding now." replied the radio operator.

"LT, go on up and relax; you did a hell of a job." Bear ordered and held back for a few minutes.

Chapter 51 Aircraft Carrier Group, USS George H. W. Bush

Within minutes of receiving the message at Norfolk, a message had been dispatched to the *George H. W. Bush*.

"Sir, we just got a message from Norfolk. They say the Soviet sub has surfaced, but they are not in great shape. They were greeted by three Soviet warships, but all is under control, for the moment. We should get there by sunrise, if possible. They are taking on water and the systems on board are malfunctioning. And they supplied their coordinates." the radio operator stated as he entered the Combat Bridge where he knew he would find the Admiral.

"Thank you, Lieutenant." the admiral said, and after he turned to face his executive officer, commanded, "Launch fighter cover and rescue helo's; here are the coordinates."

"Right away sir." responded his executive officer.

Minutes later, two F/A 18 Super Hornets were catapulted off the *Bush* and minutes later, four Seahawk rescue helicopters lifted off the deck. It would take almost to daybreak for the carrier group to get there. After the Seahawk helicopters left the deck, four more F/A 18's were launched to supply additional air cover. They were two hundred and fifty miles away from the boat. The helo's carried a repair crew to try and salvage the *Terminator* and supplies for the crew.

"Admiral, should we head toward the *Terminator*?" the executive officer asked.

"First, have radio try and make contact with them. I want to be sure it is safe to bring this task force anywhere near that boat. Once we have confirmation, then turn south and make best speed to that boat."

"Aye, sir." replied his executive officer.

"They may not have heard about what has happened. As soon as we get them on board, bring them to the main briefing room and don't let them hear anything from the crew. Your pilots and crew have been briefed on what not to say?" the admiral ordered.

"Yes, sir, they have been briefed as to what not to say." his exec replied. "I will have the team escorted to the briefing room first and then to medical before going to their temporary quarters."

"Fine, Captain, just fine." the admiral replied, looking very worried.

Chapter 52 Final Warning

Jerry Hancock, U.S. Secret Service, and Mike Olson, on temporary assignment to the secret service from the Maryland Highway Patrol, were sitting at a small café on concourse C waiting for their flight back to Norfolk, Virginia. It was 3 a.m. and they had a flight at five on American Airlines. Because Chicago was one of the busiest airports in the country, they wanted to be sure not to miss this flight. It had been a long couple of days. They had followed leads that went nowhere, one right after another. All dead end leads, the best they could say about this trip was that they did enjoy some great food and the weather had been perfect.

"What do you think of all this mess, Boston and where next?" Jerry asked, not really expecting an answer.

"What do I think of this mess? I think we are dealing with some real crazy dudes and they should be found and removed from the face of the earth." said Olson.

"Easy to say, but not easy to find." Jerry commented.

Jerry's cell started ringing, and since he had all the important numbers programmed to have a special ring, he immediately knew who was calling. "Hello, Mr. Randel. What can we do for you at this wee hour in the morning?"

"We have a new lead. Code two please." Josh informed Jerry.

"Roger, standby, Josh." Jerry replied.

Ten seconds later both phones linked up in an encrypted mode, so no matter who attempted to listen they would only hear static, known as white noise.

"Jerry, we have just learned that one of the warheads is located in Chicago, somewhere near the airport, not O'Hara airport but the airport located in downtown Chicago, Midway International Airport. We need the both of you to go over there and see what you can find. And do it quickly, our deadline is supposed to be 10 a.m. today. What time is it now out there?" Josh asked.

"It is 3:15 a.m., we have about seven hours, and I will bring in the local police to help." replied Jerry.

"Get going and good luck, we need it." Josh said and then hung up.

"Let's go! We have a lead. Collect your bag and let's move out. We only have seven hours before Chicago is vaporized, like Boston." Jerry said to Mike.

Washington DC, FBI Headquarters

"Good morning Director, this is close to your final call. You know we will set off the last two warheads if you do not comply with our demands and time is running out Mr. Director."

"Ok, we know you will destroy two more cities. And then what will you do? You are in the country, and may just die with the rest of us. Why not just give it up and we will promise a fair trial and…."

"No way man, we just killed two hundred thousand of your citizens, there is no way in the world we would get a fair trial or anything but the death sentence. Yea, it could take years before we are put to death, but our lives would be confined to one of your maximum secured prisons. As your country would say, No way man, we get the money and our freedom, or we blow Chicago, then Dallas, or maybe Dallas first and then Chicago. Get your candy ass President on the line and have him decide. I will make it easy, $50 million in cash or a half million dead. Your choice, Mr. Director. Now, get that candy ass president on the phone. He can make a decision. I will call back in twenty minutes. You better have him online. Good-bye Mr. Director."

"Goodbye" the director started to reply but the line went dead before he finished. "Lucy, get the White House on the line; I need the President now."

"Sir, the President is not in the White House. They evacuated late last night. They may still be on Air Force One, but most likely they are at Camp David or at the cave, what is it called, Noraid, no Norade, oh, I don't remember, but I will call him anyway and see if we can reach him." replied Lucy.

"You do have the emergency number on Air Force One? There is always someone on duty on board just in case they need to fly out quickly. Just make the call. I need him on the line in twenty minutes, or those terrorists will blow up Dallas or Chicago." the director continued.

"Yes sir." Lucy replied and then started to dial the phone. "Hello, this is FBI Director Donald Wilson's office calling; the director needs to speak with the President immediately. I will hold."

"Tell Director Wilson that the President is asleep and wishes not to be disturbed." was the reply Lucy received after a couple of minutes.

"Tell the President that his presence is not requested, but required right now. It is a matter of life and death." Lucy insisted. She did not take any crap from anybody, especially a weak minded aide to a President that did not deserve to be called anything but an ass.

"Well Miss, he told me not to disturb him for any reason. Now goodnight, miss."

"Wait; are you telling me that this President would rather sleep and let another city and more of his citizens get blown up by terrorists? You get him up now or he will regret it."

"Miss; are you threatening the President?" the unknown voice on the other end of the line demanded.

"Look mister, I am the secretary to the Director of the FBI and he is in communication with the terrorists and they want the President on the phone in fifteen minutes or they will blow up Chicago or Dallas. Now get him out of bed and on the phone, NOW! Or we will send over several very large US Marshals and FBI agents to arrest you and the President for causing millions to die."

"Yes, miss, you cannot do that, you cannot arrest the President.

"Watch me. We have enough evidence to arrest him, his wife, you and his damn dog. Now get him on the phone and quit wasting time." Lucy was standing and yelling at the aide on the other end; she was not taking any lip from the aide.

"I did not understand the gravity of the situation. I will be right back with the President. In handcuffs if necessary; please hold."

Minutes later, a weak voice came on line. "Miss, here is the President."

"Thank you." When the President came on the phone, she continued "Mr. President, we are sorry to get you out of bed so early, but the Director needs to speak to you now. We are in communication with the terrorists. I will put you right through, hang on."

"Mr. President, this is Director Donald Wilson of the FBI; I just spoke with the head terrorist and he has made a demand to speak with you and nobody else. He will be online in a minute or two. The situation is what my secretary told your man; we have a very serious problem out there. They are going to detonate either Dallas or Chicago if you do not agree with their demands. You have to make a decision when they call. Can you make that decision, sir?'

"Yes, I can make that decision, Director." the President stated. "I am the President; I am here to make a decision, if necessary.

The phone started to ring just about then, "Hello, Director Wilson, to whom am I speaking?"

"Hello Director, this is Viktor. Is your President on the line?"

"Yes he is; standby, I will three-way him in."

"Mr. President, it is a pleasure to be speaking with the man that can make decisions. Now will you please forgive me for making this a short call, but I know you are tracing this, and well, I will not be here in a few minutes, anyway. But here are my demands again. We have lost a few men and so they are not in the need for any money and they had no family. Besides, they did not believe in our cause; they were just going along for the money. So here they are; you may find out soon anyway, so I will help you. Wait; is the Director still on the line?" Viktor asked, pausing for a moment.

"Yes I am Viktor."

"Ok, you can hear this part but then when I say hang up, I want you to hang up the phone and Mr. Director turn off all your monitoring devices, you are not to record this conversation. Your President and I have to discuss payment. Understand?" Viktor stated and then waited for a response.

"Ok, I will hang up, only if the President agrees to call me right after you finish chatting, so I know what is going on."

"Agreed, now here is your part, Mr. Director and Mr. President. We want political asylum. There are to be no charges against me or my men for the accidental deaths of your citizens, and of course, we need new lives and $50 million dollars in cash. The choice is that or countless citizens dead from another accidental explosion. Your choice, Mr. President. Make the right decision. Now hang up, Mr. Director."

"Call me, Mr. President." stated the FBI director

'Ok, Director Wilson." replied the President as a very unhappy director hung up.

"Mr. President, forget what I just said with the Director. You will understand this a lot better than your American people will. I am Muslim and so are the remainder of my men. The ones that you have captured, the ones that are down in South America resting on the beaches and chasing all those disgusting women are not with our cause.

We do not care for the money, but we will take it; we are prepared to die for our cause and will do that today. We just wanted you to know, because we know your past, and cannot imagine how stupid the American public has been getting you into the White House. Now our real demand is for you to get $50 million US dollars. I also want you to deliver it yourself with no security or weapons. We also want Air Force One fueled and ready to leave the country with you on board along with the pilot, co-pilot and one steward to care for our needs. We will be flying to Germany then on to Iraq. Of course, you have the right to stay or leave with Air Force One. You will be coming along so they will not shoot us down. If you do not agree, we will destroy two of your cities. We, just so you know, have many more of our followers around the country ready to die for our cause. Now, it is your choice, Mr. President. I will call back in twenty minutes for your decision or can you make the decision now? Oh, I will give you the detonator and codes as soon as we are wheels up. We will fly out of Dallas. You have five hours to be there with the money and a fully fueled airplane, sir."

"Why Dallas, you said you have a warhead there?"

"Because, very simple, if you do not comply we will detonate Chicago and then Dallas. And you will be rid of us along with your citizens and of course you will die too. Leaving your country without a leader, prime for my people to come out of hiding and take over your country. Too bad I will also be dead and not see that, but I go knowing we have won."

"And if I do not show up?"

"You know the answer to that, Mr. President. Boom!"

"We do not negotiate with terrorists, Viktor. I cannot in good conscience agree with those demands, but I also cannot let you kill the citizens of this country no matter how they feel about me. You do have us over the barrel as it were. I will comply with your demands; just do not detonate those warheads." the President said and hung up.

Minutes later the phone rang in the Director's office. "Mr. Director, I will get the money together. We are to make the exchange at Dulles International Airport at noon today in terminal 2, gate 6c. Nobody but the agent making the exchange, the pilot and crew of a commercial airliner with no passengers will go. The plane is to be fully fueled and ready for a trans-Atlantic flight to England then on to Afghanistan. I will be in contact shortly with the money." the President lied.

"Thank you sir, we will get the rest ready." Director Wilson said and then hung up.

"He is hiding something," Wilson said to Lucy as she walked in the office with a fresh cup of coffee. "I just don't know what."

Chapter 53 Coming Home

"Captain Henderson, welcome to the *George H. W. Bush*. We need to debrief your crew and have someone bring you up to speed on the status of the nation. I understand two Soviet crewmembers stayed on board to help bring the boat back to Norfolk. Is she safe enough to do that?" Captain Bruce Wilkerson of the *George H. W. Bush* stated, "Is everyone else here?"

"Yes, sir, all except Captain Viktorov and his crewman who stayed on board to help with bringing her back. And, yes, the ship is safe. We sent all the missiles to the deep. They were not fueled and the warheads were removed and are unarmed. Captain Viktorov was able to talk the Soviet warships out of blowing us up. It seems he went to school with the ranking commander of that little task force. They agreed that the boat would be sinking soon and they need not waste any munitions on her."

"Is she going to sink, Captain?" Bear acknowledged concurring that the boat was in such bad shape it may not make it to any port. "Good. Ensign, would you close and, go ahead, lock the door?" Captain Wilkerson ordered. "And wait outside; we are not to be disturbed."

"Aye sir." responded the Ensign.

"Commander Lanstrom, Captain Henderson and your crew, we are deeply appreciative for everything you have just completed. The President has sent his personal congratulations and has asked me to pass it along to you. But on a more serious matter, we are not out of the woods yet. As they say in the south, I will not beat around the bush but come right out with it. We have had a nuclear explosion in

Boston, there are at least two hundred thousand confirmed dead. Many more are in critical condition and still more with lesser injuries. The terrorists are the soviet crewmen from that boat out there. We have captured several and several more have been killed, some by their own people. We know there were ten total warheads. We have recovered six. One exploded in Boston and another outside of Denver, killing several hundred people including the Vice President and the entire crew of Air Force 2."

"When did this happen, Captain?" Henderson asked.

"A couple of days ago, that is not all. The final two warheads, well, the terrorists are so confident in what they are doing and are so sure that we will pay the ransom demands that they have told us which cities they have targeted."

"Which cities?" Lanstrom asked before Henderson could say anything.

"Chicago and Dallas." replied Henderson.

"Holy crap, any luck in locating the warheads and the terrorists?" asked Lanstrom.

"Not yet, but we are hopeful. The only real problem is we are running out of time. We have about four hours before one of those detonates. The President was supposed to talk to the terrorists not long ago, but we do not know the decision that was reached. Do we pay and pray, or sacrifice a lot of our people? The President had a tough decision to make and we don't know what he said. But it looks like he is going to do what they asked. We're just not sure what it is."

"He should do as they asked and let's hope they will work with us and not be set off." Henderson said and then completed his thought. "And once we get the warheads, we go after them with everything we have and put them where they need to be, under a pile of dirt, or at least behind bars."

"I agree, Captain, but right now we don't know which way it is going. The President has not disclosed to anyone the decision that was made with the terrorists."

"What else do we know about them?" asked Henderson.

"Nothing at this time." Captain Wilkerson.

"Captain, I have some very good connections back in the CIA and FBI which may be able to help us. And can we get a ride back to Norfolk as soon as possible?" Davin asked, looking very concerned and wanting to help, even though he and his fellow crewmen and women had not had any sleep for over ninety-two hours.

"Yes, on both counts. How many need to get back?" asked Wilkerson.

"Me, Captain Henderson, and let's see, maybe Lanstrom." replied Davin.

"Me, sir. What can I do to help?" asked Lanstrom.

"Lanstrom, maybe just relaxing on board would be a good idea, Davin, just you and I need to get back. Make your call and Captain Wilkerson will work out the details for a quick ride back to Norfolk." said Henderson vetoing Davin's request to take her.

"Ensign, take Mr. Pierce up to commo and set him up for a secure call to the states, Norfolk Naval Yard. And get with the Air Boss and have him locate two jet jocks that need some R & R back in the states. Tell them to get ready for departure in one hour." Captain Wilkerson ordered the Ensign that was standing outside the door.

"Aye, sir." replied the Ensign.

"We have two F/A 18 Super hornets in Alert 1, they are fueled and ready, there are two hot shot pilots that need some time on the beach. Mr. Pierce, go make your call. Then have the Ensign bring you down to flight ops so we can get you suited up for a very fast ride." said Captain Wilkerson.

"Be there in fifteen minutes, sir." Davin stated.

Forty-five minutes later, Davin and Captain Henderson were being launched off the super carrier *George H.W.Bush* for a supersonic flight back to Norfolk.

Chapter 54 Dallas International Airport, Air Force One

Sitting in a special security area of the airport that was designated for Air Force One, the President, pilot, co-pilot and steward sat waiting for their only other passengers. On the floor, beside the President, was a big black suitcase with $50 million dollars in cash. A second $50 million had been given to Director Wilson to take to Dulles and wait for the terrorists that would never show. The airport was secure, but all the Secret Service, airport police, special security, and airport personnel had been told to leave. They were to stand guard around the airport but to let the terrorists pass without stopping them. They were only to make sure they were not carrying any weapons.

Twenty minutes after Air Force One had landed, the fuel trucks were pulling away. Four men were walking toward the ramp looking around at the empty tarmac. They started up the boarding ramp and entered Air Force One without being stopped. The Chief Pilot met them at the top of the ramp and asked if they were armed. After getting a no reply, he did a quick body pat down and let them pass to the main cabin, where they met the steward. The President of the United States sat behind the steward. His big, black suitcase was on the floor beside him.

"Mr. President, shall we close up and get airborne?"

"Let's get our new friends safely buckled in and have a drink first." The President replied, and then said to Viktor. "The case has your money; we will take off once I have the codes, the detonator, and your assurance that those warheads are not going to explode."

"You have my word, Mr. President and the remote detonator is right here. I will hand it over as soon as we take off and I know this plane only has the eight of us on board. Boris, take Mikel and search the plane for any hold outs."

"We are the only ones on board. You have my word, Viktor." The President commented as he looked intently at the terrorists that held the United States of America hostage and smiled.

"Hope you don't mind if we check for ourselves." replied Viktor.

Minutes later, they returned. "All clear Viktor."

"OK, let's get this bird in the air." Viktor demanded.

"Colonel, have the steward leave the plane and button it up and let's go." the president ordered as he then buckled his seatbelt. "You better take a seat and buckle up; you do not want to be standing when we start to roll."

They rolled down to the end of the runway, received clearance and started their take off run. Seconds later, Air Force One lifted off without anyone attempting to stop them, either on the ground or in the air. After turning east and starting for Europe, they were joined by two Air Force F-35 fighter jets. Viktor and his men had no idea they were being escorted. The jets were located above and behind Air Force One, where they could not be seen from any window in the Boeing 747. The pilot and co-pilot flying Air Force One knew they were there and would be there until they touched down in Germany. They would re-fuel in route by an Air Force tanker and again by a Navy tanker off the carrier *CVN-70 Carl Vinson* on tour off the coast of England. Air Force One would not need to be refueled until she reached Germany.

The President would be reported as being at Camp David for the next seventy-two hours, unless he did not return. Only then, would the true story be released.

"Mr. President, I really did not think you would show up. But you are here and did bring my reward. But don't you think you could drop the charade; should I call you Darrell or your given name?" Viktor commented looking at the black suitcase on the floor.

"Darrell will do just fine, Viktor, I have never answered to anything else."

Dulles International Airport

Director Wilson had his agent wait until one hour after the drop time. He then called the President and was told he was not available and would be out of contact for the next couple of days.

"Director Wilson's office, how may I help you?" Lucy asked after two rings of the phone. "Yes Mr. President, he is here; I will put you through, hang on."

"Director, the President is on line one."

"Thank you, Lucy." Then the Director spoke to the President. "Sir, Viktor did not show up in Dulles."

"Director Wilson, they will not be showing up at Dulles. Please take down these addresses." The President read the addresses to Wilson. "Got them, good, now go pick those warheads up before someone finds them and causes an accident."

"Where are you sir?"

"That is not for you to know right now. But Viktor and his men are here with me, and we have diverted a major disaster. Get the warheads and return the money to the Secretary of Finance as soon as you can. She will make sure it gets back in the system. I will be out of contact for a few days. Do not worry, it had to be done."

"Where are you, sir?"

"Air Force One, Director." he said and hung up.

Wilson immediately got a team together and headed to Camp David only to discover the President was not there and the agents at Camp David were under orders not to disclose anything over the phone, secure or not. Wilson was obviously very upset and wanted to arrest someone but could not because the agents were only doing what they were ordered to do.

Director Wilson called his team in Dulles and ordered them home. He also ordered them to bring the money back to headquarters. His next call was for two nuclear teams to pick up the warheads. The nuclear teams would have the warheads secured within an hour.

Wilson did not like to be tricked, even if it was the President doing the tricking. But once he heard the entire story, he knew the President did not leave willingly. It really looked like the President was really a kidnapped victim, or, at least, that's what it seemed like. But, it still smelled funny; something was not right with this whole thing.

Chapter 55 Norfolk Naval Yard Airport

"Navy Flight of two inbound for landing." LT Commander Jessie Stuart called approach control as they were heading in.

"Go ahead aircraft calling."

"Navy Bullfrog 1 and 2 request immediate landing, VIP's on board."

"Bullfrog 1 and 2, land in sequence runway nine right, turn to 210 degrees and descend to one thousand feet, we will set you up for a direct approach. Traffic 12 o'clock high, Air Force One and two escorts, no factor."

"Thank you Norfolk."

Ten minutes later, the two F/A 18 Super Hornets taxied to the parking ramp and saw four black Chevy SUVs waiting.

"Wow, is that your team, Davin?" asked his pilot.

"Yes, hell of a ride, Bullfrog. Thanks." Davin commented as he unstrapped himself.

"You are welcome, Davin. Next time we will make it a joy ride and show you what this will do."

"You are on, my new friend." Davin commented and climbed out and down the ladder when the ground crew placed two ladders up against the plane. "Was that Air Force One above us heading east that we saw up there?"

"Yes it was; we had orders to avoid, and she is under Air Force escort."

"Kind of strange for Air Force One to be up and heading east with the crisis happening all around, don't you think." Davin commented.

"Yes, but ours is to follow orders, most of the time." his pilot commented as he stepped to the ground.

"Davin!" Connie yelled and ran over to him and gave him a big hug. "Hey Josh."

"We have some problems, Davin. Let's get over to the war room and I will brief you and Bear. Your pilots are ordered to come too; we may need them."

"Did you hear that, Bullfrog? Come on, we need to be briefed. The ground crew needs to refuel your planes. Let's go." Davin said to their pilots, turning back to Josh looking concerned but relieved he was back on the ground after that fast flight from the carrier.

"Where is Anne?" Bear asked.

"In the war room; climb in." Josh said as he climbed in behind the wheel.

"What's going on, Josh?" Bear asked as he and Davin climbed in the front seat of one of the SUV's, looking more worried than he had several days ago. The flight crew boarded the second SUV and they headed to the war room.

"War room and your questions will be answered." Josh said as he started the Chevy and put it into reverse as the doors closed. The ride was quiet and tense; Josh would not answer questions. He stayed tight lipped during the ride.

Fifteen minutes later, they pulled up to the parking lot next to the war room. Quickly and quietly they approached the building; they were greeted by a heavily armed Marine, who upon inspection of everyone's identification, picked up his microphone and informed the guard on the inside to allow the five men to enter the war room without delay. "Go ahead, sirs" he said as he snapped to attention and saluted them.

Upon entering the war room and seeing the looks on everyone's face, they glanced at each other with worried looks. After grabbing cups of coffee, they sat down.

"Ok, what the hell is going on that caused us to speed back here and not even get a chance to take a piss before we were rushed in here?" demanded Bear.

"Captain, we appreciated everything you and your crew did to save the entire world from possible destruction, but the story does not end there. Since we lost contact with you, the terrorists that had caused you so much trouble out on the high seas raised their ugly head back here. First they contacted the FBI and made some demands that have been met, but not without more problems. They did tell us where the other warheads were and they are, as we speak, being retrieved and disarmed. But not without first setting off several that resulted in killing the Vice President, most of the cabinet and over two hundred thousand Americans when they detonated a warhead in Boston. Everything possible is being done to recover the dead or injured, and assist the city in recovery." After pausing to let that set in to the new arrivals, Admiral Scott Hamner started again after some brief comments and grim looks from Bear, Davin, and the two pilots.

"That is just the tip of the problem. This morning our President was required to deliver an undisclosed amount of money to the terrorists to get the location of the war heads. He was required to bring it to Air Force One which was staffed with a minimum crew. The terrorists were allowed on board and the plane departed the country heading east. We are keeping a fighter escort on Air Force One for as long as we can or until it lands."

"Wait a second, did you say the President went with them, willingly or not, but he is out of the country.?"

Just before they were leaving, the Admirals phone rang; picking it up, he listened and then slowly placed the receiver back in the cradle. Turning to his guest he said, "Air Force One was met by six Iranian fighter aircraft, that forced our two F/A 18's to back off and not continue to escort. They know that we escorted them and that may or may not have any influence on what happens to the President. Right now the President is in hostile territory and in the hands of the Iranians."

"Yes, the President is in Iran." Admiral Hamner stated and then added, "At this point, we don't know if he and the crew are alive or dead."

"Before we go on, I need to take a short break." Davin said, and after he glanced over to Bear, gave him a nod indicating that he wanted to talk privately. Both men got up and walked to the men's room. Five minutes later, they returned and sat.

"Ok, now, we have the President and Air Force One held captive in a hostile country. What are we going to do about it?" Bear asked after sitting down again.

"Right now, nothing. Until we hear their demands, our hands are tied. Why don't you get cleaned up and come back in the morning. I believe we will know more by then."

"Ok, but if anything comes up, call me right away, sir." Bear asked as they started to leave the office.

0930 then next morning

They reconvened in the Admirals office with grim looks and questions unanswered.

"Good morning ladies and gentlemen; we received this video this morning from the Iranian government stating the President is safe and would be their guest for a short while. The air crew and Air Force One will be departing Iran tomorrow morning. They had the balls to even thank us for the money and indicate they may need more before the President is returned. They also stated that if there is any attempt to rescue the President, his head will be removed and sent back to us in a box long before any team could reach his location. The video showed the President in a large comfortable room, unharmed and seemingly safe. He was not allowed to talk."

"Ok, we have the warheads, so the country is safe at the moment, the Speaker of the House is temporarily acting President and Air Force One is heading back tomorrow. What do you want us to do?" Bear asked as he looked at Admiral Hamner.

"That, Captain, is a very good question, and I am glad you asked. We have decided that you and your team have done more than your share in saving this country and we are only going to ask you to stay in contact with my office. We apologize for your rapid return from the *Bush* but at the time it seemed a good idea to bring the two of you home quickly. Take the next week and just relax. There is nothing we can do until we get more information from Iran and are able to debrief the flight crew. Oh, yea, just a little extra info you may find interesting. The Air Force One that was used is a movie mockup. There is no functional system on board, so we did not lose any classified information or systems. The Iranian Intel service discovered this as

soon as they stepped on board and noted that in the video they sent to us. They were

not happy about that, but did not harm the crew because of it. Now, we will have to

take the bird apart to make sure they did not hide anything on board."

"Nice touch, Admiral. We were lucky in that respect. Ok, Davin is your boat

in Florida?"

"Yea, what have you got in mind? I thought you might be tired of boats for a

while. Oh, by the way, we have put Seal Team 6 on alert, and you will be taking

charge of them when you get back, and we have the intel we need to mount an

operation."

"Admiral, I'm a submariner, not a seal, those guys are tough as nails."

"True, but as you said, you are a submariner, and they need to get to shore

somehow, and it is either by sub or by plane. So you will run the op; when we gather

the intel, you will be briefed. But for now, get out of here; I have work to do."

"Now back to my boat. Yes, it is in Florida. I thought you did not want to get

on a boat so soon." Davin answered.

"True, but yours does not sink; at least I hope it doesn't." Bear replied.

"Ok, Admiral, you can find us off the coast of Florida on Davin's boat for the

next week. We will have a sat phone, and if we are needed, just call this number."

Bear stated and handed Admiral Hamner a business card with the sat number on it.

"Thank you Captain, Mr. Pierce, we will keep you informed; now, get out of here." Admiral Hamner said. He stood as he held out his hand and received Bear's hand in return.

Chapter 56 Epilog - Let's Get Wet

Five days later off the coast of Ft. Lauderdale heading out the inlet cruising east at twenty-five knots, the crew of the fifty foot Cigarette boat, "*Searcher*" were relaxing under a blue cloudless sky, as Davin expertly controlled his boat past the breakers. Once they cleared the no wake zone, Davin pushed the throttles to the max and his boat almost jumped out of the water.

Connie, Josh, Stephanie along with Anne Rackham and Todd "Bear" Henderson were sitting in the stern of the boat sipping on cold drinks, beer and a couple of margaritas. The plan was to cruise out to Bimini, about a two hour run at fifty miles an hour. There they would refresh, refuel and grab lunch. The ride to Bimini was uneventful. The seas were nearly flat, just a small swell over the Gulf Stream, which ran north a few miles off the coast. Davin had to slow down a couple of times to let his friends get up to relieve themselves or get another drink; actually, they slowed four times. They arrived off the coast of Bimini, slowed to nearly crawling speed and entered the channel. Slowly they approached the dock, where they found an empty spot, tied up, flew a yellow quarantine flag and waited until they were cleared by the harbor's custom inspector.

"Davin, I'll order fuel and you guys head up to the restaurant, order me a beer and steak, medium rare, with a baked potato, just butter, nothing else, thanks." Josh said as they climbed onto the dock.

"Your usual beer, Josh?" Stephanie asked as she looked over her shoulder while tying a small wrap over her thong bikini bottom and grabbed a shear blouse also.

"Yes, Beck's Clear bottle." Josh responded and headed over to the fuel station. Becks Clear bottle beer was not imported to the States because its alcohol content was higher than what was legal to import, So anytime Josh was in the islands, he loved to take down a few of the best beers he knew were here.

"Go ahead guys, I will be right up." Davin said, turning back toward his boat.

"What's up, Davin?" Connie stopped, turned and asked.

"Nothing, honey. Just need to check something, go ahead."

"Ok, don't be long. Should I order a steak for you too?" Connie asked.

"Yes, and two beers." Davin yelled back as he slipped into the cabin to get the satellite phone, which started to ring just as he grabbed it. "Davin here, to whom am I speaking?" he said with a smile.

"Is this Davin Pierce, former Military Intelligence First Sergeant retired and now working as a freelancer with the Company and presently sitting on a lounge on your boat in the Bimini Harbor?"

"Yes, and since you know that much about who and where I am, you must be connected with the company also, or one hell of a good guesser." Davin agreed with a puzzled look and a small smile. "Who are you and better yet, where are you?"

"Who? I will answer later; the where is, well, in a minute you will know that."

"Ok, switching to secure." Davin said, and then he toggled a switch on the front of the phone and entered a six number code. "Done, are you?" This was a dumb question, as he shook his head knowing full well the guy on the other end would

not hear Davin unless he had gone secure also.

"I'm here, Davin. May I call you Davin?"

"Ok, now who the hell are you and why call me now? I am on vacation from

everything, including the company." Davin insisted, "My beer is getting warm and my

steak is getting cold."

"What I am about to tell you needs to stay with you, not to be shared with

anyone on your team especially Captain Henderson and his bride to be. You can tell

Mr. Randel. And, is that understood, Mr. Pierce? You cannot even tell your wife or

the future Mrs. Randle?"

"Sure, but if you think any of my team could be a security leak then you are

misinformed and don't know my team very well."

"Not what you think, Davin."

"Huh, what do you mean?"

"My call sign is 'Wild Thang" and I work for the company as an operative.

My cover is a Navy pilot on the *Enterprise,* presently in Norfolk Naval Yard. My

name is Dean Henderson and Bear is my older brother. I have been tasked by the

SECNAV to organize a bachelor party for the old boy and need you and the male

members of your team to participate."

"Cool, how can we help? You are one sneaky bastard, Dean."

"Ok, I can take that cause I am one very sneaky bastard, and well, our budget

is covered by parties that wish to be secret at the moment, and the party will be held on the hanger deck of the soon to be decommissioned *CVN-65 Enterprise* on

April 24th to the 25th. We start at 9 a.m. on Saturday morning and will continue all

weekend. We already have the food, drinks, guests and party favors ordered and

arranged to be delivered on the 22nd. My shipmates will decorate and prep everything.

Your assignment is simple, almost anyway; you and Mr. Randel need to get him to the

boat on time and not let him know why you need to visit the ship."

"The *Enterpirse*, wow, that ship has a lot of history. But that is only ten days

from now, that is easier said than done. But, I believe we can handle it."

"She arrived back in home port on the 10th of February and is scheduled to be

decommissioned in 2013, so we may have one more cruise on her before then. But

until then the Admiral and SECNAV have authorized the use of the hanger deck and

flight deck, and various cabins to hold this little party. However, back to what we need

to do, you have the easy part; keep them busy till the 23rd and then find an excuse to

visit Norfolk, where the ship is going to be decommissioned, and get him, not her, on

the ship. Get him on the ship and we will take it from there. Your ladies need to divert

her to somewhere else. I understand the wedding is on the 26th at 5 p.m.; we also need

someone to ensure he makes it there. We have staterooms designated for all of you, on

board. We have a tailor on board to ensure his and your uniforms and or suits are

perfect. So you do not need to bring anything except yourselves and the good Captain.

Do you understand you mission, Mr. Pierce? Your phone will self destruct in ten

seconds."

"What?"

"I've always wanted to say that, Davin. Look, just get him to the ship, and we have the rest covered. And, when it is time for the wedding, all, we, that is you and me, get him to the church on time." Dean said with a chuckle.

"Hell, you don't ask for much, do you?" Davin stated still a bit confused but enjoying the assignment for a change.

"Well, sorry about letting you in so late, but I had to wait till you were alone, and besides, you were out of contact for a while with my big brother. The company is not very happy that you were a stowaway on that floating bomb, by the way."

"They will get over it. And I am not going to ask or say that the use of company equipment for personal gains is against the law. How many laws are we breaking now and will be breaking, no wait don't tell me, just keep us out of jail. Is the shore patrol in on this? I hope so."

"Let me handle that; let's just say that we have everything under control." Dean commented. "Now, if you and Josh can handle the Captain, then my team will handle the other side. See you in Jacksonville. Oh, yea before I go, turn on your fax machine; I have something to send you which will help you over the next few days."

"Ok, it's on." Davin said as he flipped the switch and powered up the satellite connection. "Before you go, have you heard anything about the President?"

"Yes, and no, he is still missing, Air Force One has returned, the crew is fine and on a mini vacation after being fully debriefed."

"At least the crew and AF One are back. How is the government holding up?"

"You know the VP, Speaker of the House, and most of the cabinet were killed in the Denver explosion. We tracked AF One to Germany and they spent some time in the billets there to rest before they flew back to Dulles. You know that was not the real AF One; it was the mock up used for drills, flyable, and as a movie prop, but no classified equipment on board. That was a good thing; at least we did not lose anything classified. The last we know is that the crew flew to Iran and after refueling and a short rest, very short, they were asked to leave the country immediately, leaving the President there."

"What are we doing to get him back? I really didn't like the guy but he is our President and we need to get him back."

"Nothing, just talking. We don't know his exact location; but when we do, we turn it over to Team 6. But, back to the update; all the warheads have been retrieved and disarmed. The boat that you guys drove to the middle of the Atlantic has been disarmed and will soon be returned to the Soviets. On a side note, your civilian helpers, Jessica, Ian and William were awarded large cash dollars, allowed to never pay taxes ever, and she was offered a job with the Department of Defense to work in NCIS as an analyst, which she accepted. William and Ian were also promoted and are going to receive a commendation, level not yet determined, because the Medal of Honor is being considered for the entire crew. This will be determined soon; as we don't have a President to sign off on it, we have to wait."

"Never pay taxes!" Davin responded.

"Naw, just kidding, they did get money, promotions and she starts at NCIS in two weeks, but they still have to pay taxes." Dean chuckled.

"The captain, his family and the junior officer have been given new identities and new lives. Both were declared dead and buried at sea as a cover up. The captain got his daughter political asylum as requested and is living with her dad for now. But she can never get a job with the government or any high tech or defense contractor or get a security clearance, at least for a while."

"That is great, thanks for the update. Anything else you want to tell me?" Davin asked.

"No problemo my friend, just keep Bear busy and get him to the boat on time. I'm counting on you and Josh to get it done."

"Got you covered, Dean, see you on the 23rd." Davin said and started to hang up but heard...

"Davin, What do you think of Anne?"

"Awesome lady and a history that is unbelievable."

"Don't have time to hear about her past right now; she will tell me when she has time. Take care." Dean said and hung up his phone.

"Wow, this is going to be tricky." Davin said to himself. At least he thought he was alone.

"What is going to be tricky?" Josh asked as he came down through the hatch.

"We have an assignment."

"From whom?"

"From Dean Henderson, Bear's brother." Davin stated.

"Dean, how the hell is he; haven't seen him in years."

"You know him?"

"Yes, great pilot and good agent, oops, should not have said that." Josh commented, "Now what is this assignment?"

"I know he is an agent, he called me on a company phone and we just had a fully encrypted discussion and assignment. Wait a second." Davin said as he picked up the fax that Dean had sent. "Wow, look at this; don't know how he knew or why he is helping us, but look." Davin continued as he handed the four pages to Josh.

"Damn!" Josh said as he looked at the deep water satellite photographs of the remains of a very old ship, complete with grid coordinates and depths of each piece, cannon, anchor, what looked like ballast and other pieces of a ship that had been underwater for over three hundred years. "Wow, Davin, this has just made us, what, made this an easy dive of recovery. If we can reach this stuff and are able to recover it, wow! Look at this!" Josh said as he pointed to the outline of six aircraft. "Do they want us to figure out if they are the missing Flight 19 from Lauderdale from 1945?"

"Yea, cool; we dive tomorrow and see what we can bring up. We did bring the metal detectors, right? What's the depth of those planes? As for the assignment, we are to keep Bear busy until…" Davin explained the plan and finished by saying, "To get to the dive site, we need to leave around seven in the morning, so let's go get those steaks and cold beer."

"Yah, they are in the forward compartment next to the battery packs for the scooters." Josh commented as he continued to scan the pages. "The weather is supposed to be the same as today, a few clouds and smooth ocean. The depth says one hundred twenty feet deepest, with two at ninety feet. Do you think they may be Flight 19 or..."

"That will be determined tomorrow; what about the boat? How close is it to the planes?"

"About a half mile."

"We leave at 7 a.m. in the morning."

This is not the end, just the beginning

www.ingramcontent.com/pod-product-compliance
Lightning Source LLC
Chambersburg PA
CBHW070153260626
47160CB00002B/335